Charlotte Champion Pascoe, Charlotte Rogers, Mary Rogers

Walks about St. Hilary

chiefly among the poor

Charlotte Champion Pascoe, Charlotte Rogers, Mary Rogers

Walks about St. Hilary
chiefly among the poor

ISBN/EAN: 9783337423698

Printed in Europe, USA, Canada, Australia, Japan

Cover: Foto ©Andreas Hilbeck / pixelio.de

More available books at **www.hansebooks.com**

Walks about St. Hilary,

CHIEFLY AMONG THE POOR,

BY

CHARLOTTE ·CHAMPION PASCOE.

" She stretcheth out her hand to the poor, yea, she reacheth forth her hands to the needy."

" In her tongue was the law of kindness."

EDITED BY

C. G. B. R. AND M. R.

—

1879.

PENZANCE :
BEARE AND SON, STEAM PRINTERS,
21, MARKET PLACE.

TO THE READER

HE MSS. from which this volume is compiled were given to her sister, Miss Willyams, by Mrs. Pascoe, on the eve of her departure from St. Hilary, the home of fifty years.

They were addressed in the form of letters to the friend of her youth, Mrs. Benjamin Wood (*née* Michell, of Truro), and were begun in 1836, and carried on at various intervals during the ten following years.

In September, 1875, Miss Willyams thus writes of them :—"Some of these 'Walks' were transcribed and forwarded to the writer at Carnanton, and, at her death, sent for revision to our cousin, Charlotte Rogers. I have undertaken the remainder with the hope of furnishing a correct transcript, from which to procure a few printed copies for gifts to the attached friends of my loved sister. To the devoted friend, Mary Rogers, who was to her almost as a daughter, I must leave the arrangement, as I fear my failing powers may be unequal to the task." This proved to be the case. The venerable sister did not live to see the work accomplished, although she reached the age of ninety-one.

It only remains to be added, with regard to the following pages, that such memorials of love and kindness need no apology or commendation from those who have now, to the best of their ability, fulfilled the pleasant labour of arranging them, and whose tender and life-long affection, both for the writer and her subject, must be their plea for presenting you with these "Walks about St. Hilary," by a beloved kinswoman and friend.

C. G. B. R. and M. R.

September, 1879.

WALK I.

Frog Street.   A Ghost !   Mary Bosence and her sister Kitty.

T is not in compliment to you, dearest Maria, nor to Queen Charlotte, that
I record first a walk to Frog Street, a title no one knows how bestowed,
and far from graphic, unless you happen to inspect narrowly the rivulet
that flows between the pathway and a richly-flowered hedge, and should
spy clusters of embryo frogs which nestle among the water-cress, and it must be
owned do not much whet one's desire to gather it.   I may venture to say it was
not indebted for its name to any native wit, for then it would have been "Quilkin"
Lane (that most ingenious combination of letters signifying frog in Cornish), far
less to 'Un Avis Williams, whom three years ago, everybody, and I among the rest,
used to visit for the sake of the monthly rose that covered her cottage from end to
end ; her bright little vixen of a canary, and the surprising set-out of the chimney-
piece with curiosities brought from beyond seas by her bachelor son, who then
resided with her.   Frog Street must have had a more sophisticated sponsor than
any of these ; not improbably, one of the visitors at the great house on the hill,
to the proprietor of which these few cottagers have been tenants, time out of
mind ; aye, even beyond the time when it was occupied by Chancellor Penneck,
whose ghost, residing in and about the great, walled grave, at the end of our
church, is said to show his temper occasionally, by raising the wind in a terrific
manner.

So much for the direction of our walk ; its object was to enquire after the health
of Mary Bosence.   This is not her present name, indeed, but it seems to be the
charter of valuable servants to retain the name which their good character has
rendered honourable.

Mary was nursery maid at Tregembo for many years,—one of those domestic
factotums who think and feel, as well as act ; and who, when they marry, carry
into their cottages the wholesome habits of gentleman's service—order, cleanli-
ness, and reverence for their betters.   I do suppose that Mary never seriously

A

displeased her mistress but once, and that was when she received the addresses of
Robert Carter, a handsome young miner, although a widower with a child or two.
But my sister Anne is a just woman, kind to Mary in her distress, whom she has
heartily forgiven; I therefore do not mean to make *her* my text for a few animad-
versions on the unreasonableness of those mistresses who take upon themselves to
resent the settling in life of a favourite servant. To such I say, they have no right
to be angry at the favourite's lending an ear to the addresses of an honourable
suitor, unless they are prepared to whisper in the other ear, " I mistress, take thee
maid, to have and to hold, for better for worse, for richer for poorer, in sickness
and in health, to love and to cherish, till death us do part." Few mistresses, I
suspect, would witness with the affectionate endurance of Robert (when he returns
from Bal at Huel Vor, ten miles out and home) the utter helplessness of poor Mary
from a spine case; fewer still would incur the burthen of maintaining one to wait
upon her. Mary's handmaid is her own sister Kitty, who left her place immediately
on hearing of the affliction in this family, and has ever since sustained in it the
several posts of nurse, mother, and housekeeper. "She asks for nothing, ma'am,
of us," said Mary, "but her living, which is poor enough; and a pair of shoes
now and then—that indeed, she does not *ask* (but it is sad to see her diminishing
what she had looked to against age and sickness); so, when he sees her shoes are
coming poor, Robert goes and buys her a pair." Kitty must not expect any help
from her late master; so indignant is he at her abruptly depriving him of the services of a valuable cook, that he has peremptorily forbidden her to enter his doors.
Who can blame him when they consider that her successor may not fry his fish, or
mash his turnips so much to his taste? for saith not that master of the heart, Lord
Byron, "some men will set a house on fire in order to roast their chesnuts."

We had not visited Mary for a long while on account of the small-pox, fearing
the infection for Kate;* and coming in we had met three of her children, hand-in-
hand, in the lane, all marked, some pitted in the face. One would think with five
children lately suffering from this malignant malady, and with a spine case herself,
that regret for the loss of beauty would hardly have found place: she smiled,
apologetically, I own, as she observed of a prettyish-looking boy, "*he* is the most
marked of the whole, the only good-looking one, too."

---

* A niece and adopted child, the writer's constant companion.

WALK II.

May, 1836.

A runaway horse. Happy old age. Little ones in charge. A burned child.

FTER a congratulatory visit to the lying-in room, at Tregembo, we called in at Mary Hodge's. Sick or well, Monday or Saturday, she is always in what is called "apple-pie order," though I could never understand the appropriateness of the phrase. This one thing is certain, it does not imply either *tartness* or *crustiness*, as far as Mary Hodge is concerned. She had been sadly frightened by the running away of the Tregembo cart-horse, or, more properly speaking, carriage-horse, who, conceiving himself too fine to draw a cart, had taken to his "high-mettled heels" all the way down Relubbus Lane. Mothers ran out, terrified to death ; every one of them sure that her own youngest was under the wheels. Happily, the indignant steed was brought up by his coming in contact with the angle of a cottage-wall, which shook so that they said the "geranjas" within were upset, the pots broken, and the good woman sent to bed from fright.

On our homeward way, we dropped in to see 'Un Hannah Allen. This sweet, mild-looking old woman deserves the compliment paid to her by her children, who prefer being charged with her maintenance to seeing her abandoned to the Workhouse. These good people do not *know* it, but what a sweet lesson they are daily reading to their children, who, you can see, dearly love "Grannie ; " and how surely will the benefit be paid back into their own bosoms, when they come to want the indulgence which they now accord so unostentatiously.

In such cases, however, let the daughter-in-*law* have her due share of praise, and that a very large proportion ; for, besides suffering in common from this invasion of their slender means, all the attendance which age requires, all the forbearance which its slowness, its infirmities demand, fall to *her* share.

Shame upon us of higher condition, that it should be commonly asserted, "No two generations can continue to dwell together in unity." If this be true (as I fear, with few exceptions, it has been proved to be,) all I can say is, "Let them pay a visit to 'Un Hannah and Betsey Allen." Next door to these worthies dwells Betsey Simmons, but she had gone to market to buy a pair of shoes apiece for six *such* tiny beings, so young and helpless. Helpless! Never judge from outward appearances. The eldest of the batch, about seven years old, was left in charge of the house; the baby, a cripple boy (no better than a baby), and two little girls of that age when they are said to be "just got out of the way," but which appears to me the precise time when they are always *in* the way—able to run about, and to catch up knives, and to dabble with the fire. On this occasion, little Kitty and the cripple were packed into the window-seat, brandishing a knife from one hand to the other, and then scuffling for its possession. The young housekeeper, meanwhile, lighted the fire with a piece of tallow, which she stuck burning into the just-opened drawer, making repeated excursions to and from the cradle, to borrow a handful of straw from the baby's loose paillasse, and leaving a train of combustibles each time. Yet, no doubt, the mother found all safe on her return; whereas, I have known the finest house in this county (Nanswhyden) burnt to the ground, though every room but one, and that from whence the fire proceeded, was avowedly provided with stone arches, to guard against such a catastrophe. Sometimes, however, such instances of reckless trust, as that which I have just recorded, prove fatal, as in the following sad story.

Left to take care of his little sister—charged against touching the fire,—Jem put on the child's bonnet, sent her out to play, and carefully secured the door. On the mother's return, he lay on the floor, it is hardly hyperbole to say, burnt to a cinder.

The predominant feeling, strange to say, in so young a breast, was remorse; for the dear child had always been remarkable for his regard to truth. "Mother, I have told a lie," he shrieked out at the sight of her, alluding to his promise of not going near the fire. "I have told a lie, and for that I am burnt." "He prayed fervently," said the poor mother, "like any full-grown Christian, for mercy, and at length became calm, remarking that all would be burnt up one day—the bed, the world itself, and there would be an end of all. Well, that don't matter, mother, do it, if all go to heaven?" He enquired if he might sing, inviting his mother to join him. "No, my child, I cannot sing," said the broken-hearted mother, who shed bitter tears at the relation of the same. He sang a verse of a hymn by himself. "I think, mother" ('twas "mother" every moment with him), I believe,

I shall die ; so much people comes to look at me to-day, there must be something strange in me. Ask father to pray for me. If I go to heaven, I shall see little David ; and, mother, you will mind to pay for my schooling, wont ye ? If I had lived, I should have come to spell and to read, and to writing, but now there is an end of all."

WALK III.

MAY, 1836.

A bed-lier. Jenny Priske. Righteous indignation misplaced.

E went to see poor William Pearce, who has been a bed-lier for nearly twenty years. I must not pun, though many do suspect he took to lying in bed, prematurely, in order to entitle himself to the full-pay allowed under such circumstances by the friendly club. Whatever he may have been, poor fellow, he is no deceiver now. His wife was just able to hobble about with an inflamed leg that had confined her to the bed, the only bed in the house, which serves the poor invalid for couch by day, and accommodates the whole family at night. Yet his eyes and lips ran over with thankfulness. What a reproof to the pampered and luxurious !

We dropped in at Jenny Priske's in order to disburthen ourselves of the remaining pudding. The first person I saw on opening the door was her eldest son, fresh from bal, with a face as black as his behaviour, if village gossips may be credited—the tale is too revolting to be entered upon ; I could not bear the sight of the wretch, and no doubt looked as black to him as he did to me. He was one of my Sunday scholars—a great sullen, duncish, ragged-headed boy. I used to compare him and his younger brother—so slight, pretty-featured, and nimble-witted—to Ariel and Caliban. I do not remember to have met a more violent contrast in two brothers. "How is Henry ?" said I, in a kind tone, partly, I fear, to make my coolness towards the offending Samuel more pointed. "Ah, ma'am,

I wish you could tell *me* that; the poor fellow has been gone many weeks up the country to look for work." "I thought work was plenty, so many new mines." "Why, work *is* plenty; but, the truth must be told, the poor lad was quite out of heart, to hear so much about—— It is a shame to speak of it; but"——

Here I broke in, this being the invariable preface to very disagreeable details. "Oh! for pity's sake don't say anything of that shocking affair; it makes one sick at heart to think of those unnatural parents" (glancing angrily at S——); "but, in regard to poor Henry," I added, with severe emphasis, "let it be remembered the innocent will not always be permitted to suffer for the guilty."

Thus, mounted on the stilts of righteous indignation, I reached the end of the lane, not recollecting that "the wrath of man works not the righteousness of God." Pity I had not thought of all this ten minutes sooner; I should have avoided an act of great injustice, and my victim might have washed his dirty bal face in peace, a job from which he desisted during my speech, because, as I then thought, he was glad of even that screen to cover his shame. I have since learned that the person I addressed was not Samuel, but John, a third brother, of irreproachable walk and conversation. And I found to my discomfiture, that Henry, the nimble-witted, the Ariel, has been the defaulter; Samuel, who I insultingly compared to Caliban, is the prop and stay of his one-legged old mother. Grant I may be the wiser for this lesson!

With a view to surprise my poor couch-captive, I called on my way home for our little mutual favourite, a delicate morsel of a thing, two years and half old, whom Kate and I make a plaything of. The best bonnet and Sunday shoes were soon put on by friend Mary, of whom you must hear more anon, and I carried off the little Betsey, as lovely, and well-nigh as diminutive, as a thing from fairy land. The pretty story I want to tell you of friend Mary must wait a more leisure time.

I am now called by my companion to read Mrs. Jamieson's *Female Sovereigns*, of which number we have discussed the imperial Semiramis, the queenly Zenobia, the voluptuous Cleopatra, and, far from least, the lovely and loveable Joanna of Naples.

WALK IV.

A valuable horse. Dibdin's Songs.

CALLED in—I should rather say, I struggled for entrance—at Anne Trenawden's, being stoutly resisted by two famishing pigs who blocked up the doorway. Three children, scarcely less boorish and dirty, were abreast, endeavouring to push through the same narrow passage a wheelbarrow, full of potatoes. I am afraid I felt glad, for I hate a mess, when they told me, "Mother was gone to Goldsithney to get a croom o' rice for dinner." The poor woman had called at the Vicarage a few weeks ago with a begging paper, whose object it was to raise money enough for the purchase of a horse to replace one that had "muirly died of old age, and which," she added, "was a good beast more ways than one, for he had provided her and her children with the means of living for many a year." The husband himself, past hard work, had employed the trusty animal in bringing home coal and sand for the neighbours till, as we have seen,

"The sand of his hour-glass stood still,"

like that of the degraded racer.

There is much plaintive, as well as playful philosophy in those old songs of Dibdin's, if one could but extract some gems from the heap of terrible rubbish that surrounds them. There is "Tom Tackle" for one—

"So brave and so noble, so true to his word,
That if merit bought titles, Tom might be a lord,
Who was ne'ertheless pitiful, scurvy and mean,
And the veriest scoundrel that ever was seen ;
For so said the girls and the landlords 'long shore,
'Would you know what Tom's fault was ? Tom Tackle was poor.'"

I remember, too, a sweet little bit at the beginning of a song, of which, I believe, I have reason to be thankful I do *not* recollect the succeeding verses—

> "Come, never seem to mind it,
> Nor count your fate a curse ;
> However you may find it,
> Still someone else is worse."

WALK V.

Pearce and the parson. Pride in humility. A sick miner.

HAVING lost for a while the old companion of my walk, my poor Kate, I challenged her uncle to go with me the rounds of the Higher Downs. Poor Pearce, for one, was glad enough to see the parson— and his shilling—as well as to listen to his good prayers ; only, unhappily, he thought it right to proclaim his devotion by long, " minute " groans, which his wife, though not hearing a syllable, echoed from the outer room. I cannot imagine why, sectionists especially, think this sort of accompaniment helps devotion ; it puts an extinguisher on mine, having the same effect as a whimpering tone has on my charity. It may be wrong, but I like Grace Trevaskis's ways better, though I could not say there was not a mixture of pride in the motive that induced her to shut the door in our faces. She *said* that she did it to keep the chimney from smoking ; but I suspect she did not want us to see the contractedness of the dwelling—in which her tall, gaunt form could hardly turn round or stand upright —nor the ladder and hole through which she climbed to bed. After a while, she suffered herself to be soothed into civility, and related her little history ; how she had maintained, and finally buried, her mother, at four score and four years of age ; how, after this, being herself no more than fifty-two or three, still young for marriage, she earned her "little living" comfortably.

Here were four nice cottages in a row. Jane Johns, once our washerwoman, was in a peck of troubles. Work was plenty, she allowed, but men were plenty, too ; besides, her husband was falling into the miners' consumption, and one of his "woollens had shrunk a nail of a yard all round." It is a blessed thing when evils can be redressed and sorrow alleviated at the expense of half-a-yard of coarse flannel. Jane thought she never could have looked in my face again after her poor sister, unknowing to her, had been buried in a shift which I had lent her for her sickness.

'Un Amy Wills, a worthy old soul, I do believe, but with the physiognomy of a cat just stepped upon, would have been mightily tiffed if we had not looked in upon her, though we only disturbed all the family at tea, and put them into a fuss to get us seats. Whether I call or not, I am sure to be greeted, as often as we meet, with a reproachful, "How are ye so strange ?" Now she could not add, in her usual taunting tone, "I heard of ye going along;" and it is worth while to escape her angry looks. After all, she must be a kind-hearted old woman, and a good peace-maker, or they would not have been sitting so cosily round the tea-table ; for once, when she was absent for only a few days, her son, with whom she resides, and her daughter-in-law, quarrelled and separated, the wife alleging that her husband "lashed her with a rope as big as his arm," by which, if her tale was true, he ought to have been suspended himself.

WALK VI.

A benediction.   Bugbears.   Mary the friend, and the other Mary.

VISITING poor Pearce, in our next walk, we carried him some rice-pudding, for which good deed he hoped we should "receive four-fold into our bosoms," a benediction whose literal fulfilment would be as inconvenient as that of the Frenchman who prayed that his benefactor, together with all his amiable family, might be everlastingly pickled, meaning preserved.

"Honor's leg was," she said, "charming, wholing as pretty as could be," &c. She did not give so favourable a report of her son Samuel, whose dislike to learning is quite· insurmountable. "He would as lief take a serpent into his hand, as a book," she said.

How figurative the poor, the country poor, are! I suppose we are all poets by nature, only we are rubbed down by custom and habit to the vulgar currency of prosaic phraseology, so that our language loses all originality of character. A town nursery-maid threatens her refractory charge with the chimney-sweeper, with his bag, or the coal-heaver; whereas Mary, whilst tying on a clean "pinnie" to my little elfin pet, declared that if she did not get dressed to go with the gentry, a bird should carry her away. Little cared the small thing for the frock we afterwards put on her at the Vicarage; she liked better to chase the cat, but Mary the mother, and Mary the friend, expressed all the joyful surprise we had intended, especially the latter, who saddles herself with the obligations as well as the cares of the family with whom she resides.

I never beheld so pleasing a specimen of friendship, in the rough, as these two Marys offer, though I am at a loss to imagine what can be the cementing principle, unless it is their native dissimilarity. Even in respect of age, they seem mis-matched, though there is no saying. Mary the friend is of that homely-featured class, who may be of any age from fifteen to fifty. It is a silly, injurious notion that heroines must needs be beautiful. A Russian lady, who knew the Elizabeth of

Madame Cottin, assured me she was an ungainly-looking being, and kept a shop; and one writer of fiction has the singular courage and good taste (Sir Walter Scott, of course) to describe his tip-top heroine as being short, thick-set, and baby-featured.

The two Marys had worked at the same "bal" for years, perhaps sat on the same stool, "warbling of the same tune," albeit most unlike "to a double cherry;"* for Mary the less was pretty, and exceedingly young-looking. This is friend Mary's artless account of their friendship : "When we first worked together to the mine, she had but twopence-half-penny a day, so you may think how young she was, but we were neighbours afore that ; and so she grew up a companion like, and came nearer than a sister to me, or else, I reckon, I should never have come away from my own parish and natural friends. And now that she is married, I do not know how to leave her neither, being as it is so lonely for her and the children at night, when William is away at 'bal.'" The generous creature did not advert to another motive for remaining with them ; but I learnt that William had had what the world calls a run of ill-luck—in mining phrase, "bad speed of late," and could not pay his way without occasional help from the poor spinster's mite.

WALK VII.

JUNE, 1836.

Fair-day.   Mary Wills.   Vagabond children.

E passed through Relubbus, and were everywhere reminded of the "deserted village ;" scarcely a creature to be seen, except a cat here and there craving with hunger, who had been, probably, locked out of the house to save crockery-ware, when its inhabitants set off for the fair—St. James's Fair at Goldsithney, the grand carnival of all the parishes round. Kate and I indulged in many moral, and I dare say

---

* Midsummer Night's Dream.

splenetic, reflections on the all-prevailing dissipations of the age, particularly when we heard from Spinster Mary that Matron Mary had set off for the fair with the baby and my little sick pet. Mary, spinster, with all the burden of the ménage left on her shoulders, could hardly forbear joining our philippics, and she had good cause. She had lately lost a day's labour and the night's sleep, to watch and soothe, and carry up and down the little Elizabeth. This tells against the doctrine of instincts !

We also called in on Mary Wills, purely, I must confess, with the unamiable object of discovering whether *she* had also gone with the idle stream. We found her weeping over her work. Her son had promised, she said, to be home by St. James's Fair, and he had not come. Poor soul, I wonder she is not cured of expecting any good from *him*, for a more consistent little reprobate, through every stage of his childhood, I never knew ; and, I am told, his more mature villanies drove his poor mother from house to house, and will ultimately, I fear, drive her from her present comfortable asylum as housekeeper to an old bachelor. This boy's early delinquencies were of no common cast. He and his sister (who, let me say, died afterwards a 'hopeful penitent) went about the country laying contributions on the benevolent by the most ingenious fictions of poverty and misery. When invention was exhausted, the little vagrants took advantage of any affliction in the neighbourhood, personated the orphans of a poor man lately killed in a mine, &c. By such expedients, I have known them return from Penzance, clothed and pampered, whilst the real widow and orphan remained cold and hungry. I cannot think that the mother connived at these frauds, *i.e.*, further than that every parent is negatively accessory to the crimes of her often-neglected child.

Mary had, and still retains, much of the gipsy *insoucience*, that is the French word ; the Irish call it *deil may care* ; but we have no name in English to express the absence of house-wifely concern which makes Mary Wills differ from all her neighbours, and puts me in mind of an " about-a-go " fortune-teller. Yet I never remember in all my dealings with her that she ever asked me for anything but " another pamphlet," the boy having destroyed a religious tract she set much value upon. I should like to have Mary's skull examined by a good phrenologist.

WALK VIII.

'Un Sally Fox.

THIS morning we paid a visit to our old friend and favourite, 'Un Sally Fox, and found her wonderful mind still triumphant over what she calls "the bit of body," though, if you could see her lofty forehead, her fine Siddonian countenance, the free action of her lengthy arms, you would say it was

> "A frame to set a soul in."

I have boasted much to one friend and another of 'Un Sally's intellectual superiority, till she got the name of my sublime old woman; but, however I may have raised expectations, it has in every case been outdone by her actual presence and conversation; above all, by her parting benediction which is quite patriarchal; I have seen it draw tears from the stern, and make grave the giggler, and I *have* known it extract a confession in favour of Christianity from the habitual scoffer. "Do you know," said the artist whom I took, many weeks before, to *see*, not to *hear*, 'Un Sally, "that I cannot forget that old woman of yours. I never was so surprised as by her parting words; they are constantly recurring to my mind." We found her to-day, pondering, as usual, still painfully unsettled on the grand question of ultimate acceptance at the Throne of Mercy—the penalty of deep thinking. All her visions, whether sleeping or waking ones, are tinctured with spiritual dejection—timidity, perhaps, I ought to say—for I am glad to observe that her endless allegories and visions, trances, &c., have all a happy ending, for example: She was walking along, seeming to her, in a pleasant place, where were throngs of singing birds; only a few of them, however, flew up towards heaven, carolling with joy and gladness as they rose and rose, and winged away out of sight, "to show (who knows)," observed 'Un Sally, "that it is given to some more than other some, to keep on their way rejoicing. Some Christians fluttered and warbled, whilst others creeped and mourned and drooped;" to the last sort she belonged, she said. At another time, the emblem was a stream of water that continued to gain upon her,

D

in spite of her efforts to escape from it. It crept up higher and higher, colder and colder, and just when she thought she must be engulfed (for there was near no help in man), the stream abruptly flowed away in another direction. The similitude which took the strongest hold of her mind was that, seeming to her, some person presented her with a ball, such as children play with; this, like everything else, was to be the test of her spiritual destiny; accordingly, she sought to make it bound upwards, but failed. Resolved not to be daunted, she tried with her other hand, but still the ball refused to rebound. "Well," she continued, "for all that I will try this once more." She did so, and "oh, what a *coose* (a mining phrase) it went up! You know," continued 'Un Sally (who, I suppose, had never heard the word perspective), "that as a thing gets further away from the eye it looks smaller in size, but in the case I am relating, the figure did not decay (diminish, she meant), but was visible till it entered into the very heavens." According to her interpretation, it was a token that the prayers of the devout would prevail in spite of all impediment.

Necessity is the mother of many inventions, and a comical race they are, thought I, as I entered the family apartment below. In default of an elder sister, Betsey had placed the baby upon Tommy's lap to nurse; and, poor innocent, he had clutched it round the waist, grinning and jabbering behind his victim, after the manner of the monkey's dealings with Gulliver. Poor Betsey! she might well complain of the "sight of work she had," with four helpless ones including 'Un Sally, and nobody to lend a hand but Tommy.

Tommy is a great casuist in his way, "I wish you was dead Granny," said he the other day. "Wish I were *dead*, my son!" rejoined 'Un Sally reproachfully, "that is not very mannerly, and why for, pray, dost thou wish I were dead?" "Because, Granny, I am certain you will go to heaven."

When I told her of my sweet L. M's* death, describing her as one taken away in the bloom of youth and beauty, she quietly remarked, "no vain sacrifice." How greatly is the good old woman to be envied, whose very dreams are full of the one thing needful; the one thing desirable, although nothing could well be more comfortless than her earthly position!

---

* Mrs. Marsh, who died May 5th, 1836.

WALK IX.

Snuff. Spoiled children.

SALLIED forth with Kate, (who is restored to her locomotion,) to the Workhouse, just as we used to go in olden time to the Nunnery at Lanherne, with our little offering of snuff, &c., a small matter of novelty going a great way with recluses of whatever rank or order. I daresay I should be the same if shut within four walls ; but, oh ! I must be changed in my tastes and subdued to my destiny, before I could think the replenishing my snuff-box the acme of human felicity.

It was pleasant to find 'Un Conny and Mary, and the two 'Un Pollies more content with their lot, and, in consequence, less full of their merits and their distemperatures. They spoke, too, more charitably of the children of the establishment, especially those of them who had had children of their own, but it seems there has lately been an irruption of fine, headstrong, disorderly ones, between the ages of twelve and two, "who got such a head," (the broken-spirited mother said in extenuation), because, as often as she went to chastise them, the thought of their poor father, killed in a mine, came between her and the offenders, so that she never could make up her mind to punish them except she was in a passion, and then, she said, with an air of self-approval, "she gave it to them unmerciful."'

WALK X.

_____

Sick rich and poor. Earrings. A lone woman.

 WIDOW, Jenny Curtis, having called at the Vicarage a few days ago, for "something to put inside the maid's lips, quite sure that she had got the fever," I stepped across the downs to enquire how the matter stood; Kate had one of her headaches, and was as muzzy as the weather, so I went alone.

I found Jenny elbow deep in soap-suds, washing up their crum o'clothes, and learnt from her that her daughter had resumed her labours at the mine two days before. How soon the poor are down and up again! In our line, what with care and remedies, and lying-a-bed, we should have been as weak as water after such an illness; hardly able to crawl across the room, instead of jigging, and bucking, and cobbing at the "Bal." Another of Jenny's daughters who stood by her, a girl of about fifteen, was as nice a fair modest lassie as you could see, till, taking off her bonnet, she revealed a pair of gold drops, which reached from her ears half way down her throat. In the lower walk of society these ornaments are, in an especial manner, odious to my taste, almost immoral, and I ventured to say as much to the two Jennies. The young one looked sheepish, while the matron Jenny vehemently protested her individual innocence. *She* never approved, not she, of such finery; 'twas all done unknowing to her—"the maid was treated to them, (and what female can gold, especially gold earrings, despise?)—and stole a march one fine morning to Penzance, twelve miles out and home, in order to purchase them with the money given her by three of her cousins. "How much was that?" I asked. "A shilling." "Well, there is a shilling if you are willing to sell them to me, and I will tell you the purpose I want them for. We are puzzled to think of a punishment in the day school, as the mistress is not allowed to beat the children. I mean, therefore, to collect together all the finery (especially earrings) that may come in my way, and any very naughty girl will be decked out in it before the eyes of her schoolfellows."

I observed the hand gradually raised to the offending ornaments, and then "mother" was applied to for help to take them off. Thus, the shilling which I had intended for the good of young Jenny's body, will, I hope, prove of benefit to her soul. She, at all events, will see the matter in this light, for "ever since she had them things in her ears," her mother told me, "she had trembled to come athirt the crofts at night, for doubting the old one was behind her; and (how Wesley would have delighted in such a convert!) would not, to gain the world, go to bed without taking them off and placing them in the furthest corner of the chamber." We smile, alas! but is not this the mode in which we all tamper with our darling sins? They are harboured, even gloried in amid the noontide of worldly prosperity; when the dark hour of sickness or sorrow comes on, they are put far from us, only to be resumed on the first returning dawn of health and fortune.

Finding myself so near, I peeped in upon my female Diogenes, who this time did not close the door against me; on the contrary, she was courteous and communicative, for *her*; told me what I did not know before, that she worked on the land, doing sometimes the work of a man. I could well fancy it, as I looked at her lengthy, bony limbs, but she was between two and three score, she said, and well nigh past any sort of labour; a lone creature in the wide world; all her friends in the churchyard. This last pathetic touch she often repeated, adding, for conscience' sake, the clause of three first cousins, but they were men-kind, and what could *they* do for such as her? The worst of all was that she could not read a letter in the book, which made it "twice so lonely." A neighbour's boy came in once upon a time and read a chapter or so for the "vally of a halfpenny." "Then this sixpence," said I, "will give you twelve readings."

Truly I was ashamed of the blessings she heaped upon me, so disproportioned to the donation; and yet, on second thoughts she is right; that small coin may be to her the source of inexhaustible riches for time and eternity. I only wish the lady I once heard declare she would at any time give five guineas for the effluvia of a strawberry in winter, had been a witness to poor Grace's raptures. Her benediction followed me to the next door, but poor Jane Johns is not given to these grateful paroxysms. She comes of the horse-leech's kindred, and the more you give to her the more you may. One has heard of the various modes of *granting* favours, there is no less difference in asking them. With some it has the air of a prayer, some of a petition, some of a claim, and with some of a reproach.

E

WALK XI.

JUNE, 1836.

An Ophelia.

E went this morning to Goldsithney to complain of our ten o'clock scholars, and get, if possible, their mothers on our side. A country village is a pretty thing in a story-book, but nowhere else. The children are so bedizened with dirty finery, so be-curl-papered, and stare so rudely, the women look so gossippy and *slamakin*, the men so muzzy-headed; for there are scarcely any of the latter to be seen at midday, except the few who lounge about the doors of the alehouse. On our way home we met the funeral from Marazion, and were surprised, considering the curious circumstances to which the poor girl owed her death, at the scantiness of followers; I saw but one who had any claim to be called a mourner, though the first pair of mourners, (by courtesy so-named) were the parents of the poor girl. This is her painful story. A few years since, this giddy-headed and pretty girl encouraged the addresses of a dissipated young mason, whose monied father vehemently opposed the match, but, of course, it took place, and was followed by all the wretchedness and wedded strife that had been predicted by the parents. The ill-used, and finally deserted wife, after suffering from a succession of frightful fits, became crazed, and thenceforward was neither controlled nor in any way cared for. She subsisted upon a pittance jointly paid by the two fathers. I once saw her, when driving from Penzance, peering into the dusty hedges, and I imagined her to be some sick person engaged in culling simples. I soon found, however, that she had no settled purpose, but was occupied in collecting together straw, dust, and other trash, as a matter of taste, like another Ophelia; like that heroine, she accomplished her own sad destiny by means of these artless pursuits. Being seized with spasmodic retching on returning from one of her evening rambles, she boasted to the old woman with whom she lodged, that for once she had had her fill of poppies,— pop-dock, or foxglove, no doubt she meant. Poor soul, their slumb'rous influence proved strong and lasting; she died that night.

I was very unwilling to give credit to the story I heard, that the offended father-in-law had disparaged the poor creature's modesty before the Camborne Bench, to free himself from the burden of her maintenance. But supposing the tale to be true, one could fancifully have imagined the one solitary mourner, her sister, apostrophising the traducer in the strain of passionate affection so touchingly put in the mouth of Ophelia's brother, "I tell thee, churlish *mason*, a ministering angel shall thy sister be, when thou . . . . . . "* but, no, I cannot finish the sentence, for John Davy, aforesaid, is a great ally and favourite of mine. He knows and often befriends the sick poor, and, like Job, the cause he knows not he searches out.

WALK XII.

Crazy George.   Cornishisms.

DROPPED in most opportunely at the Workhouse. Mary Wills, in a voice between coaxing and scolding, was trying to induce poor crazy George to eat his supper of bread and milk. "What! you have quarr'ld with your victuals again, have ye?" screamed she in a most unsirenlike tone. Then, seeing me, "Here's the second day he's refused to take his meat; muirly starving himself with hunger, because, he says, if he eats he shall be put to work." This was an ingenious inversion of the Apostle's injunction, "Those that will not work, neither shall they eat."

I did not feel sure of my measure of authority in George's eyes, but, thus appealed to, I determined to assume that air of confidence in my own powers, which made thousands, better, wiser, and taller than Buonaparte, receive his

* Hamlet, Act V., Scene 1.

dictates as the mandates of fate. "You ate your supper the other evening to please Mr. Pascoe," said I, laying my finger on his bent shoulder, "You must eat it to-night, George, to please me."

He instantaneously began his attack on the porringer, bolting square after square of barley bread in a manner which proved that, at all events, the obstruction was not in his throat.

What a subject crazy George would have been for Crabbe, unless, indeed, the poet has anticipated him in his "Silly Shore."

The three old women had gone to bed tired with their day's weeding. Jones surprised two of them, who will never be eighty again, thus employed on an onion bed. "Better do that than nothing, if it's ever so little," observed the notable governess. "They have been asking leave to *walk*," (an expression which, by the way, in Cornish, does not mean to advance one leg and then another, but to take a pleasurable excursion,) "and I have told them" pursued the governess, "that when they have performed their task they shall be allowed a half-holiday." Pope might have availed himself of this fresh exemplification of the ruling passion. It is strange to behold these feeble old souls, to whom one would suppose rest the only acceptable thing, toiling and moiling under a scorching sun, on their "two knees," as they would describe it. Our cottage dialect abounds with these expressions. I will transcribe a list of them which I noted down from time to time, commencing with Mary's aforesaid figure of "starving with hunger," and its converse, "no stomach to *meat*," meaning food of all kinds; "mouth-speech," "April month," "ould ancient," "young youths," "widow woman," "arm wrists," "bread corn," "nail of a yard," "two twains," "two double," "hear tell of;" and "have you not remarked," said a zealous collector of Cornishisms, when I read him my list, "that they tell you 'you are looking bad in the face?'"

WALK XIII.

The Preventive Station.   Emigrants.   A Romanist's children.

Y dear young guest, Harriet C—— (for mine own familiar Katie was gone on a visit to her mother), walked with me to the Preventive Station.   I ought, long before, to have told the boatmen and their wives of the well-being of their old commander, Lieut. Crispo, and his family, and delivered the remembrances with which I was charged to their friends at the Cove.   The poor fellows had good right to be remembered for the honest sympathy they showed the poor emigrants, up to the moment and long after they lifted the last of eleven children—from the cutter—on board the ship "Brazeba," on whose deck the poor mother had stood, gazing her soul away, and weeping till she had no eyes to gaze out of.

It is painful to think of, it must have been worse to witness this parting scene ; so I thought at the time, I remember, and let Kate and her Uncle accompany them to the ship's side without me.

When individuals leave their native home willingly, from a restless disposition, to fare more luxuriously; or, more pardonably, from a taste for the picturesque, I say, "joy go with them ;" but, to behold a poor family like this, driven from their fatherland, and flung suddenly and helplessly, as it were, on the wide waters, and only because "Tom Tackle is poor ;" this is truly touching, even when the suffering party are strangers to you.   It is true our acquaintance was accidental ; something better, let me say, for it began in the church.   A nice pleasant-looking mamma, generally with a child in each hand, took her station in the strangers' pew whenever the weather was fine enough to permit a walk of, at least, two miles. We continued to meet and part with a bow of courtesy at the church stile, till Mr. P. observed to me, "We ought to call upon these people."   I thought so too, and never had we cause to regret our walk to make their acquaintance, till the sad moment to which I have referred.

F

But all this while I have left the assembled group to hear the mistress's letter, for I judged it good policy to assemble them. The first who obeyed my invitation was pretty Mrs. Boyle, who has a gentle sweet voice that mightily sets off her strong brogue. Some voices would make music of High Dutch, though this excellence in woman is, perhaps, the rarest of her accomplishments. Little Patrick Boyle's head was bandaged in consequence of his having fallen a depth of six fathoms in pursuit of a goose. Plasters and wraps would have little availed him, poor child, if it had not been for the sollar (planks or beams fixed in the sides of the shaft to guard against similar mishaps); and even that might have failed to keep him from destruction, had his bulk and "celerity in sinking" equalled Falstaff's. Mesdames Neale, Boyle, and Ladner were so pleased with the account I gave them of the emigrants, that I promised, for Kate, that she would copy the mistress's letter for the information of their husbands.

My visit to the Station, I grieve to say, was not altogether friendly, I was obliged to tell tales of Mrs. Neale's twin girls always coming late to school, and, worse than that, having deceived both mother and mistress on St. John's Eve, by falsely affirming to the latter that they were bidden to meet their parents at Goldsithney.

Nothing could be more characteristic, I should say more Papistic, than Mrs. Neale's proceedings thereupon. Without the least touch of maternal grief or surprise at this duplicate atrocity, she summoned the culprits from the outer room, commanding them to fall on their two pair of knees, and straightway to beg Mrs. Pascoe's and God's pardon. Deeply shocked as I felt at this most profane conjunction, I thought I should only make matters worse by expostulation, and so, having performed this most orthodox duett, the twins were suffered to depart. "Exeunt, kneeling." If I could possibly have anticipated such a farce, I believe I should have found out a good Protestant punishment for the truants myself.

All the world runs riot just now. As we crossed the higher downs a Roman candle fell at our feet, almost; and, further on, a group of young boys and girls presented a pretty transparency, clustering round a bonfire kindled in honor of St. Peter, whose vigils they were celebrating.

Pity, while all these traditionary revels are so piously observed, their coeval virtues of reverence and obedience towards parents should have passed away from the face of the earth.

WALK XIV.

Jenny Priske and her fancies. Pearce. Dewing.

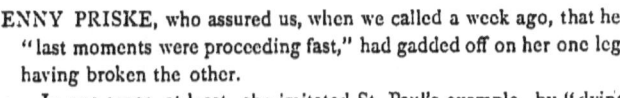ENNY PRISKE, who assured us, when we called a week ago, that her "last moments were proceeding fast," had gadded off on her one leg, having broken the other.

In one sense, at least, she imitated St. Paul's example, by "dying daily;" but she has threatened me so long, that I have become as hardened as the shepherd who suffered the poor boy to be at length devoured by the wolf he had so often proclaimed. I mean no pun when I say she now looks very sheepish whenever we enter her cottage, though, before we leave it, we are sure to be told we shall never see her alive again. I am sometimes afraid that Kate will laugh outright at these contradictory bulletins.

Poor old Betty Vincent died at last, to prove the truth of her predictions, though not for many a good year after the following affecting scene took place at her cottage. I found her sick in bed, and she solemnly assured me, in the "article of death." Among the many impressive truisms she uttered, I well remember her speaking of man, in this present state of existence, as no better than "a flea that fleeth," "a bubble upon the water, crack! and it is gone." A few days after, Betty walked up to the Vicarage to "ax a croom o'honey for a hoize."

Poor Betty has long been gathered to her fathers, but she did some good in her generation, and, after her death, her son's children, whom she kept together in decency, were wholly neglected, running about dirty and almost naked;—with their little uncovered heads bleached in the sun, they looked like a gang of white gipsies.

Poor Betty! she was spared the sorrow of beholding the ruin of the eldest girl, of whom she used to boast as a miracle of scholarship, and no wonder, for Betty declared, with a somewhat startling metaphor, that all the learning came out of her own bowels, meaning that she had pinched herself in order to send her grandchild to school, where, as she assured us, she would "lap her learning like nothing at all! and come to read her Bible over like a tale." Betty was a golden treasury of quaint sayings;—peace to her memory!

Pomp could not take the dose of physic which Shakespeare prescribes, in a more profitable form than in a visit to poor Pearce; so humble, so thankful and devout amid his sufferings and privations. I generally find him pondering over a pet text. This evening it was—"Behold, now is the day of salvation, now is the accepted time."—"Now! mistress, nothing about repenting to-morrow: No, no such thing as that to be found between the two covers of the Bible." If penitential tears could wash away every sin, poor Pearce would have nothing to fear from a wild youth and ill-spent manhood. Nor has he now, for he knows of a more cleansing stream. But he has almost wept himself blind, and, like his prototype in patient suffering, has nothing left to him but that most equivocal comfort, a talking wife.

I was waylaid by Catherine Gartrell, some of whose brother's family are inmates of the Workhouse; worse than orphans they may be truly deemed, for their great ostrich mother has abandoned them entirely, bequeathing them a legacy of shame which will cling to them—poor things!—as long as the memory of the great Betty and her evil courses lives in the parish.

To acquit myself of the promise to the aunt, I called in, late as it was, at the Workhouse. The obliging governess assured me that the children should attend our school as soon as the fixed work was out of the way, but that now the little Eliza was wanted to hold a child whilst its more able-bodied mother worked at the Farm. With this reasonable concession I was obliged to be content, and so must Kattern, but "'twas a wisht thing," she said, "to think the poor creature should come to be bound out without knowing how to mend a hole in her stocking." The Sunday School provided, in a measure, for her book-learning.

I could not but look in upon the old women, who I found, July though it was, around the fire; their withered trunks, as it were, shrinking away from the open door till the back formed a centre angle; as good an illustration of our Cornish trees growing away from the blasts of the North coast (though not so droll a one), as Mr. Fisher's simile of a goose tied by the tail. 'Un Polly Freethy, who, by virtue of good sense and politer manners, is always the chief speaker, was "sorry Miss Kate couldn't come too, feared I should find it 'dewing' out." I have often heard this phrase, "dewing," but it never before seemed to me so pretty—perhaps in its appropriation to that soft, silent rain, that rather lights, begging Shakespeare's pardon, than "drops" on the place beneath. I know no word more expressive of the thing than this of *dew*; except indeed the French, which is still more rich in association. What indeed induced them to give it the name of *rosée*, the Etymologists best know, but to me it suggests the idea of a rich Provence rose enjoying its refreshing bath after a day of cloudless sunshine. The stated return of dew also affords to my mind an illustration of morning and evening prayer, feeding and strengthening the soul of the Christian to meet his daily task, and refreshing it on its return.

'Un Polly little thought of being the occasion of such flowery meditations—all the roses in L——'s nursery garden being, in her estimation, not worth a stem of tobacco.

WALK XV.

JULY, 1836.

Dame Williams's daughter.   Adventure at the Sessions.

WALKED late in the direction of Camborne in the hope of meeting my returning truants, "Uncle" and Kate. Saturday being pay-night, there was a risk of meeting tipsy miners, a species of assailant with whom numbers tell more than physical force, so I took with me Dolly, who was pleased with the opportunity of saying "how do you do" to her mother *en passant*, and still more to distribute some strawberries among the young ones. We only met one of these, literally, knights-errant, who was propitiated by our yielding the entire breadth of the road, across which it was his pleasure to stagger. Fearing to miss the carriage, I sent Dolly with some strawberries to poor Mary Carter, and took my station at Dame Williams's, whose cottage faced the road. I found its occupant more than ever exasperated against her daughter (in service at Parson Hockin's). She wept passionately, and reminded me of King Lear, all the milk of human kindness having turned to gall. That she, who had sold her last bit of property to

G

launch this child—this General—into the world, that she should disown a mother's authority, and "take up with such a fellow!" "If it pleased the Almighty to give her strength to fetch Phillack Rectory, she would surely expose her to her unsuspecting mistress, and let her know what a snake she was harbouring."—Poor woman, she seemed writhing under the anguish of its envenomed teeth, and if she had been born poetical, would have railed in good blank verse. My truants did not arrive till long after the increasing darkness had driven Dolly and me home; when they did at last make their appearance, we met as if we had been separated a year or more.

Mr. Pascoe has related an interesting Sessions adventure. He had, on a former occasion, mentioned, with much compassionate concern, an extremely juvenile offender, who, in company with an elder brother and another boy—all of them orphans—had been brought before the Camborne Bench at a former Meeting. This little gang, after committing repeated thefts, had always, it appeared, evaded detection by sheltering, together with their booty, in an old deserted ruin, among the mines about Redruth. It was long enough before anyone thought of going there for their lost property, but they did at last, and then the young banditti were secured, tried, and would have been, to a boy, transported, but for Mr. Pascoe's earnest interposition in favour of the youngest. The plea of excessive youth even penetrated the coat of mail which generally guards the breast of a parish officer, though one of these did tell their worships at the time that, as sure as fate, the boy would return to his evil courses.

> "As old experience doth attain
>   To something of prophetic strain,"

with parish officers as surely as with star-gazing sages; so, having continual dealings with juvenile offenders, it is to be feared that their propensity to think the worst is too often borne out by the result. It was so now. The unhappy little culprit again offended, was again committed for trial, and now appeared before the Bench, accompanied by his former associates. "I forewarned you, my poor boy," said his former kind advocate, "where, if you persisted in your unlawful courses, our next meeting would be, and here I find you." The poor child gave evidence by his looks that he recognised his former patron, and that he had not forgotten his prediction. But now there remained no appeal to mercy. The sentence was a heavy one—fourteen years transportation,—and the boy was removed to his solitary cell. There, in the course of that day, Mr. Pascoe visited him. The poor little felon was lying crouched on the floor, side-by-side with his young accomplices, to whom, in trying to stir them from their lair, the keeper employed the same coarse tone and terms which a huntsman would have addressed to his four-footed charge, not stopping first to ask pardon, like Shakespeare's gentle executioner. Whether owing to the little extempore homily which Mr. Pascoe preached, or to the tears which would come with it, the boy seemed to be moved, and at length shed some gracious drops himself, accepting with apparent thankfulness the small Bible which, by a happy chance, Mr. Pascoe had in his great-coat pocket. He promised to preserve and to peruse it, his integrity being aided by the consciousness that its sale would not bring him one shilling sterling. The sentence, I rejoice to say, has been mitigated to half the number of years.

There are griefs and sorrows of which extreme youth is justly accounted an aggravation, but this of transportation strikes me as being an exception ; indeed, the reflection is sufficiently palpable that it must be much easier to detach old affections and superinduce new ones in the young mind, to say nothing of the lot common to boyhood, of banishment from home, in one form or another, with this balance in favour of the young convict, that he has previously been familiar with labour and privation, while pursuing the hard and precarious existence of a London pilferer, whereas the schoolboy or the midshipman, dissevered from the apron-string of a caressing, cuddling mamma, at once exchanges the plenty of a luxurious table for plain and, perhaps, scanty fare, and finds himself subjected to the caprices not only of one, but of many taskmasters. This disproportioned sympathy with youth is nothing new. I have heard my father speak of the outcry, raised throughout the land, against the judge who condemned to death an idiot girl for wilfully setting fire to a neighbour's cornstack ; his plea for this unpopular measure being, in reality, regard for the public safety. Under the shelter of legal impunity, any maliciously-disposed persons might employ idiots to fulfil their evil wishes to the loss of property and even life ; and who shall say, as the case seems to have been a solitary one, that the warning held out has not been efficacious ? In the case, too, of that memorable murder committed in the Marr family (I can remember that myself), how concern for the agonising terror and bloodshed, and moral responsibility of three or four full-grown persons, seemed to have merged in sympathy with the cradled infant, to whom a spasm of the stomach or the cutting of a tooth would have caused more suffering than the knife of an assassin.

WALK XVI.

Mrs. Townsend.   Dolly.   Pack-horses.

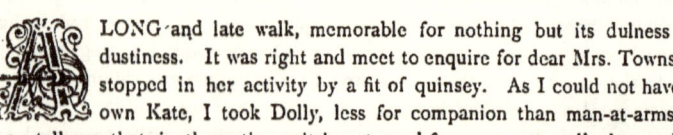LONG and late walk, memorable for nothing but its dulness and dustiness. It was right and meet to enquire for dear Mrs. Townsend, stopped in her activity by a fit of quinsey. As I could not have my own Kate, I took Dolly, less for companion than man-at-arms, for they tell me that, in these times, it is not good for woman to walk alone. Be it so, but, assuredly, nothing can be less agreeable than to have your steps dogged and your contemplations broken, by the ever-recurring fear of having your heels stepped upon. Not but that little Dolly is modesty itself, and far from needing the rebuke dealt by Tilburina* to her confidential attendant, only at rare intervals drops the jocose or monitory word, which has been the indisputable charter of waiting-maids from the time, or perhaps before the time, of the little Israelitish Maid, who spoke to such good purpose when waiting on the wife of Naaman, the Syrian.

Our homeward route was all among shafts, and mine-engines, and great heaps of rubbish. The little verdure which these had spared was so choked with dust that the poor whim-horses, just turned adrift, found it hard work to pick up a supper, though, poor things, they tried hard, with their noses close to the arid ground. It was, however, comforting to know that their ceaseless round of work was closed for the night. Not so with a poor pack-horse, which stood lengthwise across Mr. Townsend's Lane, while his ruthless master continued to load him with bale after bale.

---

* Sheridan.

WALK XVII.

The Mill.   Mary Peters.   A Concert.

UCKILY, our bread was so dark that it was thought expedient to expostulate with the miller in person, to beard him within the spray of his own mill-stream, or I might have remained another twenty years without walking to Carvis' Mill. I feel quite ashamed of my ignorance of this picturesque little valley, complaining as I always am that we have no pretty walks about the Vicarage. The indolent can always find a lion in the way, but there had been two which presented themselves to my view whenever I would turn my steps this way,—a huge ill-mannered tithe-in-kind-paying farmer, and his dog. We found the farmer as we passed down the lane, patrolling about to watch his reapers. He was civil enough, pointed out the road, and said his dog was harmless in respect of biting, but that he would probably bark after us from the wheat-field below. Thus assured, we felt valiant as Pilgrim when passing Pope and Pagan. The miller was from home, but his good old mother welcomed us with that respectful courtesy which you generally meet from " tenants of fifty years standing." They show one the more respect, perhaps, from the consciousness that they deserve some themselves. I have fancied that there is more of this dignity and elevation of character in the family of a miller than in any other calling ; perhaps it may be traced to a remembrance of that sweet old song, beginning

> " Ere around that old oak that o'ershadows our Mill,
> The fond ivy had dared to entwine,"*

and the association with the loveliest and most endeared of mills. And good "'Un Mary Peters" (for she would not be dubbed mistress), with her hospitable smile, her old-fashioned bonnet and gown, and the beautiful great loaf from which she was cutting liberal slices for her three grand-children, kept up millocracy, even in these upstart days.

---

* Old Glee.

H

I am more than ever anxious to improve my acquaintance with this dear old vestige of the past since a visit I paid to poor Jane ――――, who is so cruelly bruised and battered from having been trampled on by "a dismal great slug of a horse" on her return from the Methodist Meeting last Sunday week.

Jane is a woman of irreproachable life and conversation, and as ready, not to say the most ready, of any one in the Parish, to hold out a helping hand to a neighbour, but the truth must be told, she has not been so due a church-goer, nor could she ever be prevailed upon to attend at the Lord's Table; the old flimsy excuse, "not being worthy." But now I found her in quite a different mind. Her "Week's Preparation" and her spectacles lay by her on the bed, and she assured me that if she were ever raised from that bed, she hoped she should do better, for that the dear old woman at the mill, 'Un Mary Peters, only the day before her "misfortin," had been telling her they were surely under much condemnation for having neglected the Church and its Sacraments. For herself, the old woman said, she had left it too late to mend; her lameness kept her at home, and now when she should wish to go she could not, but for Jane, who was years younger, &c., &c. Perhaps, too, poor Jane's most heretical mischance, coming from Gold-sithney Chapel, gave additional force to 'Un Mary's arguments. I devoutly hope that their combined influence may be strong enough to bring her to attend this holy (but oh! how cruelly neglected) rite; for I think Jane is not of the class that gave occasion to the biting epigram, whose truth and wit excuse its coarseness and staleness,

"The devil fell sick,"* &c., &c.

---

* See Scott's *Black Dwarf*.

WALK XVIII.

The Cove.   The delights of retirement.

THOUGH traversing grander scenery, and in grander company, for we have been rambling over the Land's End and Logan Rocks with our guests, Lord and Lady C———, yet I gladly return to our pretty little Gull's Nest, our *Sans-souci*, Land of Beulah, or whatever other name fondness has bestowed on it to express the profound repose and delicate leisure of the place. The constant sound of what I love best on earth, I was going to say, the rock-bound ocean: the scenic variety of our little Cove, with its four or five boats moored under the window, continually coming and going, with about the same number of fishermen; a scene at once soothing and enlivening, like the company of a cheerful and affectionate inmate: the larger and more distant shipping (of which our spy-glass shows us the minutest tackle) that glide along the horizon, like the hooped and lappetted beauties of the last century, performing in the ever-to-be-regretted minuet: the no less graceful sweep of cliff to the east, which embraces all these, and adds to them by its rich vicissitude of light and shadow; and, talking of grace, let me not pass over the occasional visits of a snow-white gull, that floats and skims and balances, as if she had nothing else to do but to study attitudes. Then—as " blessings brighten as they take their flight," the consciousness that we are so soon to leave this scene of retired blessedness ! that we are to receive company, pay visits, attend the consecration of a churchyard, which is to draw crowds of holyday people, enough to vindicate the poet's exclamation,

" How vital, how populous is the Grave ! "

Then we are to receive guest upon guest, preceded by the " peace-scaring knocker." By the way, I wonder whether the bards, who express so much spleen against knockers, would have felt more in charity with their successors, the door-bells. There are not, I can truly say, two lines in English poetry to which my feelings more willingly respond, than those of the persecuted poet,

" Shut, shut the door."

Sometimes, I think I could even go further, and almost be ill to evade the dreaded incursion,—I mean on condition that the sickness should depart at the time the visitor might be expected to do so—a few twinges of tooth or head-ache would not so effectually upset one's mental arrangements as a mawkish visitor.

A sidelong glance at my Lochabar this moment reminds me that I have to bid it farewell and prepare for a guest.

WALK XIX.

OCTOBER, 1836.

The Workhouse.   Crazy Mary.

I USED to fancy that a walk to the Workhouse would class amongst the dull duties. It was a mistake—few among our Parish perambulations are more fruitful of mental interest. I am sorry they talk of breaking up these little district sanctuaries for the old and helpless, to enclose them in one huge mass of wretchedness in some central town, where none will have heart or time to enter into their little personal wants and feelings like our good Mrs. Treweeke. Her very foible is in their favour; she is no doubt fond of a little executive importance, a quality which has been improved by her former vocation of monthly nurse. Really, her ministrations to the sick and feeble individuals of her household are exemplary, and atone for that little self-importance with which she records the proofs of reverential affection shown to her by them. Some of her patients are quite her pets,—there is Mary Stevens, whose tale of woe deserves a page to itself, when I have leisure to relate it.

The nice little boy, who was an apprentice to Farmer White, little thought he was going to point a moral for my pen when he stole away from his master's work to look at that of a neighbouring steam-engine. I forget particulars, but somehow his leg was caught by some coil of this boa-constrictor, and so mutilated that amputation was necessary. To look at him you would hardly think he could play the truant, he seems so meek and steady; but possibly his sufferings, poor lamb! have given the expression to his mild pale face. Affliction (so it be not *unblest* affliction) is a mighty improver of the physiognomy.

We were thinking of bringing him on to be a schoolmaster. It was a happy thought of the parson to give him a little pair of crutches to bring him to school and church. He sits just under the desk, alongside of Uncle John, who takes him under his special protection and ghostly direction.

To relate Mary Stevens' sad tale, I must begin with that of her mother, who was, I have been told, the daughter of respectable parents at Tavistock, where, unfortunately for her, some of our Cornish miners obtained work. John Stevens, from this parish, was one of the wildest of the "pair;" and he was, moreover, a very ill-tempered and passionate man, which his poor wife must too soon have discovered. Hard fare and hard treatment soon gave the *coup de grace* to a delicate constitution, and Mary's mother fell into a decline, after giving birth to the poor girl to whom I have alluded. The father married a second wife, and there is no reason to believe that she treated Mary with unkindness, though to look upon the creature's starveling and dejected countenance, you would declare she had been reared on a step-mother's bread and butter.

Poor Mary grew up and worked in the Devonshire mines, and became engaged to a young miner, whose most shocking death, which she witnessed, brought on fits of insanity. This part of my heroine's history, when brought back to the Workhouse, was betrayed in her ravings. The mistress occasionally relates little touching anecdotes of her mental wanderings. Here is the last. During her fits she sometimes sings snatches of pretty hymns. Once, and once only, added the mistress, had she heard from her a scrap of a song. I wish the fair warblers of Moon's ballads could have witnessed the deep concern with which the good woman made this confession, and heard her account of the poor wanderer's deep compunction at hearing from one of the old women what she had done. "To see the tears she shed," said the good governess, "to think what she had been guilty of—her eyes were like pools." (This image, by the way, is scriptural.) "She could not put it from her mind; so I told her God would not lay to her charge any sins she committed at such times."

"Were they any bad words she sang, Mrs. Treweeke?" "Why no, ma'am; it was not that there was much harm in them either. I believe I can tell them pretty nigh over, for she sang them so pretty and sweet.

> " She trilled like a Linnet,
> She mourned like a Dove,
> And the words that she sang
> Was concerning of Love."

Amid her Ophelia ravings she occasionally adverts to her lover's unhappy end, of which it is thought she was a witness, for once she shrieked out, " Take him up, take him up ; he's dashed to pieces—pick up his fingers !" &c., &c.

WALK XX.

Anne and the Twains.

FEW tales of sorrow could be more contrasted in their circumstances than Mary's with that of Betsy Jones, who has occupied our time and thoughts during the past week. Mistress of a pretty cottage and garden, respected by her neighbours, a cherished wife and sister, and the mother of two fine little boys, of whom one was only three minutes older than the other ; with all these things worth living for, and despite the best nursing and medical advice, she has been this morning called to her congenial skies, for a sweeter, or more patient, or more grateful spirit, I never knew. Her first look on waking from a fevered doze was always a seraphic smile, like one returned to the body after a heavenly vision. I used to think of the " Kilmeny " of the Ettrick Shepherd.* Now, however, she belongs entirely to the world of spirits.

---

* *The Queen's Wake*, Night II.

Thomas came up this morning to speak about the funeral. She died last night. The friends wish, agreeably to an affecting custom that prevails here, to have the twins christened at the same time, but as the mother will be borne to Breage, to be buried by her relations, we have persuaded Thomas that it would be hazardous to take the children out at so late an hour. We saw them yesterday at their grand-mother's, in a bed hastily made up on the floor, so wrapped and blanketed around, their little heads, as if that was not enough, coiled under their arms.

We expected that Thomas would have been more disconsolate, but there cannot be a greater mistake than this notion. It is not when the first hideous idea of the loss of a beloved object suggests itself that the acutest anguish is felt; the fatigue, anxiety, and loss of rest attendant on illness, break down the mind to a state of passive endurance to the discipline, and when death at length takes place, the thought that there is no more to be hoped is mitigated by the thought that there is no more to be suffered. There is something, too—weak mortals that we are—in the personal occupation and importance of the moment. The chief mourner is also the chief object of observation and sympathy, the first person in the pageant, the hero of the tragedy. Our poor widower's bitterest moments are to come. It is when his little motherless boys become a burden to relations that they will be felt such to him. And what is a man to do, as he pathetically asked, when first alarmed for his wife's life. He might manage with one baby, but how shall he manage with two? I only hope that nice worthy sister Ann, who has so essentially fulfilled the duties of a tender nurse to her deceased sister, may remain, for some time at least, Thomas's housekeeper. She has a cottage in Breage with a field or two, and makes up her livelihood by going out to work; yet I should not wonder if she were to abandon it all. She has that Jeanie Deans air of straightforward integrity and benevolence, with those rarer qualities of self-forgetfulness and sim-plicity, which leads one to expect from her such an act of self-devotion.

WALK XXI.

Mary Carter's revival. The Ark. The Twains.

N my rambles through this chequer-work of joy and sorrow, I have seldom met a greater contrast than my late and present walks suggest.

At the end of Frog Street, whose damp, swampy atmosphere is enough of itself to foster melancholy and miasma, I found poor Mary Carter in the identical spot and position in which she has lain night and day for nearly two years,—a happy example, however, during that trying time, that the spirit of man (under the influence of piety) can "sustain his infirmity." But now, startling to behold, the poor creature is writhing under the insupportable burden of a wounded spirit. It appears that a spasmodic crisis in her bodily complaint had been mistaken by herself and her injudicious visitors for the "new birth," upon which certain Methodistical Pharisees gathered round her bed and discussed her experiences.

Alas! for such people, who load men with grievous burthens of visionary doctrines and mysterious precepts, and if they do not altogether shake themselves free of the oppressive load, have shoulders better fitted to bear it than those of the poor weak creature in question. The little body is giving way, too, under this frightful attack, and her mental sanity hangs by a thread,—nay, at times she is quite insane. Mr. P—— found her with the words of the psalmist literally fulfilled—her tongue had quite dried up, and had fallen out of her mouth, owing to her continual and passionate supplications for mercy,—a mercy she never doubted of before; and I found her striving to obey the injunction of her Methodist advisers to "keep fast hold of what she had got," using the action of one who had got fast hold of a rope. The still more absurd vagary of a disturbed brain was the imagination that Satan had visibly gone out of her. She said she had seen him with her bodily eyes, and he had on a cocked hat. This is no less than noonday madness, yet, after a little soothing talk, she is as sensible as ever she was in her life, and that is saying much; for there are few of her class who naturally boast of better sense. We have heard of mental wanderings being affected by entire change of place and objects, and the experiment is to be put to the proof. Mr. P———, with an indulgence for which I cannot feel too grateful, has permitted me to arrange for her removal, for the time, into lodgings in the churchtown, near our gate. I pray for God's blessing on the scheme—for here, if ever, it may be emphatically said, "vain is the help of man." She is to be conveyed hither in the "ark," which means a commodious covered cart from Tregembo, that obtained its name from the following ludicrous circumstance. Ann (Mrs. W. Pascoe) came to tea in it with all her six children, and when the time came for their departure, our servant flung open the drawing-room door, and announced to the company that the ark was at the door. Everybody stared, the proprietor of the vehicle with the rest, and waited and waited the explanation, which, however, we did not obtain until I privately questioned poor Jane as to why the carriage was thus announced. She "didn't know what to call it," she said; it was like nothing under the sun, she was sure; and having heard some one say it was like Noah's Ark, she gave it the name :—but it is time to go and give directions that Mary may be safely packed into it. ✳ ✳ ✳ ✳ ✳ ✳ ✳

The people at whose house poor Mary was to have set up her bed, have heard she is beside herself, and refuse to receive her. I deserve my disappointment for believing that every heart would divest itself of selfishness, and open to the distressed. I could be very splenetic on the occasion, but will try to take a leaf out of Kitty's book. On hearing of her poor sister's intended rejection, I sent for her, and confess, for the moment, I should have been glad for her to share my indignant feelings. Her beautiful meek reply was, "Well, ma'am, we have no right to blame,—it is for those whose duty it is to bear the trouble,—we ought not to expect it of strangers." I believe I have already recorded the sacrifice which this admirable creature makes to *her* sense of duty, by giving up a gainful service, to take charge of poor Mary and her six young children—to feed scantily, to be clothed how she can, and to toil from morn till night with Mary's family, every faculty of mind and body at full stretch—and all, not only without murmur, but without the slightest mention or allusion to what she is doing and suffering. What is heroism, if this is not? Here are three examples, at least, of exalted virtue in this one parish; and, talking of this, we have been to visit Anne and her pretty twins. Poor Anne! I believe we drew forth the first smile from her benign face since the death of her sister, by our pranks with the little fellows, who lay side by

K

side in the same cradle: making them shake hands, and look upon one another, which they seemed to do very knowingly; but Anne said she feared to let them lie face to face, lest, in spite of good Dr. Watts's exhortation, "their little hands should tear each other's eyes."

I told Anne she was like the picture of the Welsh parson, for she sat knitting her stocking, watching the babes with her eyes, and rocking them with her foot, at the same moment. It is seldom I can call a beam of cheerfulness over her countenance; she is "for ever silent, and for ever sad," like the widowed Celadon,* and with far greater cause, for besides her privation, in the death of a sister whom she dearly loved, for they were nighest of an age, it must be "cruel wisht" to pass the livelong day on the spot which so lately witnessed her mortal agonies, with no creature by but the pair of infants.

How grossly do those err who deem the poor in condition must needs be vulgar! They should pay a visit to the good and delicate-minded Anne, and have called with us a few days after on poor old Polly ———. We found her "prusing over" an old carol with a fine picture at the top, by reason of which, and her deafness, she did not remark our entrance, upon which her daughter-in-law, shocked at her want of manners, jogged her vehemently; and most reverential was the obedience of the startled reader, while her plaintive looks seemed to deprecate our displeasure. "What, you have kept your mother with you, Nancy?" I asked. "If I hadn't, ma'am," replied the kind creature, "I could never have looked for a blessing on this roof:—she is a *good* old soul." My observation on her apparent love for reading drew forth another trait of kind-heartedness.

"Yes, ma'am, I brought her home that *curl*; I gaved a penny for it I could ill spare, but she do so delight in a croom of a book." I passed my finger over the old woman's arm, to draw her attention to the piece of money I proffered her —she took it with a gesture of thankfulness, and turned her head away. "She is crying now," exclaimed the daughter-in-law, smiling through her own tears; "that is always her way when she meets with kindness." Need I say her's were not the only eyes moistened with pleasurable emotion? yet it was a scene that painfully rebuked the egotism of affluence, and made one blush for many a mis-spent half-crown.†

---

* Thomson's *Summer*.

† Never was there human being who had less reason for self-reproach on this head than the writer of these "Walks," —she did not *spend*, she only *gave*.—J. L. W.

WALK XXII.

Clowance fire.   Anne King.   Kitty James.   A victim.

HONOR PEARCE actually kept me ten or more minutes in the rain, to enquire into the burning down of Clowance, only to bring in that an uncle of hers had been a servant of Sir John's, and his uncle before him, for forty years. I could give her very little satisfaction on the subject, for Mr. Pascoe, who had gone to the spot in his magisterial character, to keep order, and prevent needless destruction of property, had not returned. I could not, however, help sharing in Honor's regret that such a venerable building, such a grey chronicle of olden times, should have been not destroyed (as appears from Mr. P.'s report), but defaced, more by the hordes of miners who came to the rescue, than even by the devouring flames. Alas! if the owner had been by, the thought might have occurred to him, how much more, in a moral sense, he had done to disparage his ancestry, than the wild hands that tore their portraits from the walls which they had adorned so many years, to cast them out of the frameless windows and doors.

But this is nothing to Honor, whose uncle, it seems, when past his labour, had, often and often, the gift of a guinea from Sir John; and once, after presenting him with two rare apples, his honour had given him a snuff-box and a guinea, seeing he had raised the apples in his own little garden. I do not like Honor the less for having the organ of veneration remarkably developed, I mean in her behaviour. She came back to me, when I was in a monstrous hurry, to apologise for not having made me a "fitty" reverence.

When I last called to enquire how her husband was (I generally call for a daily bulletin), the poor invalid and his family had been brought into the room in the Workhouse which adjoins our little day school, and upon which I confess I had set my Ahab eyes, in order to make an addition to our small room, and thus enable me to increase the number of my little sempstresses from thirty to fifty. Yet, after all, it is not unpleasing to have a few poor so sociably near.

There is Anne King, who makes out her living with one of the few spinning-wheels that are left in the land,—who keeps the Sunday school children in such tight order, and takes as great a delight in the spruceness of the aisles, and pews, and communion table, and points out their beauty with as much unction, and far more disinterestedness, than the exhibitors of Blenheim. Meanwhile, nothing can surpass the exquisite neatness of her own apartment. I wish I could say as much for her neighbour's. Alas! it will not always do to inspect our national houses in detail,—yet the Painter of Nature must lay on his shadows as well as lights, and if you shrink, dear M., from my chamber of horrors, pass by the next Walks, for horrors have dodged my steps at every turning.

One is apt to compare every comfortless human dwelling to an Irish cabin; but I really think the latter would lose in comparison with the hovel we entered to-day, to visit a sick woman. The domestication of the family pig at least implies that there *is* a pig, and the shutting him up with the family, that there *is* a door, both of which luxuries seemed to be wanting here.

Who that saw Kitty James in a high pew at church, dressed in a rich silk pelisse of as tender a blue as her large roving eyes, with bright rings on her delicate slight fingers, would have thought—or rather let me say who would not have thought—of her coming to this? Her father, a hard-drinking farmer, did not live quite long enough to leave his widow and family penniless. There was enough from the wreck of a good hereditary property to keep on the farm, and to give each of the children £100 on their coming of age.

This small certainty had its baneful effect on the idle and vain. Kitty always slighted the apostolic rule of working with the hands, and could not even submit to the small labour of straw bonnet making, so that the money and time spent on her apprenticeship were wholly thrown away.

During her subsequent times of distress, when she would gladly have turned a bonnet to turn a penny, I gave her straw plait to make a hat for our little Harvey, and positively there was neither form nor feature, poll or brim, to the thing: when it was brought home, it threw the kitchen-folk into convulsions of laughter. If poor little Harvey had assented to his title of " Goose-Gibbie," the head-dress, with the addition of a cock's feather, would have suited him exactly. The tempting lure of £100 induced Jack Dawe to marry this ill-starred beauty, and to treat her with kindness; that is to say, he indulged her laziness by taking much of her work on himself between *cours*, so that his health gave way, and he died.

One anecdote characteristic of my heroine's habits, at this period, I well remember. Long ago as it happened, I can never lose the frightful impression of the poor man's swollen face, as he lay under the operation of a supplementary salivation, his helpless wife standing gazing at him. Her reply to my enquiries how this effusion came on was as follows, "I'm sure I can't think,—he was taken dreadful in the night, his head swelling, and his poor mouth running like anybody under *salvation*. So I had nothing to give him but two of the doctor's pills that was left in the box, and I gave them to him."

Poor Dawe, of course, between the doctor's blunders and his wife's, was a corpse before another day dawned.

I wish I could think I had finished the history of poor Kitty—its sequel has been a tissue of poverty, destitution, and disgrace; such a one as

> "Nature's sternest painter, but her best,"

would have better delineated.

WALK XXIII.

Snow and kindly frost. Grace Trevaskis and church-going.

 NOVELTY—the ground covered with snow, the pools cased with ice, and light, powdery showers, falling at short intervals, insomuch that the few who besides myself ventured their noses out, expressed their surprise at seeing me. Yet fenced as I was with cloak, veil, double gloves, and list shoes, I felt warmer than I had done before many a bright fire in a drawing-room. "Frosty, but kindly"*—these words were running in my head all the way; from whence taken, I know not—Shakespeare, most likely—and

---

* Adam, in *As you like it.*

L

applied, I think, to cheery, healthy old age; but, at all events, they chimed in with my sensations and reflections, and, I may add, my errand, which was to take a piece of surplus beef left from that which Mr. P—— bestows every Christmas on the poor widows of the parish. Grace Trevaskis is no widow, but an old maid, therefore she did not score, but surely a desolate spinster, "with all her friends in the churchyard," and possessing little of the sympathy of her neighbours, is a widow and mair; in which opinion, by the way, I am borne out by the no less authority than he (I forget who) that pronounces widow, "Vidua," to mean a woman who has lost her husband, or never had one. How many smart things occurred to my mind, in favour of spinsterhood, in my walk to Grace's! But it is more to my purpose to take up the thread of my thoughts on the kindliness of frosty weather, which, though it partially blocked up doors and windows, imparted, I thought, to the cottages around, an appearance of heat and comfort, suggesting the idea of the inhabitants holding holyday around their bright fires within; for there is no working on the land this weather—fine, to be sure—as if the frost suspended the appetite as well as the means of satisfying it. Of this I thought not; I only considered how much more comfortable an appearance it presented than the late storm, of whose angry visitation I observed vestiges in shattered roofs, kept together—and hardly so—by ropes and stones, or anything that came to hand.

As I passed Jenny Curtis's, the next door to Grace's, these sadly discourteous words issued from the open door—"You be a big liard;" followed by volley after volley of the same sort of *bon mots*; but I could see no one. As I looked in I pronounced an audible and severe rebuke, which must have been the more astounding as, under favour of my list shoes, they did not hear my approach. I did not shew myself, but, having shot my bolt, and, as I hoped, hit my bird, proceeded on to Grace's. She was at home, cowering over a handful of fire, and employed in mending her shoe with a needle and thread. "There was no work to be had on the land." I looked about in vain for any eatables. Alas! I found there was nothing halcyon in a frosty holyday. Pussey (for who so destitute as not to be able to keep a cat?) seemed no less rejoiced and thankful than her mistress, at seeing the turn-out of my little basket. Grace said she "did not come with the rest, for she was a poor beggar, and, more than that, she was never married." Her modesty stood in the way on both occasions, probably, for anybody may be married in these parts—such brides as I have seen!

I questioned Grace about not seeing her at church, hers being that old-fashioned sort of God-fearing, command-keeping faith which formerly brought people there. "Where," as she said, "could anybody go better? Mustn't they be brought there first and last? and didn't St. Paul declare that the church was the right thing? But then, St. Paul said, too, that everything must be done decently, and it was a hard thing to go in dirt and rags to the House of God, to be mocked at by the youngsters."

I wished to discover what Grace wanted to make her "fitty-like," but I could only draw the confession from her piecemeal, for, like the unjust steward, "to beg she was ashamed:" whilst confessing her wants, one would have thought, by her averted, shy looks, that she was confessing her sins; though on other topics her eyes encounter mine with frank confidence. I do honour this trait of a delicate, generous mind. But to return to the wardrobe: the gowns—of which she had once a good store—were cut down to bed-gowns, so that there were none, and the cloak had long given place to an old working jacket; so it was beyond dispute, what she averred, that she was in no church-going trim. "Your height, too," I said, "makes your clothes more expensive." "It is so," she replied, in a tone of humble resignation, "but 'tis God that gives the growth, so we must not complain." This put me in mind of a man who came to me at the outset of my medical career. He much complained, he was in such a low way, so patient that, when his wife abused him ever so much, he could not return a railing word. Thirty years ago, I would have given my dower for a few of Grace's despised inches; but now, if I go to market for supernumerary graces, it shall be to him who has on hand so large a stock of patience and resignation.

As I was re-passing Jenny Curtis's door, a soft, contrite voice issued from it, "I beg your pardon, ma'am, for the words I spoke;" and, in the downcast, curtseying little figure from whom it proceeded, I recognised, I thought, my little earring friend. She took my rebuke and subsequent homily mighty well.

On returning, I just called on pretty little Sally Gilbert, whose tiny room was half-occupied by the carcase of a huge pig, a delightful sight, although it was the primary cause of an odious puddle, through which I had to wade, at the door, and was anything but aromatic—such is the magic of association! As there was only a narrow partition dividing this cottage from that of Hosking, I could not but call in there, too. Kate's first-class scholar, Elizabeth, sat by the fire, mending her frock; the lively Peggy held the baby, and smiled as kindly, if not as sweetly, upon me, as she used to do before that bal boy knocked out a whole side of pearly teeth, and she ran up to the Vicarage to complain and be doctored. I passed a man engaged in breaking the ice for his horse to drink, and then two boys pelting each other with snow-balls, and so ended my frosty walk.

WALK XXIV.

DECEMBER, 1836.

A Thaw. Little boys frightened from their sport.

THE snow was, yesterday, yielding to a slight thaw, which made walking less agreeable ; but it still lingered over the distance, and beautified the prospect, giving an interest even to a pile of refuse or a stone hedge. The cottage gardens looked pretty, too, with their green cabbage-heads studding the snow like emeralds set in crystals. I envy those masters of language who, by a stroke, can represent the varieties of nature's lovely face, as when Burns tells us

> "Ilka blade
> Droops wi' a diamond at his head."

Who does not feel as if actually brushing away the dew from the green sward on a summer morning.

Near Relubbas, by the side of a pool, were three little bits of boys, with their bits of shovels, as round, as pretty, and as mischievous as a group of Cupids. They had continued to break the ice which had formed over this piece of dirty water, and were splashing each other with its contents, amid peals of laughter that, to borrow again from the rustic bard,

> "My heart was sae fain to see them,
> That I, for joy, stood laughing wi' them,"

and, giving vent to my raptures as one does to children, I exclaimed theatrically, "you little icicles." Whether frightened by a word they did not understand, or that, in my crimson cloak, I seemed to them the Frost King come in person to vindicate his rights, I know not; but the trio took to their little heels, one of the splashers shrieking at the top of his lungs till he reached his mother's door. Thither I followed him to make my apology, and found him crouching down inside the table, from which place of security he stole at me very fearful glances as I conversed with his mother. On leaving the cottage, I perceived another of the fugitives, who, at first, had put a bolder face on the matter, drumming, however, at *his* mother's door to be let in, and increasing his clamour at sight of me. I hate, above all things, to be a spoil-sport, and generally am apt to pique myself on being a favourite with children, so that I felt utterly mortified, on the whole, at my adventure.

1837.

WALK XXV.

St. Erth Vicarage. A naughty girl. Phillis, the spaniel.

KATE rode to Lelant Vicarage, and Spernow agreed to meet her, on her way home, at that of St. Erth. Thither I always "go with cheerful feet," for, besides old recollections which people the way-side, it is the prettiest walk we have. I always think that I know when we have passed the boundary line between the two parishes, by the size and colour of the very primroses—their hedge-rows are so much richer than ours, and the ruthless hand of avarice has, here and there, spared an old hollow tree, fit for nothing but to look picturesque, but which greatly relieves the monotony of a parish road.

There are also one or two prettyish-looking farms as we pass along, but the sweetest passage is just above Trewinnard Mill, with that lovely bit of woodland to the right, bounded by those outlines of Tregonning and Godolphin. Godolphin Hill! there is picturesque beauty in the very name, setting aside its brow of majestic and fine plum-bloom, and the assurance that the time is not long passed when wild deer bounded over its heathy sides. It was when passing by this spot, gladdened by the view, freshened by a clear, wintry atmosphere, and elastic from a sense of perfect health and a tolerably easy conscience, that I said to myself, "It would not do to feel happier than I do; that would be heaven, not earth." I love to linger through St. Erth village; everything seems so exactly what and where I left it—the bridge; the churchyard gate, through which I have so often passed with those who, if they have left their like behind them, *I* never looked upon them; the Cellars, a miscellaneous shop at the head of a flight of steps, in comparison of my notion of which, for the variety, costliness, and magnificence of its stores, Howell and James's would seem a joke to me; Goodman's public-house, with the same identical porch and sign; Miss Grace Jenkins's stone house, with doors and windows all in the precise and miniature line, like herself and her maid Avis—in short, as I said, everything looked so exactly *in statu quo*, that, if one could do such a wrong to Godolphin as to suppose it guilty of expectorating

flames and sulphur, it would be natural to think the old village had shared the
fate of Pompeii. I could even, in that case, imagine I recognised an acquaintance
of forty years standing, in the cat who sat on a door-sill, curled up into the form
of a hedgehog, with a physiognomy between sleepiness and curiosity, only that
she lazily turned her head from this side to that to observe the passengers, as one
has seen an old lady planted, from breakfast till dinner-time, in an arm-chair near
the window, looking ever and anon over her spectacles and the blind, with a who-
may-you-be expression of face.

But the charm of identity was rudely broken by the inhabitants themselves, who
appeared to me the most discourteous, uncouth crew I ever met—*they*, at all events,
were not the same; whether it was their new trade of mining had spoiled their
manner, or whether their strange looks reminded me that what I best loved had
passed away, as Shakespeare (who always supplies a fitting verse to every purpose)
says,

> " Thy news makes thee a most ugly man."

Not prejudice itself, however, could mar the sweet countenance of that lovely
young mother who now fills my beloved aunt's place at the Vicarage, or make the
pretty Johnny, who gambols over the nursery floor, less pretty in my eyes. I am
really thankful that such as they *are* have succeeded to such as *were*, so that I
can admit them into the same picture-gallery without offence to my feelings.
A propos to grouping—As Mrs. P——— sat at my feet on an ottoman, confidentially
communicating a painful domestic circumstance, the little Johnny caught a glimpse
of her tearful eyes, and, taking advantage of her low position, which put their
two pretty faces on a level, threw his little arms about her neck with repeated
kisses, as much as to say, " Never mind them, dear mamma; Johnny will take care
of you." She said he cried whenever she struck herself, so that, instead of thinking of her own grievances, she has to comfort him. Pray God this disposition
may always accompany him. I couldn't bear to think that the sweet Margaret
should ever be otherwise than she now is, the happiest of wives and mothers. She
has married with her fresh, *unpalmed* sensibilities about her, and he is fully sensible
of his treasure. " Happy are the couple that are in such a case," and I may add, in
their case particularly, " Blessed are the people who have the Lord for their God."
As I passed the corner of a cottage in the purlieus of the village, I heard a very
contumacious little voice exclaim, " I waint, that I waint; I'll burn them, that I

will." Walking up to a dogged-looking girl who leant against the wall, swinging her work-bag to and fro, I addressed her in the hypocritical phrase common upon such occasions, "I hope it was not *you* who uttered such shocking words" (she hung her guilty head), "and, above all, I hope they were not spoken to your mother." The girl seemed aware of the offender's charter, that he shall not be obliged to incriminate himself—she persisted in keeping silence till I touched the chord of her imaginary wrong, when she passionately exclaimed, "Mother wouldn't give me a halfpenny, and she gave Samuel one." "But who gave you that nice pinafore and frock," I asked, "and that neat work-bag, which you wickedly threatened to burn? and, tell me, who is it that says, 'Honour thy father and thy mother?'" Although the culprit held her peace, I was pleased to observe that she was not offended, by her following close upon my heels, till I got out of the village, and entered the way-field to the Vicarage, that scene of touching recollections, where I have played at tea-things under the oak that used to rain cups and saucers o'er merry little heads, in company with her whose beautiful image is as fresh to my mind, after a separation of five-and-thirty years, as if we still sat packed together in its old hollow trunk.*

Among other sketches which memory presented to my heart was a couple,† the most loving that ever came together, walking along, arm in arm, followed by their harum-scarum niece, and the more discreet Phillis, the most sagacious of liver-coloured spaniels. When I have lost sight of my uncle and aunt at the junction of many roads, she has taken her seat till I came up to the spot, indicating, I have imagined, by the turn of her head, which path they had taken. Her mode of begging entrance into the room was one common to parlourised dogs, that of scratching at the door, but one day she surprised her mistress by demanding entrance, in this manner, to her bed-chamber. On being admitted, she ran up, and laid at my aunt's feet a sick chicken, having observed that her mistress had nursed such while labouring under a fit of the gapes; but, lest you, my dear, should feel symptoms of a similar affection of the jaws, I spare you the rest of my auld world stories. My walk out and home, in a word, was delightful; I would borrow Mr. Fisher's phrase, and call it an "integral" walk, had I not splashed my stockings, both going and coming across the swamp.

---

* The author's sister, Mrs. O'Brien.
† Her uncle and aunt, Mr. and Mrs. Willyams.

"Would you like to get sixpence easily, as you may any day, by only placing a few flat stones across the stream yonder?" I said to the miller's boy, who was unloading his horse at that pretty mill. He replied, "Yes," with that frank readiness, that "where-shall-I-go? what-shall-I-do-for-you?" look, which Sir Walter brings before you in his mountaineer, so that I feel assured I shall, in future, pass dry shod, nor ever again be exposed to the girlish impropriety of skipping over running streams, and balancing upon treacherous stones.

WALK XXVI.

FEBRUARY 21, 1837.

Edward Briant. Church-goers. Armless. 'Un Sally.

WE were out this morning from ten till two—positively I should be ashamed of consuming so much time in walking, if we did not turn it to account by calling upon all our cottage acquaintance by the way-side; and, after all, it is at least as well to trifle away one's minutes alongside of a hedge, as within four walls. Our call at the Workhouse I have already mentioned; from thence we cut up through Trewheela Lane, in order to enquire what was become of dear old Edward Briant, the endearing adjunct being drawn from my pen by the recollection of the old man's due attendance at church, as long as breath and limbs would carry him thither. He was emphatically a good church-goer, for he walked more than two miles out and home, every Sunday, and in all weather, to attend it. How few such humble worshippers are now left in the land! I know but of one besides, and that is Ellick Roberts, who fills Uncle Edward's place; all the rest of the world are professors or profligates, the godly or the godless; they are either too good or too bad, far too enlightened or too brutish to follow the worship of their fathers in an assembly where everyone is expected to be decent, and no one is eminent. The generic description of the good old church-goer, as far as I have observed, is sobriety, humbleness of mind, reverence for authority, and mostly taciturnity, especially among *men*kind. I knew one talking old woman, who, when she was too infirm to attend the church, chose her residence in a joyless, rubbishy spot, because she could see the steeple from her window. In another fifty years, the existence of such a creature will be no more credited than that of the Kraken. I have widely wandered from Uncle Edward, whom we found more than usually ailing ; only just come down stairs, with his nose almost touching the grate, the "martyr-bend" of his meek head having increased to a bow since I last saw him. I imagine he will not much longer try the filial piety of his granddaughter, who, with the permission of her husband, has determined to support and watch him to the last, rather than suffer him to be removed to St. Erth Workhouse, as under the late act of *in*justice, I had almost said, for what else is a retrospective law ?

En passant we peeped into Catherine ———'s cottage. Between fifteen and twenty years ago, she was among the *élite* of my Sunday school, one of my own class. We saw five out of the six little girls she has had in sequence, but the mother herself was "out about the potatoes," an answer which we pretty commonly receive at this season.

Mary King, however, *was* at home, and she had good reason to be, with her little crippled, diseased infant, an abscess on its back, and both its feet turned inward, so that they can never serve the purpose for which feet were intended. I hope it is no breach of the sixth commandment to wish the poor innocent in heaven. The supposed cause of this deformity was that engine of all mischief, a rude boy, who let off a cracker near a thatched out-house, and set it in a blaze, a short time previous to Mary's confinement. I seem to have cut into a vein of the horrible, for my next call was upon Ann Curtis, who exhibited, with motherly pride, the beautiful hand-writing of her armless boy. He holds the pen in his left stump, and guides it with his lips, and this tempts me to tell *that* story, too. Anne had a sad drunken husband, and her roving and predatory habits had acquired for her the nickname of "the prowler." One day, she left the youngest child in the cradle, the door unbarred, and—the pig unfed ! Horrible, most horrible ! but I must go on with my story. A neighbour stepped in on some errand, but, finding Anne from home, was departing, when a low moaning from the inner room arrested her steps. She feared to enter it ; there might be Charley on the bed, and he was a perfect

savage in his cups. She was turning to go, when a child—a more horrible apparition than that presented to Banquo—passed her with two bleeding stumps, which
he deliberately plunged into a vessel of water, which stood in the centre of the
kitchen, plashing them to and fro, with the greatest *sang froid*,—how long, the
spectator could not say, for she lay fainting against the wall, till another accidental
visitor dropped in, and raised an alarm. As a sample of the father, he clapped
his hands on hearing of the accident, exclaiming, "The boy is a gentleman for
life—the parish must look after him." The less brutal mother exhibited some
traces of remorseful sorrow, and thought, I believe, that she made the boy the best
possible *amende*, by deserting the rest of her children, from that time forward, for
the greater part of the year, in order to exhibit the little mutilated fellow at fairs
and markets, and at coach-windows, to the peril of future generations. This
vagabond life was pursued by mother and son till a short time before the last
illness of Charley Curtis, the father, respecting which, I find the following
memorandum in an old pocket-book :—"Mr. P——— visited a spent-out sot,
dying of a stricture. His poor mutilated son lay at his feet, disabled from a
drunken broil of the preceding night ; yet did the wretched father constantly
endeavour to neutralize the clergyman's admonitions to the younger sinner, by
offering excuses for him. We shall not often meet with such zeal in their Master's
cause among the children of light." The mother, I remember, drew a pitiable
picture of the impotent rage which her husband displayed towards this very lad,
when, after endeavouring to strike him with his dying hands, he would weep from
disappointed rage. But now, I rejoice to say, John is very steady,—"brings in
his gettings ;" he is postman to a mine with a salary of two guineas a month, and
reads and writes of evenings. What a fine, flourishing specimen I reckon I shall
have for my scrap-book !

We stopped a minute at the door of poor Bettens, sinking fast into the miner's
consumption, and finished our round by knocking at 'Un Sally's door. "Nobody
in, sa-ar," cried a little voice, which proved to be Nickey's, who, like his betters,
had his private reasons for declaring himself "not at home." He was deeply
engaged in the contraband employment of roasting slices of potato on the fire,
and evidently wished us at Jericho for interrupting his cookery. I was restored to
favour, in the end, by giving him sixpence for as many bantam eggs, which were
hoarded in a tumbler, over the chimney, in furtherance of "a new hat agin Christmas." 'Un Sally had a new dream to tell. She had been ill, but her "sickness

assuaged," she said, and she fell into a sleepy way. She imagined herself on a public road, where were throngs of people, none of them caring to look upon her; so she passed alongside of the hedge, as usual, "mourning her cause," when she perceived a person approach, who, they told her, was a great physician for the soul, but whom she knew by intuition was the Saviour of mankind. He had a pen or pencil in his hand, but she did not notice either book or tablet. Advancing with passionate eagerness, she pronounced her name, Sally Fox, when the man turned, and, looking graciously upon her, said, "*That* name I have written down already." Her tone and action, when relating this part of the vision, were quite Siddonian—'Un Sally is at least the tragic muse of *humble* life.

The circumstances of our visit to "the oldest woman," &c., I did not dilate upon, because it was quite uninteresting; at least, the only sensation excited by it was that of fear, lest we should fall through the various holes in the floor of her chamber, an eminence which we attained at the risk of our necks, by means of a really perpendicular ladder, which would have defied access to any person less versed than Kate and I are in scrambling over the Cove rocks.

The old woman was a perfect vegetable; at least, the only sign she gave of animal life was the extending of her hand after her daughter had "insured her" who it was who stood by her bedside, and bidding us to sit down upon the bed, for there was nothing there to hurt us. Of *spiritual* life, alas! there was no gleam. "The dull, cold ear of death" itself would not be more deaf to the blessed name which I tried to ring in her ears. Nay, the time will come when that will be roused at His voice! But, who knows? she may have done her work before those evil days come upon her.

WALK XXVII.

Mary King. An inexpensive mode of doing good.

HERE is no sweet cottage smile that I love better to be greeted by, than Mary King's—altogether, I do not think I ever met such perfectly guileless manners.

We were unavoidably speaking of some frail parish sister, and naturally slid into philippics on the degeneracy of female manners. "How *are* they so?" asked Mary, in that half-pitying, half-reproachful voice, which showed that she was a dove, and not a dragon, in virtue; "I can't fancy how they *are* so" —then, with a rich blush, "I was married a twelvemonth before he there" (pointing to her eldest) "was born." She then related a little story of her own courtship, which I might have divined, without being the conjuror she would have taken me for, if I had said, "Mary, you admire your husband more now than when you married him.

"'Once a man, and twice a child;' and worse than a child, a fine deal," said old Polly Freathy, from her bed at the Workhouse, proving, by the way, that *her* second childhood had not extended to her vigorous mind. I threw her into ecstacies by the gift of a new pair of spectacles; her eyes had long survived the old ones. As soon as she had saddled her nose to her satisfaction, she seized her Testament, and, plunging at once into the Book of Revelation, broke out into a Doxology, which, but for the sacredness of the text, would have made me smile.

"Glory! Honour! Power! This puts me back forty years! Blessed be His name!" &c. I have been more fortunate than Moses in the "Vicar of Wakefield," in my bargain of spectacles; these had, in truth, no silver rims to beguile my judgment, but were all as rusty as an anchor, so I got them cheap, and in no conceivable way, probably, could money have been better spent. Many a "small prent" Bible is laid on the shelf; many a jacket left unmended; many (for some will work, whether they can see or not) an eye is made worse by straining it, for want of "a fitty pair of spurticles." Then, there is the collateral benefit for which I always stipulate, that the superceded pair shall be given to some younger person, who is beginning to feel the want of "glasses." I am really proud of having hit on this means of doing good at a small expense.

WALK XXVIII.

THE COVE, MARCH, 1837.

The charms of spring. Gulls.

PRING! This was the first spring day—to the *feelings*, I mean. We talk, we sing, all the year round, of the charms of spring, but, in fact, know little about it, till suddenly, in a walk, or through an open window, it steals upon our hearts by means of a hundred "sweet influences." Perhaps, the most tangible of these (query) is the first discovery of a few half-opened primroses, peeping out, as I saw them two days ago, in Trelease Lane, from out the embanked roots of a hedge-row tree, like infancy smiling from the mother's lap, &c., &c.; but that is another feature of spring, that it makes us do our best to be poetical. * * * * * * *

I spied "Uncle John" sunning himself, or, as our miners term it, "eating the sun," under a hedge, after his morning's labour of driving the horses at the mine, and completed his felicity by giving him the portion of tobacco that fell to his share. As the boy wished to be a king, that he might swing all day on a gate, "and eat fat bacon," so Uncle John probably could imagine no better use of royalty, than the privilege of lying in a sunny hedge, chewing his quid; while I, for my part, wish to be a queen, that I might bestow a handsome estate on Benjamin, and build you a cottage, either among the wild thyme on the cliff-side, or in the valley, which (sheltered and wooded as it is) commands a pretty little framed-in view of the sea and its passing sails. Now I think on't, I will build them *both*, and then you can take up your winter quarters in Glen-Lou, and return to your cliff dwelling in the month of June, to bless your eyes with the view with which mine, as I write, are ever and anon feasted ; for, be it known, I have resumed my perch at Bessey's Cove (where I hope soon to take up my permanent station) for a day. Vellanoweth had almost spoiled it, by making a road for his carts to bring up oreweed, just opposite our window. I was sorely vexed with him, in spite of his beautiful old Cornish name, but he has shown so much good taste in his line-of-beauty sweep, from the green summit down to the beach, that I have made up my quarrel with him. Then, the carters' cadence, mingling with the voices of the fishermen, and their hollow-sounding preparations for going out to sea, adds considerably to the life of the scene—not to omit the gull, whom I should have left out, if she hadn't, at this very instant, sailed past the window. They certainly must have taken the idea of the *waltz* from the elegance of her attitudes and motions, only that our gull is too wise to·make a teetotum of herself. The posture-master has unquestionably borrowed his light from that graceful, self-sustained flight, giving at once the impression of repose and vigour, pastime and purpose ; for while our visitor sails over the Cove, with all that air of elegant leisure which belongs to the high-bred dame, I observe she has generally some good house-wifely object in view—a pool full of "miller's thumbs," or, haply, a straggling sea-fish, or (if all the truth must be told) those portions of the fish which I do not like to name, nor the fishermen to bring away from the shingles, the idea of which it is difficult to associate with that of a creature, whose pure ivory whiteness should have been nourished by ambrosia, at least.

WALK XXIX.

A Tragedy.

WE went, this morning, to Goldsithney, in search of a poor woman, whose husband had beaten her truly "within an inch of her life." Report *did* say she was dead, but this, luckily for Jack Bawden, was not the case, and *unluckily* for society, who have thus lost a fine warning, and retained a pernicious member. We knew very well where the woman lived, for she had been a patient of ours, but, as she had escaped, at midnight, from the ruffian's hand, we had to find out with which of her relations she had found shelter. At length, we traced her to her brother's, Captain Edward Williams, up at Wheal Carline, in what was formerly the 'count-house, and there received from the sister-in-law such a harrowing relation of the case as Tragedy herself, with Shakespeare for her amanuensis, could not have improved upon. The narration, in fact, reminded me of some among his tales, and showed that he had not exaggerated the effects of an evil temper, exasperated by jealousy. Not Desdemona, nor Hermione, high dames as they were, possessed a higher value for the jewel of their sex, than poor Betsey Bawden, or showed more conjugal devotion. Often, her sister-in-law said, she had cheerfully brought forward the best in her house, to give to her husband and his riotous companions, when she and her children had gone hungry to bed. Latterly, the wretch had taken mightily to a young man called Carter, brought him to his house at all hours, and woe had it been to his wife if she had not received him cordially. It was on this object that his jealousy suddenly fixed. After maligning his innocent wife at the alehouse on a Saturday night, insomuch that he drew upon himself the indignant rebukes of his not-over-sober companions, he rushed home, in order to vent his madness in the dreadful manner which it is painful to relate, and difficult—for my memory has let slip some of the graphic touches, which made it so interesting from the lips of the kind protectress.

Betsey Bawden, it seems, was lying on her bed, surrounded by her children and

P

mother-in-law, about midnight, expecting the return of her husband. She was in her clothes, for it had been her custom to retain them till his return, at whatever late hour, since the time that he drove her, almost naked, into the night air, pursuing her with a knife, which, once or twice, came in contact with the bone of her stays. On that occasion, she owed it to the kindness of a distant neighbour, that she did not perish from cold. The wonder is that she should ever return to the doors from which she had been thus expelled; but—they enclosed her eight children, and maternal love is stronger than death. This happened several months ago. Think of the wretch's refinement in cruelty; at the time of which I am writing, having announced to his wife that he intended to kill her, he sent down his boy for a bason of water and his "own knife." It was a thing (blade and handle) of a foot-and-a-half long, made by a blacksmith, under his own express directions, a short time before. He commanded the child also to bar the door, lest his mother's cries should bring assistance. One could hardly believe that a child of ten years old would obey these directions, if one did not allow for the stupefaction consequent on extreme fear, and the poor things, it seems, had long lived under a reign of terror. With frightful premeditation, the man placed the water by his side, knotted a strong cord into a scourge of nine knots (the poor always "mind their quantities"), doubled it, made it secure by coiling it round his right hand, while his left grasped her mouth, lest her cries should bring help. In this situation, he bade her own her guilt, which she, meekly refusing to do—indeed, the detail is too revolting to write down, what must it have been to witness! The old mother, past eighty, tottered to the spot, and threw herself across the daughter-in-law, to defend her from the ruffian's blows, some of which, dreadful to say, she received herself; the eldest daughter hung on his collar, entreating mercy for her mother; but such feeble resistance could not long suspend the work of blood. After flinging his mother over stairs, and turning her into the night air, when all the assistance she could afford was to cry murder, the brutal parricide returned to his occupation. I forget how he disarmed the daughter, whose tenderness for her mother seemed to have risen above the fear which kept the other children (even to the youngest) silent and motionless. I think he had her down in some way. It is impossible (for if I had the heart I have not the power) to record what followed in the strain of indignant eloquence, worthy of Paulina herself, with which Mary told it. Two traits, I remember, one particularly touching, and another particularly shocking! Between the dreadful acts, he took draughts of water to allay the thirst which, it seems, his victim's blood was insufficient to slake, exclaiming, with a fiendish laugh, "now, this refreshes me." The affecting trait, which to hear made poor Betsey Jenkins's heart overflow at her eyes, was that, four distinct times, the poor soul obeyed her husband's commands to kneel before him with meek submission, but, when told she might purchase his mercy by confessing the truth of his accusation (owning to the guilt she knew not), she steadily refused. I believe these were her words, as she knelt before him with clasped hands :—" How can I confess this lie, with nothing but death before me ? I see you are intent on my murder! how can I own to the sin which I know not ? as soon could I deny my Saviour as tell you I deserve the name you call me by: that babe on the bed is not more innocent of this charge than I am, and I think I speak it with my dying breath."

And yet, the worthy creature afterwards told her sister that she never lost all hope of life; she thought she was not yet fit to die, and that God would surely send her help before she was quite murdered, bitterly mangled as she was, with scarcely a sound inch in her body, her ears nearly wrenched off, and her breast-bone so crushed that she has yet hardly breath to tell her sad tale. Such meek confidence in divine help is never deceived, but, in regard to the manner of deliverance, we are often mistaken.

It might have been supposed that the old woman's shrieks would have brought a rescue; they did alarm the few neighbours, and draw some to the spot, but so great was the popular terror of the bloodthirsty savage within, that even men, as they called themselves, were not willing to venture in. There was one exception, however—blind Peter (my blessing on him for it), importunately besought the bystanders to give him a stone, with which to "break abroad the door." Had his prayer been granted, no doubt the villain would have stabbed him. After this, blind Peter deserves a chapter to himself, and his story is well worth telling; but, to proceed with the one in hand, or, more properly, to go back with it :—Jack Bawden's brother left the tavern, where the wretch had so villified his poor wife, at the same time as he did, and seeing how he was irritated by the testimony which everyone present had borne to her exemplary character, observed to his own wife on his return home, "Peggy, I am distrustful there will be mischief this night up at Jack's." Peggy concurred in opinion, and, as well as his nephew, insisted upon accompanying him thither, late as it was. They found things in the state in which my narrative left them; consternation without, and a death-like silence within. Robert Bawden stood under the window, calling to his brother by the family name of Jack, and was answered by a peal of curses; but there was one ear that blessed the sound. "From that moment," said Betsey, "I felt my deliverance was at hand." Yet, so stupified was she, that it was many minutes before she could avail herself of the opportunity to escape afforded by her husband's conversing with his brother at the window, or comprehend her daughter's vehement gestures to seize the happy crisis; but, from the moment she felt she had got free from this man, she thinks her feet hardly touched the ground. Her hands befriended her no less than her feet; they at once found, and drew back, the bolts. Her road to her brother's was quite straight and open, but it is probable that she lengthened it, in her distraction, by scrambling through hedges, &c., for thorns were extracted from her flesh for some days after she arrived at her brother's door; "in a whisht condition," the narrator might well say; streaming with blood, half her clothes torn away, her cap entirely so, her hair in strings, hanging over her death-like face—up in that desolate, rubbishing, shaft-windy place, too! what could anyone have thought, if they had met her, but that she was some vexed spirit, returned to haunt the spot, or upbraid the author of her murder? But, it was in a far different temper that poor Betsey told her tale, and laid her mangled body in her sister's warm bed. On the day we called there, she had just crawled out to try if she could reach home to see her younger children, but she fainted by the way.

The man, I should have told, absconded the following morning, not believing, as he confessed to his brother, that the woman could have survived his ill-treatment, but had probably died by the hedge, while making her escape. I can hardly restrain the wish that he may long be tortured by this apprehension, so much do our passions need the restraining words, "Vengeance is Mine."

WALK XXX.

May 2, 1837.

Blind Peter.   The motherless twins.   Tom Floyd.

HAKESPEARE calls samphire-gathering "a dreadful trade," but methinks the term more properly belongs to the occupation of mining, for, besides the chance of breaking his neck, our miner lives in constant peril of consumption, not to mention his peculiar temptation to hasten his end by intoxication, and it is ten to one that he meets a premature death—he may truly say with St. Paul, "in deaths oft;" for, grant that he escapes with his life, mutilation in every revolting form threatens him!

What horrors of this kind, during a residence of twenty years, have we witnessed! The loss of sight is by no means an uncommon case. Sometimes, it is partial, as in the case of our Sunday school assistant-master, John Floyd, but poor Peter lost the sight of the blessed sun at one stroke. He was, when the misfortune befel him, engaged to a very pleasing, but of course very young, girl, for the miners and miner*esses* all marry early. If I remember right, their banns had been published. Her friends—and who could blame them?—wished to break off the match, but Mary was staunch to her vows, and happily the large family which the prudent ones prophesied never arrived; they have only two little girls, who are well out of the way, so that the mother is enabled to resume her occupation at the bal. Peter himself can do a few things—dig the ground for potatoes, and take the potatoes from the ground, &c.—with the help of his little girls; and he can walk to Helston, with their guidance, in order to receive his first pay of one shilling a week. His income is further eked out by the voluntary contributions of his brother miners. At their invitation, he attends the surrounding mines on pay-days, hat in hand, and receives without solicitation whatever they can afford to drop into it. I know this, because little Jennefer is sometimes kept home from the garden, and Mary from the school, to "lead father." They are a pretty-mannered, gentle little pair, bobbing up and down at every word, and side by side, like what they call "a

Q

peer o' stamps," and so exceedingly timid that Jennefer, in her confusion, still calls me "Miss," as well as Kate. I have had my eye on Jennefer, ever since my first visit to the father's cottage. She couldn't be more than three years old, when, hearing me make an observation to her mother respecting her "foolish necklace," she slipped from the room, and returned with the offending ornament quite hidden under the neck of her pinafore. If I remember right, she was, on our next visit, rewarded by one of Kate's nice dolls. I introduced the history of Peter, at this time, to eke out the scanty adventures of this day's walk; run, I might more properly call it. The weather was stormy and uninviting, but we had not seen the twin orphans since their mother's funeral, and fancied their worthy protectress, Anne, might deem it unkind. Anne, however, was not at home, we found—she was gone to Marazion on some house-wifely errand, so that Thomas was obliged to marshall us upstairs, and draw the coverlet from the faces of the little Gemini, who occupied the very bed and pillow on which I had lately seen their poor mother's pale, haggard, patient face, and where she drew her last painful breath. It was a touching sight. One of the twain did not look so thriving as her brother; they said he had had the thrush. There was great discussion as to what they should be called : my heathenish suggestion was Romulus and Remus, the diminutives of which, Rom and Re, would have done nicely for our nicknaming neighbourhood; Mr. P—— proposed Valentine and Orson; somebody said Joseph and Benjamin, or Ephraim and Manasseh; but the poor are never fantastical, I think, in these matters; besides, we afterwards heard that poor Betsey had named one infant herself, after a brother who died two years before.

The family were disappointed, that they could not carry the babies to be christened at the time of their mother's funeral, agreeably to a strange and, I must say, very affecting custom which prevails here. She was taken to Breage (five miles), to be laid by her relations, and the weather was too wet and boisterous for them to be exposed to it. Accordingly, they were baptized in this church on the following Sunday, and Thomas himself, looking most woe-begone, "stood forth" for them. We just peeped in on Thomas's mother, who lies dangerously ill at her little farm of Lower Chenoweth. After a long illness, she had at length taken to her bed, being able, she said, to drag her old clay about till then, proving the ascendancy of spirit over body, which makes the distinction, according to my notion, between the vulgar and the refined.

There was a visit, which we paid a few weeks ago, to which I did not advert, at

the time, though few have awakened more eventful recollections. At the end of
ten or twelve years, I can still recall the shudder with which I used to hurry by
the desolate dwelling, once inhabited by Jenny Tucker, contaminated by her
crimes, and finally the destined scene of a coroner's inquest on her body, which
was thought to bear the appearance of having been poisoned. He who had long
been the partner of her crimes, the husband of another woman, was the only
person at whom suspicion could glance in the affair. They were known to have
desperate quarrels, sometimes, but suspicion could *only* glance ; there was not
evidence enough to delay the interment of the blackened and defaced corpse,
respecting which, I recollect the following singular occurrence, related by Mr.
P———, at the time :—When fetched hastily to the poor creature, I think he
found her dying, or having just expired, but the countenance which lay before him
seemed not that of Jenny Tucker, though he knew it to be herself. "Who is she
like ?" he enquired abruptly of the woman who, sitting on the coffin-lid, watched
by her, or rather, waited by her, to perform the last offices. "Tom Floyd," replied
the woman, with a tone and look of corresponding horror—both spectators repeatedly affirmed that it was more than likeness, it appeared *identity.*

Some have imagined that the intense emotion, the concentrated feeling, of the
soul in dying, will communicate its impress to the countenance. Certainly, it is
not uncommon to hear the remark, how very like he or she, in their last moments,
looked to such a person. The vulgar idea in this case seemed to be that the
murdered should resemble the murderer. After this, for many years, I heard but
little of Tom Floyd ; certainly no good.

Among the baskets brought to the Vicarage for flowers, this autumn, was that of
the woman inhabiting old 'Un Sally's cottage. I always admired the pretty
geraniums, through the casement, as we passed to the Workhouse, and made
them an excuse to call.

Whilst I was talking with the woman, a man entered the room, who seemed
quite out of character with the cottage and its appointments ; he was more fit, I
thought, for a banditti's cave—for height of stature, and handsome features, he
might well have been chosen their captain. He seemed unaccountably agitated
at sight of us, and, as if to pass it off, took up a jug, and began to water the
window-plants. The woman looked surprised. "Don't water that, soase ; 'tis
just planted, and well watered—my patience! what makes your hand shake so ?"
Aye, indeed, thought I, what is it that thus palsies that dreadful hand, whose

congenial employment is assuredly not watering flowers; but I was really glad to edge off as fast as manners would allow.

The old shaft-house (so called from a hideous chasm, which yawned so near it that there was only room for a narrow passage between it and the cottage door) has fallen to the ground, for want of a tenant. Only one person, and he was half a villain, and the other half madman, had the hardihood to live in it, after the tale I had related. I confess, between terrors ghostly and bodily, I should always avoid the road, were it not a short cut to my favourite walk: and St. Erth Vicarage, without this abbreviation, is almost beyond the limits of a foot journey.

WALK XXXI.

THE COVE, JUNE 27, 1837.

Seaside flowers and insects.   Youthful recollections.

WHAT a hideous chasm between this and my last walk! An attack of erysipelas in the head has done me this good, that it has brought me hither to recruit. It was not my purpose to recall anything so disagreeable as my late illness, except to make it stand in contrast with a walk over the cliffs that divide our rocky dwelling from Pengersick Castle. I was far too frail to think of reaching that interesting ruin, made more interesting to Kate and me by a walk thither, last year, in the company of Mr. Fisher, that phœnix of rock and wave companions, who, by the way, was captivated by our scenery, the simplicity of our *manière d'être*—our little dinner-table, under which our four pair of knees almost met. He fell in love with that "omnibus" of household work, Dolly; was so delighted with Harry and his cat, Dido (who watches his boat, from the time it leaves the strand, till it returns at night), that he has written to say he must try and join us during the present vacation. It will be very agreeable to think such an event possible, but, to use a rustic phrase, " I don't put nothing upon it." Nor do I intend to quarrel with my venison, because its flavour is not heightened by currant jelly sauce. This is the season when the cliff sward is most enamelled with flowers, the minute and elaborate beauty of which, I fancy, is nowhere equalled. The exquisite little blue butterfly, I think they call it Alexis, with a fine green embroidery on its nether wings, flies about in great numbers; he scarcely stirs the flower on which he lights, and seems to feel intensely happy, verifying, by his rapturous gestures, Kate's observation, that this is the paradise of insects. Her quaint remark, when observing some of the caterpillars, that "Adam had done well to imitate the obedience of these little beings, and stuck to his allotted vegetable," is rather too fantastic to record, only that the vow is upon you to pardon and, when you can, relish our nonsense.

I have more yet to add: we gathered samphire to eat with our cold veal; we eyed wishfully some water-cress that grew half-way down the cliff, and we admired the sails, from the tiniest fishing-boat, up to the portly vessel (which Kate told me I must call a barque, it being the generic name for all vessels of three masts): in short, there was nothing our eye took in we did not admire, except a steam-vessel, with its diagonal pillar of smoke. One almost wonders the ocean does not spurn this great unsightly monster from her pure and majestic bosom.

It is not often that I cavil at any expression of yours, especially when it has—and when has it not?—poetry and feeling in it; but, I said to Kate, I have a great mind to carry home a nosegay of these flowers (in spite of dear Mrs. Wood); they would become our cliff cottage better than ixias and roses. You remember the little anthyllis, of every color and shade, that carpeted poor old Carthon, and which, in those days of grammarie and romance, we named Titania's honeysuckle? It is now in its prime here, and powerfully restored to me those long-departed scenes, "when first it moved remembrance."

Were you of the party (I think not) when, by a concerted scheme, and a hot circuitous road, we conducted to a bank, covered with these flowers and nestled amongst rocks, styled by us "Titania's bank," a party of young friends, affecting to wish, all the way, as we scaled the cliff, that her fairyship would regale us with tea—not out of buttercups filled with dew, but a good substantial tea-kettle meal?

Except Mrs. Siddons's scream, in the mad scene of "Venice Preserved," nothing has made a livelier impression on my memory than dear Elizabeth

Reynolds's shriek, on arriving on the brink of the little sheltered dell, and seeing, "withouten hands," all the spirit-reviving apparatus of a hearty English tea! The centre of the bank was covered with cakes, bread and butter, cream and treacle (a conjunction always entitled "thunder and lightning" by the sea-side, and nowhere else), cherries, "ripe cherries," and strawberries. In an angle steamed a large black tea-kettle, placed, gipsy fashion, over an extempore fire of dry turfs and sticks. The Being of grosser element, meanwhile, who prepared all these good things, kept out of sight. If I remember rightly, Louisa and Sarah acted the Titania part; to play Puck, and to take my guests as far, and make them as thirsty, as I could, was mine. Alas! shall I ever cease to be a child? It is no use to deny it, I should enjoy such a stratagem now, as much as I did thirty years ago.

As we passed the Station, we saw the preventive-boat go by, in her best holyday trim, filled with happy, fresh-looking Jack Tars, to help at the ceremony of our Queen's Proclamation.

WALK XXXII.

JUNE, 1837.

Consumption.   Polly Freethy.   St. Peter's Eve.   Miners.

THE poor young creature—Tucker by name—who was lately brought home to the Workhouse, is assuredly dying. She owes, perhaps, her chief interest to her complaint, consumption; yet she showed she was not devoid of sensibility, by weeping, when I adverted to the mistress's great kindness. There is no knowing what is passing in her poor mind, for she is habitually silent, and now wants breath to speak; but she shakes her head, with an air of sorrowful assent, when admonished to improve the short time which remains to her. The happiest thought remaining to her is that "much has not been given." She entered on service, stigmatized with a mother's shame; fell into the hands of a godless master, to whose brutality she ascribes her broken constitution; and, without merit or friend to recommend her to decent service, has since had reason to regret even the shelter that his roof afforded her. Bating the sufferings of disease, the Workhouse must be the happiest asylum the poor orphan has ever known. Her bed is clean, and tolerably warm; the food, such as it is, ample; and the mistress ever ready to bestow that sympathy which is more than diet and sleep to the destitute: moreover, I supply her with *liquorice*, which, absurd as the anti-climax sounds, is the greatest comfort she knows.

Two doors off is poor old Polly Freethy, at length a confirmed bed-lier. For a long time, she bore up bravely against this penalty of a protracted life—her tall figure has been a perfect triangle for years, to the added terror, no doubt, of her little bunch of scholars. When forced to give up her school, and take refuge in the Workhouse, she continued to exercise her scholarship and needle. Instead of burning her nose over the grate, and grumbling that it was not duly replenished, like her aged compeers, we generally found her making a couch of the window-seat, with her poor bent back thus stayed, mending a night-cap, &c., or poring over an old *curl* (carol), which she always read with a loud voice. I think she was glad to see me, for we talked of old times, when I used to visit poor old Ralph, her husband. He was an awesome man—sick, and poor, and old, as he lay, I felt really afraid of him. He is the only being I remember, who came up to Sir Walter's description of "*douce* Davie Deans," and, if I had then (twenty years ago), read "The Heart of Mid-Lothian," I should have believed I saw the old covenanter on his death-bed. One little incident I cannot help recording, to my own confusion. Paying him a visit, in company with my sister-in-law, Miss Pascoe, he said, pointing to an open Bible, that "there was a passage he wished explained." I felt alarmed at the thought of expounding before so great a critic, but obeyed the summons by approaching his bed. "Not you," he cried, waving me off with the official majesty of a prophet, "let her come near," meaning poor Sally, who confessed afterwards that she quite quailed at the summons; however, she needed not, for the querist himself assumed the office of interpreter, and gave us a little homily on the words, "the wicked have no bonds in their death."—Ps. lxxiii. 4.

To return to the Workhouse. Old Polly's reminiscences of her husband seemed, I thought, tinctured with a little wholesome terror; but she had had "a peck of troubles since his death." Jenney and Effie—I forget their real names—both married, and, at no long distance of time, died, leaving their old mother alone.

Her son built her a room at the end of his new cottage on the higher downs. He is one of Madame Trevelyan's* mud tenants, to whom she presents a Bible each, and whose little shrubberies she enriches with a grant of fine shrubs, which they take pride in shewing off, and calling by all manner of names.

Poor old Polly's gaunt form was so doubled up in her little tenement, that it never recovered the perpendicular; but her spirit, as I have said before, bowed down as it was by sorrow and want, retained its energies, as many a luckless scholar could testify.

June 29. I might have given you a *nocturnal* walk, for a change, dear Maria, but I feared, for the first time in my life, the night air and wet grass. I declined, therefore, to join the party to the Point, and so missed seeing the fireworks set off round the Bay, in celebration of St. Peter's Eve (for what reason, the oldest inhabitant could not explain), and I had the less reason to regret them, as Kate returned "bedabbled with dew," and went straight to bed.

A few years ago (but the attraction then was the revels of Midsummer—St. John's Eve—when the Bay and its Mount are circled with living fires), Grace† and I walked to Cudden Point at a still later hour. It was pretty enough to see the flickering of torches, which our Bachantes, running at full speed, carried, and the more substantial bonfires on the heights. My handmaid was delighted, but I, somehow, thought the glowworms, which gemmed the furze bushes all the way along the cliff, much more attractive, and they were to be seen every night—the one reason, perhaps, why no one cares for them.

The manner in which, in our country, folks congregate at the funeral of a person who has died a violent death, is an example of the love of the uncommon. What droves of women and children there will be to witness the interment of a poor miner, whose death took place at a mine mis-called Wheal Prosper! As he was hacking in an old shaft, the ground gave way above him, so precipitately as not to afford him time to recover his standing position. His nephew, who was working near by, could hear him speak from beneath many thousand tons' weight of earth, and distinguish the directions he gave about the part of the heap he would have the best chance to extricate him from. Alas, the more exertion the young man made to this end, the faster the earth fell in. "I can do no more, Uncle," he

---

* Note by Miss Willyams. "Madame Trevelyan," afterwards Lady Currington ; a most accomplished lady, and a most kind benefactress to her simple Cornish tenantry.

† A much valued servant.

said, "I must go for help." "Then I must trust in the Lord for help;" and, probably, these were the last words the poor man uttered, for, when a party of miners at last reached down to where the body lay, it was without a symptom of life. The deceased left nine children, most of whom, in defiance of this warning, will pursue the same "dreadful trade."

The very sports of the miner, like those of the leviathan, are full of terror. No later than Midsummer Eve (a week ago), a lad whom I know well had his cheek shattered, and his eye blown out, by the untimely explosion of a kind of firework which has been invented by the mine-boys. They bore, I apprehend, a succession of holes in the rock, which they fill with gunpowder, and then set fire to, having provided a sort of safety valve, which, in the ardour of play, they sometimes neglect—not unfrequently, indeed; for it was only this time last year that a poor lad fell back a corpse in the arms of his brother, owing to a precisely similar inadvertence. But warning avails nothing to a miner: they are all fatalists, and, in nine instances out of ten, you will find that the doomed victim, or some of his family, will have dreamed of the coming misfortune.

WALK XXXIII.

JUNE 30, 1837.

Emigrants. Vessels in danger.

UR hour-glass runs golden sands, and every minute that passes seems a precious grain lost to us. This sounds fanciful, but it is not fancy; witness this morning, when, musing on my perfect happiness, I said to myself, what could be the drawback to it? I looked this way and that, and found I could not recall it, or mend my lot; and then I looked upward in devout acknowledgment, and prayer that so rich a portion might not prove a

s

snare to *us*—for Kate and I, in point of taste and sentiment, are the Siamese twins.

There is to be a move in the Preventive Service for which we are sorry, because, by the removal of her father to Scilly, we shall lose the good offices of the pretty, gentle Dora—Dora Neale, what a sweet name! and she is as sweet as her name. I want to get her a Cornish place, to rescue her from the improvident habits of an Irish mother, and still more from the ignorance and error of, I cannot say the Roman Catholic *faith*, for error implies its existence, and these poor people seem to have no religion at all. They are too remote from a chapel (the nearest is at Falmouth) to attend its worship, and may not enter a Protestant church; therefore, Sabbath they have none. Yet Neale (so we were told by one of the English boatmen's wives) has a most papistical disdain of our churchmen, taunting them with their "few points of faith," he himself holding eight hundred and thirty. When our old friend Mr. Crispo (the emigrant) commanded at the Station, he used to call together these discordant professors, on rainy Sundays, and always of an evening, to hear a good Christian homily; but since then the men have been less fortunate in their presiding officer, and we have had a loss, in our way, of that single-hearted couple, of whose further progress through the backwoods of Canada I am longing to hear. I do not think their character and mode of life is much changed. Mrs. C———, with her one servant and nine children, must have lain down as weary, and risen as full of care, at Prussia's Cove, as in her log-house, and seen as few strange faces—perhaps fewer, for she writes me they have neigh-bours now within reachable distance. Then, Miss C——— and Sophia cannot, in whatever quarter of the globe, but lend a hand to keep the children and mend the clothes; and John and Francis have well exchanged the culture of a few weather-beaten cabbages for the more profitable exercises of cutting and chopping. Their mother gives them the character of excellent axe-men, and says they supply the house with fuel, which is no baby's play in such a climate.

There is another feature of emigration (I was thinking yesterday, when I heard an arrangement for a party on the water, between our landlady, Kate, and Dolly) which equally belongs to this primitive spot—a community of labours and pleasures. On the present occasion, however, Kate and self took fright at the idea of sea-sickness, and so the maids went without her.

They sailed, in the first place, to view the "Bishop's Rock," which they say (sad augury for Episcopacy) is tumbling down, and then proceeded to Porthleven, where, to their unexpected delight, they arrived in the bustle of a fair, and—

rather a queer conjunction!—a Sunday-school tea-drinking. They returned very late, Kate and I, *à la* Canada, boiling our own tea-kettle, and trying to soothe the rugged heart of Captain Will, through the open window, by a moonlight duett and an occasional nod of sympathy. He, after sniffing about for something to eat, with the amiable demeanor of Bruin in the fairy tale, fetched himself out a block of wood and a care-soothing pipe, and sat sullenly watching the coast all along to Porthleven.

In pursuing my parallel between the emigrant's life and ours, I omitted one of the most prominent affinities ; I mean our dependance on the day's sport for a dinner.

These hot cliff suns have proved fatal to the provisions we brought with us ; we have been obliged to give them to our Esquimaux, and in return to purchase their turbot and mullet. Our host and his sons are not genuine fishermen ; they derive their maintenance from lobster stores, the contents of which are duly called for by a smack, and conveyed to London, &c. Now the first of all sorts which they catch in a net called a trammel, are generally used for bait ; only that they favour Dolly with the *élite*. Let me make your inland mouths water :—yesterday we had a turbot, which was hardly dry from the salt water before it was put into the fresh, and the day before some red mullet, with livers large enough to vindicate their knighthood and *soubriquet* of sea-woodcock.

July 1. I can hear the sea murmur, in my little white bed, along the hollow roof (for I think I have told you of the curious place of concealment, between the roof and wall, contrived by the old Smuggler King, in order to outwit the exciseman). Last night, it was something above a murmur that lulled me to sleep. This place is so quiet that an impulsive movement, or an elevated voice, makes one think something has happened. Thus it was this morning, when, sitting composedly at work, I was attracted to the window by hearing a sudden exclamation from Cornish (one of our young fishermen), who, with uplifted arm, was running down the cliff, crying out, "She is surely on the Stone !"

We could only watch with lively anxiety the motions of the seemingly fated vessel. Our little congregated band of fishermen appeared to think that, if she had not already fallen on the sunken rocks, she would never be able to thread herself free of them, and promised us that, as soon as the danger was apparent, they would "row to the assistance of the crew." But it was decreed otherwise, and the vessel (with the souls on board no less unconscious, perhaps, of their late deliverance) bravely pursued her course. This is the second vessel for which our experienced seamen have had serious apprehensions, in the course of the last few days. Both were in danger past the skill of man to escape, but they have escaped, unconsciously, perhaps, to themselves. "Oh, that men would therefore praise the Lord."

In a former walk to the Cove, I think I mentioned that my all-observing companion had spied the mast of a vessel, in what she thought an unnatural position, and which, in the event, proved to be a wreck, drifted on this coast; where from, whither bound, no soul has been able to guess. The hulk took up her final station off Great Cudden, from whose point her masts were sometimes visible; but now every vestige has disappeared, and her history will remain a secret till that day when "the sea shall give up her dead."

You will think we never *walk* here, I write so journalwise, but indeed we do; we visit the boatmen's wives, pay a charity visit to a sick gude-wife, bring some moths from the valley, and leaves for Kate to print off. Following Kate's idea of the Insect Eden, I should say this is the Paradise of Weeds, and, for the self-same reason of loneliness, the Paradise no less of Birds. The blackbirds and thrushes will perch on a tree on either side of you, and challenge each other to a trial of vocal skill, for as long as you will stay to listen; and the sweet little yellow-hammers will perch on a hedge-row twig long enough and near enough for you to take a lesson from them.

And now tell the truth, dear M———, are you not glad that this is Saturday afternoon, when Kate and Dolly and I must soon set out for the Vicarage, in order to receive the master, on his return from a week's Sessions? Whether he will consent to our coming hither again next week, is yet in the breast of absolute authority, and not even to be guessed at; but, at all events, I can say with Lord Byron, "I have been blest."

WALK XXXIV.

THE COVE, JULY 8, 1837.

A farewell.   An escape.   Spinny's history.

E have had an adventure! One of Kate's squirrels gnawed his way through his cage, and escaped over cliff. The alarm was given; all the chivalry of the place were in arms—dogs, cats, and fisherboys. Some of the latter jeoparded their lives by plunging into the most precipitous parts of the cliff-brake, where they supposed the fugitive had taken shelter (for Miss Kate is mighty popular). One man had his feet held whilst he hung perpendicularly over cliff, in order to grope among the tangled weeds. As a last resource, a muzzled hound was caught by a young farmer, and put on the scent; but all in vain. The refugee had, perhaps, found some snug cleft in the rock, where he sat more at his ease than the poor Baron of Bradwardine under similar circumstances; for these creatures are little nothings, though they make a very imposing appearance, with their plumy tails arched over their heads. It would have been a sight to see him bounding from rock to rock, under the inspiration of recovered liberty. This was the "*tree* squirrel;" the other is on his native element, "the *ground*," and is much tamer. When Captain Will came home at night, he was greatly concerned to hear of Miss Kate's misfortune, and in the true spirit of the old smuggler, to whom difficulty is motive, vowed (I wish he might not *swear*) that, "dead or alive, he would have him in the morning." He went to bed, and, like Captain Hall's old sailor, slept with all his might, in order to be up early: and so he was; and over the hills before the sun, "a-chasing the wild *dear*." At four o'clock, he knocked at the cabin window, bidding Harry rise and come out, "dressed or undressed," to help him catch the squirrel, of which he had caught a sight. Poor Harry, knowing with whom he had to deal, obeyed to the letter, and positively pursued the fugitive without stocking or shoe, "thorough brake, thorough briar," till the runaway was taken in the tank, and rescued from the double danger of drowning and being devoured by Harry's cat.

T

WALK XXXV.

The Dove.   Penair.

SEEING the cutter pass, which was to convey poor Neale and his family to Scilly (in exchange for a sick preventive-man), we all three walked to the Station to take leave. What a lovely thing was this preventive-cutter ! She seemed almost conscious of her beauty as she lay at anchor under the Station ; so beautifully proportioned, so slight, so delicately trim and neat—her fair " woven wings" half furled, yet seeming only to wait an impulse to spread out and "flee away." I give him credit who named her the " Dove."

Before I take leave of those two good things, yourself and the Cove, I will just tell you that we expect a visit to-night from Mr. Penrose, author of one of the most celebrated series of the Bampton Lectures—*you* know them, I dare say—and he has written something else since. He is lionizing with his sisters at the Land's End, and has a mind to rub up his old Penair acquaintance with me. I was *very* young when I knew him first, and he was prodigiously tall, with a mouth like an ogre. Playing with Julia, his cousin, in a hay-loft (two little girls we were then), he strode up to us, and, before we had recovered our first surprise, he threw us into a second by popping us one after another into a great corn-bin, stepping in after us, and shutting down the cover ! It was well it was not a mistletoe bough affair —how it would have puzzled the curious to account for three such incongruous skeletons ! Mrs. Penrose (his lately deceased wife) was the Mrs. Markham whom future generations will have reason to bless for juvenile histories of England, France, &c. Did you ever hear why she assumed the name ? Her father, Major Cartright's seat was called Markham.

WALK XXXVI.

An old sailor and his ship.

"CHANGE came o'er the spirit of my dream," I may say with Lord Byron, for I find myself in the midst of a busy seaport town; I hardly know how, though too surely I know why. Dear Kate's health has long demanded such a change as a migration from the bland south to the elastic north coast, and here we have the last in perfection. The air is clear and springy, and the walks inviting and prolific of interest. Sometimes we go to the strand, and wander amongst the vessels which have been hauled up for repair, after the injury they sustained in the late gale, so destructive by sea and land.

This morning something went wrong in the labours of one of the proprietors of a vessel under repair. He was an old captain, and of course expressed his indignation pretty freely at these repeated *contretemps.* "Do not swear, my friend," said Mr. P———. "I tell you," he replied, "it is enough to make a parson swear." "I hope not, my friend," rejoined the former; but I believe the old seaman was unconscious of his own repartee.

Away further off was a little thick-built man in a dreadnought, who, between age and tobacco, had hardly a tooth left in his good-humoured round head, but his merry eyes contained all their youthful fire, and he answered our questions with ready frankness.

"Why, your vessel is like the Irishman's knife, my friend; new blade and new handle," said uncle.

"You say truly, sir,—and more than that, for the blade is where the handle should be. The old planks that came out of the bottom, I've made serve for her deck."

"Was she new when you bought her?"

"New!" repeated Jack, turning an eye of fondness on her, as he might on the wife of his bosom, on hearing her complimented on her young looks. "New, master? I'll tell ye just how new she is. Ever since I have had a wish to be owner of a vessel—and that's as long as I can remember—I've saved every bit of plank that came honestly in my way, and all that I could reach in the way of purse I bought, for I knew well enough it would all come handy. There they are, every plank of them; all heart of oak."

WALK XXXVII.

A great "traveller." An apparition.

HE observation is common enough, and true as common, that Nature teems with beauties and wonders, if we would give ourselves the trouble to look into them. There are also moral wonders of which we take as little heed, and but few turn aside to draw from their concealment. For my part, I have a positive taste for inspecting and dissecting, as it were, the minds of the honest people I encounter on my rambles, and feel myself as well repaid as the disciple of Withering, who pokes his sagacious nose into every bank and hedge.

Walking up the Terrace Hill this morning, I encountered an old woman, who, wanting the usual keys to sympathy, the appearance of sickness or need, I addressed with the usual prologue, the weather.

"Aye, madam, it *is* fine weather, but *slottery* under foot."

"You seem a good traveller, however,"

"Like enough: I have travelled afoot as much as most,—I s'pose I have walked to every place in the county, I may say; why, I've travelled ninety-two miles in twenty-four hours, and took never a wink of sleep, only just a dish of tea, from St. Ives to Mevagissey and back again."

"You know Mrs. S———and Mr. R. H———," said I, rather for something to talk about, than any doubt of the fact.

"Know Mr. H——— and Mrs. S———?" exclaimed Betty; "yes, fie! and poor Miss Mary and Dr. H———."

There is a mischievous tenacity of memory in some folks—the doctor, so dubbed by Betty, now stood high in the squirearchy of St. Ives; only second to his brother-in-law, the member for that ilk; and had probably almost forgotten himself that he was an army surgeon; and yet I think he would never forget having been, as I have heard him say, professionally witness to the cutting off of one of the two handsomest legs in England. The much-extolled limb belonged to the Marquis of Anglesea, and was amputated after the battle of battles—Waterloo.

To return to Betty's less symmetrical, though equally useful, supporters.

"Travelling as you do, night as well as day, and quite alone, don't you sometimes feel fearful?"

"Never in my born days," stoutly replied Betty Quick, for that was her characteristic name; "never but once (she lowered her voice); it was by Rose ———;" here again I lost a gem of a name; but, if I have forgotten place where, I can remember time when, as Betty, like all describers of apparitions, began with, "It was coming on to night—not quite dark, either, for I could plainly discern what I shall hereafter make mention of. Right afore me, and about the distance of yonder brambles, I saw something right across the road. I can't say I felt altogether afraid, to say *afraid*, so I walked up to it, thinking it was some sort of cattle, but withal it seemed to fill the lane—full of men," I fancied she said, and repeated these words enquiringly, "Full of men?" "No, no, it was nought of mortal kind that I saw that night," repeated Betty, somewhat piqued; "I stooped down my head in this fashion, and then I could discern that it had the snout of a swine, and—"

"Probably, it *was* a large animal of the pig kind," I said.

"What animal could that be," retorted Betty, angrily, "when the very nose of un filled up the lane? No, no, 'twas no animal; 'twas the Evil One hisself, as you shall hear; for I called out with a loud voice these words, 'In the name of the Holy One, can't I pass?' Upon that, the form gathered up his fore-legs, and stood along the other side of the hedge, and, as I passed, neither groaned nor growled, and you may depend I did not know whether I was in the body or out of the body, and, if ever the hair stood up on end on anybody's head, so it did upon mine, and yet I couldn't say altogether I was much afraid ; but a young man who passed there that night, with the fright of what he saw, never left it alive."

"Why do you suppose God sent such an apparition ?" I asked.

"For a trial of faith," answered Betty, thinking, and justly, that a fable is nothing without its appendant moral ; and, our roads diverging, we parted.

WALK XXXVIII.

1837.

Pierce.   Mary King's garden.   Jenny Priske.   'Un Sally.

I AM glad, and I hope thankful, to walk again among mine own people, after an illness trying to body and spirits ; but I find poor Pierce, my nearest sick neighbour, has fallen a victim to it,—that is to say, it has given the *coup de grace* to a constitution worn down by near twenty years of sickness. I was struck at seeing his vacant pillow, from which, at our entrance, he always raised his head to make a meek bow ; but I felt glad it was so, as I told his wife, poor Honour, who, with her wonted ingenuity at perplexing the Queen's English, told me she had "no more doubt of his spiritual death than that knife there, and this thought had dried up her tears, if there were any to dry." That most impracticable *A B C D-arian*, her son, sat on the side of the bed all of a scrump, and looking as if he had by no means made up his quarrel with his horn book ; however, he and the girl have promised to attend the Sunday-school, and I was glad to hear Honour expressing her determination to keep the family to-gether. She is really a good intentioned being for a queer body as she is.

Mary King's husband has enclosed their bit of flower-garden in front, from which I already see crocuses and wind-flowers peeping. She says her husband works by moonlight, but that she tells him "that the boys will soon be coming on to bear a hand." The first shade I ever saw cross her frank, sunny face, was when she enquired with solemnity whether we had observed "the element, and how *ghastly* it looked, like a thing on fire, the night before last? She had heard, but couldn't vouch for the fact, that a bright star had been observed right afore the moon."

How often have men's hearts failed them for fear at these elementary variations before the time! Our household had encountered the cold nights, as well as Mary, to gaze at the strange Heavens. It gave me more the idea of a large sublunary conflagration, than any meteorological influence.

The poor, I know not why, are tenacious of a compliment to their healthy looks; Mary laughed at mine, and said, "she believed 'her face did put upon her body,' as the saying is (a saying, by the way, new to me, observer as I am of cottage metaphor) for that she wasn't no great things."

We called, *en passant*, on poor Jenny Priske, whose son has taken away, on his marriage, every chip of furniture, except the three-legged stool on which his poor one-legged mother sits in the chimney-corner. Jenny's *bon mots* do not much enrich my pages, yet it is out of the abundance of her heart that she incessantly repeats the burthen of her sad song, "very weak; very weak, indeed."

Dear 'Un Sarah's indomitable mind rises even above the depressing malady under which she still suffers. She had, as usual, her allegory, her gracious benediction, her appropriate phrase; and all strikingly dramatic. I never see her without thinking of Mrs. Siddons, though it is to be doubted whether even our tragic muse maintained so elevated a bearing on the bed of death.

We looked in at the Workhouse, which has lost, since we last visited it, one sorrowful, suffering inmate—the poor girl Floyd—who, by the way, gave, in her last agonies, another example of the "ruling passion." She lamented she could not see "her dear mistress," and begged Mrs. Treweeke to "take the candle, and look upon her." No sooner had its beams fallen on her convulsed features, than, seeming to have gained her object, she bowed her head and died.

Among our victims to influenza, there is not one I regret so much as old Philly ———. Her daughter-in-law, whom I met yesterday, returning from her sale of oranges, gave me a little account of the dear old soul's last moments. They came on very suddenly, she said, for that on the eve of her death she threaded her needle, with this startling observation:—"My child, I have fastened my thread, but I shall not live to sew it out." "You shall not sew for *me*, mother," rejoined the affectionate daughter-in-law, "sew for your own soul," and took away the work. At night, the old woman lay down as usual, but not to rest. After a few hours, she called Anne to her bed-side, saying, "Pray for me, my daughter." "My faith is weak, dear mother, and my prayers feeble, but, such as they are, you are welcome to them," said I. As the poor mourner told the tale, her tears bore witness to her affection. "If it had pleased God, she wouldn't be without the dear old soul on no account. She died in my arms," she added, with affectionate exultation.

Anne had had a dream, too, which had comforted her heart. "Seeming to her, she saw the dear old woman sitting up in bed, from which she had said, in a tone of kind reproach, "How are ye here, mother, when you know I buried you, to the best of my power, a week agone? I am afraid it is not well with your soul." "Yes, my child," said she, "it is well. I *have* been admitted inside of Heaven's Gate; I have a place to stand within it, and, though it is no bigger than your little fringle yonder, yet I catch the wind of the Saviour's mantle, as he passes along the Courts of Heaven." "She then," pursued Anne, "told me that she was permitted to return to tell me this, and furthermore she promised I should have comfort in my ' going out and coming in ;' and so I have found it," continued Anne, brightening with the thought ; "so I have found it, ma'am, ever since."

WALK XXXIX.

A scene at the Workhouse.

> " Cold blows the wind to-night,
> Cold are the drops of rain ;
> The first true love that ever I had,
> In greenwood he was slain."

THIS is a snatch of what the good governess at the Workhouse calls the old "tragedy tunes," that the poor girl, Mary Stevens, whose history I have already related, chaunts forth in her—fits, they call them, but there is vastly too much method in her ravings for the effect of spasm. She is either possessed or—I do not like to write the word—a deceiver. If the latter, she is sworn sister to Caraboo, and hardly less adroit at the trade.

I ventured to hint my imaginings to the good governess, who told me the overseer (a shrewd man, and eke an old smuggler) had dropped a hint to the same effect.

We were advised to drop in at noon, if we would see her in a fit, and the exhibition took place very opportunely, just as we arrived. The evolution of bowing the back, distorting the fingers, and absolutely turning the eyes inside out, were gone through—the last-named, I confess, somewhat staggered my incredulity. She looked so thoroughly demoniacal—so like the possessed in Raphael's picture of the Transfiguration—and there is something extraordinary in the change of colour, from bright to livid, extending to her hands ; while, on the other side, the caution of her language, which is known to have been habitually wild and low-lived ; her exclusive praises of those who were present,—even to old Polly Freethy, whom she is known to hate cordially ; and the malicious pleasure which gleamed from her eyes, when she knocked off the poor old creature's bonnet, who was officiously endeavouring to hold her knees, expressing that she was " only sorry it was not her head "—were, in spite of myself, continually corroborating my suspicions.

v

Time, that best ally to truth, will shew; but, if it turns out that I have wronged the poor creature, I shall be ready to expiate my uncharitableness by going on pilgrimage without boiling my peas.

WALK XL.

Parish map.　Economy of time.　Phrenology.

S we puzzled our way across the Higher Downs to Woodstock, I thought how much I should like to have a map of the parish, and how vastly more useful the study would be of local geography, than that of the distant world, with which we may never come into contact.

Our object this morning was to find out Nancy Harry's new little cottage, which she has so often reproached us with never having "looked upon." No wonder she should be proud of this monument of a husband's sobriety, industry, and skill; she never seems tired of repeating that every inch of it was his own performance; walls, planking, fireplace, even to the setting-in of the window-frames and panes; "and never lost an hour's work, neither."

Time is a material that some contrive to "put ten times so far as other some." Why it is so, I have often heard asked, but never had satisfactorily answered. Is it, I wonder, by taking heed to the 'tis buts? 'Tis but an hour to bed-time, 'tis but ten minutes to breakfast or dinner," or, "'tis but just to warm my hands;" and so our capital of waking hours is squandered, and there is nothing to show for it.

Ninety-nine out of a hundred miners would, on returning from "night core," have gone to bed, or lain down under a warm hedge, "eating sun," or smoked his pipe, that premeditated waste of time; while Harry, this very morn, had finished his wife's day's work of drawing potatoes, to enable her to return to the wash-tub, at which we found her, and then adjourned to the nice little square of garden-ground, to prune the young trees that bordered it. What a pity there are no boys, the havage being so good.

Three little blue-eyed girls sat in a row before the fire, and the fourth, a "maid," was taken up from the cradle to be shown off, and repeatedly pressed to the mother's bosom with a thrill of tenderness that did one's heart good to see. But the poor thing had been ailing with her teeth-cutting, and nothing would quiet the pain but the "doleful community," if you can guess what that is; but perhaps I told you this, among other *malaprops*, before, and you already know that the remedy is neither a Quaker's Meeting, nor a community of Trappists, but simply Dolby's Carminative.

We went this morning to bespeak a turkey of the good-wife of Trevabyn. A forlorn-looking old creature sat by the open chimney, tearing abroad a faggot of furze. I enquired her name. Hosking by her husband, but he was gone, she said, and her children were all married, and had others to care for, and now she was getting old; her arms had gone to nothing, and her feet covered with chilblains, &c., &c. The crippled, feeble movements confirmed her words, and I thought that one who would grapple with such ills, rather than be beholden to charity, was worth knowing, so I said, "Where do you live, my good woman; I mean, where is your home?" "I have no home," she replied, "but what the Almighty has spread over my head." She meant the Heavens, and the sublimity of the sentiment seemed strangely at variance with her most ungraceful efforts to make an oblong faggot of furze pass cross-ways through the door. It was a stubborn trial of strength between the door-frame and tough furze-stalks, till the mistress came and adroitly turned the faggot up on end. I wish Dr. Spurzheim had been there; he would doubtless have detected the organs of higher and lower individuality in the wizened head of the servant, and the fair, laughing brow of the young mistress. "He" or "she is extremely clever," is used—such is the penury of our language— to express indifferently the Prime Minister and his cook, Madame de Staël and her *fille-de-chambre*.

I myself know a learned man who maintained, in the face of the whole family, that a pair of bellows had but one aperture, and that was in the snout; and I met two others, both D.D.s, shuffling away briskly from a cloud that was sailing off, still more briskly, before the wind, in an opposite direction.

So, then, if my clever man had been destined to bellows-mending, he must have starved, while our two doctors would have made sorry Generals, thus flying from a retreating enemy.

———

WALK XLI.

———

Gratitude.   Crazy Kitty.   A good riddance.

IT would be worth walking to Goldsithney only to hear this declaration from the lips of the mother of seven children. "Sometimes I think I am hardly like a mother, I have had so little trouble or sorrow with my children—five of them boys, too—no broken limbs, no rude words, no bad behaviour ('their father wouldn't bear it,' she said in parenthesis, unconscious that she had furnished the master key to this lock of seven wards), so all I can say is, I can't never be thankful enough."

The same sentiment, connected with still more touching circumstances, flows from the lips of Kitty Bray, not long discharged, cured, from the Bodmin Asylum, thanks to the kind, eccentric Dr. Potts. He and Mrs. Potts seem, by her report, to have been kindly interested about her, and no wonder. If you would hear another tale of misery—the parish annals supply little else—this is hers. Twenty years ago, when we first came here, Kitty Johns was a comely, well-grown, sensible young woman, and very "well to do," for her little shop had all the custom of the churchtown. Perhaps she meant to do better, but she made a sad mistake, when she retired from business to marry Bray. He was a man (to borrow the phrase by which her friends would have described him) of an "ugly temper,"—a most significant expression, if you know all it means to convey. It describes one who · is wicked for wickedness' sake, who has a vein of maliciousness, who does not need to be drunk in order to beat his wife, thrash his children, and waste his substance. It describes one who, reversing a fair maxim, regards vice as its own reward, for he is only happy when he has broken the peace of all around him.

The continual grating of such a disposition on one of tenderer texture at length plunged poor Kitty into a sort of crazy melancholy, as harmless as that of her namesake, and almost as picturesque. She did not ask an "idle pin of all she met," but used to follow us with the plaintive entreaty that her poor head might be laid open, and the mischief looked into.

A sufficient sum of her maiden savings had been rescued from her husband's grasp to maintain her awhile at the Asylum, and were there applied with, as I have said, the happiest results. Kate is cured, and, what is better, the wretch miscalled a husband has absconded, no one knows whither; so that, by the aid of a charitable, eked out by a parish, subscription, Kitty is not only restored to her wits and her family, but also to her shop, where we find her, "close-packed and smiling," behind her little counter, whenever we go that way, for she likes a call from "my ladyship."

"When I think of what I have been, and what I am," said she to me the other day, "my only trouble is that I cannot be thankful enough."

WALK XLII.

Betsey Peters and the vicissitudes of her life.

HIS morning we met poor Betsey Peters, with a basket on her arm, and exchanged "good morrows." I feared to say more, she looked so intensely sad, as if another word would have been an intrusion on a sorrow which words could not reach.

She is one of those "never-smile-again" mourners of whom we have specimens,

W

from the king on his throne to the afore-named "' crazy Kate,' roaming the dreary waste," and yet, only a few months ago—such is human vicissitude—there was not a more substantial, influential person in the Parish of St. Hilary, not excepting the parson and his wife, nor even Captain Tom Francis, the owner of that new stone house at Goldsithney, and possessor of the patronage of more than one mine.

Long before I came to the parish, she was the greatest dealer in tobacco and snuff for two miles round, and, I believe, an honest one, though she would take especial care that the scale did not turn in the estimation of a grain of snuff, and would divide and sub-divide her (very) brown paper, till it scarcely covered its contents. In her haste to grow rich, she must needs also keep a school. Pity I did not walk (with my pen, I mean) in those days. What tragic-comic scenes have you not lost in this novel attempt to wield, at once, the Caducius of Mercury, the Ægis of Minerva, and the thunders of Jove. I suppose no mortal ever exercised so wide a dominion out of so small a space. I can think of nothing like it, unless it be Buonaparte governing the whole world from his little Island of Elba, which he did *not*; wherefore Betsey (I forget her maiden name) may be pronounced incomparable.

Perhaps you would like me to describe her person. One likes to know what sort of a body it is which enshrines the master mind, and hers is worthy of its tenant, which is by no means generally the case. Her face and her features, in spite of their roundness, are strong and firm-set, her complexion is dark and unchangeful, her figure tallish, and more than stout in proportion, measuring indifferently, from her shoulders down, about one and a half of her own yards, that awful yard which, while it dispensed tape to the customers, could also reach the row of little heads that were ranged along the forms, as regular and close as the ha'p'oth of pins in the window, where, after the fashion of village shops, stood tops, and twine, and eggs, and combs, and tumblers full of thimbles, and balls of cotton festooned with stay-laces of all hues, with here and there an orange or a biscuit, meriting the character the farmer's boy gives of his Suffolk cheese, "too large to swallow, and too hard to bite," and, hardest to forego, the sparkling crystals of a lump of sugar candy. Ah, many is the time that the relentless Betsey, when seemingly occupied in sub-dividing an atom, and returning half of it to the quivering scale, has nevertheless contrived to rap the sconce of the luckless urchin who was caught casting sheep's eyes at it. Yet it is said to this day that no one brought on the children so cleverly, and general was the regret of the mothers when, emancipating her smaller slaves, she married the aforesaid Peters, a mere *oaf,* who not only wore her chains, but submitted to have them daily "clanked about his ears," a metaphor, by the way, strong and original, addressed to the patron of the Truro Borough by one whom you loved, and who loved and admired you, dear Maria.

But how shall I get back from such a flight to poor silly John Peters, now better known by the title of Betsey Peters' husband?

This rare couple had an only child, a son, who quickly imbibed the lesson taught him, both practically and theoretically, by his mother—he heartily despised, and cruelly maltreated his father, whom—if it were not too shocking to write the word —he is reported to have beaten. As soon as he grew up to big-boyhood, he stoutly resisted even the authority of his awesome mother, crossing her will and vexing her soul, till, like another Frankenstein, she became horrified by the being of her own creation. By the time he had arrived at the age of fifteen or sixteen, she had tried, in fruitless succession, a Sunday-school, a writing-school, a boarding-school, and one or two different trades. The last step was to apprentice him to a respectable saddler at Marazion, but his idle, vicious habits baffled all her plans; he would neither make bridles, nor submit to wear one; he would be nothing long but a lawless vagabond, and in this character it was that he came to the frightful end that I have to record.

Passing the little isthmus that joins the Mount to the mainland in a neighbour's cart, and, it is to be feared, in a state incapable of guarding against the rocky inequalities of the road, he was thrown under the wheels, and killed, it was said, not on the spot, but that, rising and reeling a few paces, he fell down and "word spake nevermore."

His mother heard of the dreadful catastrophe, and followed his remains to the grave, without those indications of vulgar sorrow which have been compared to the cow's lamentations for her calf, which, a few days gone by, she remembers no more, and is agreeably engrossed by the surrounding daisies and buttercups, as if naught had happened.

You can see that Betsey's is a life-long woe, a sorrow in fee; one that—making bold to amplify a thought of Shakespeare's—is for ever upbraiding the overwrought heart for not breaking. What was it now to her that she possessed half the deeds of the cottage-building miners, in pledge of payment for a long arrear of debt? What was it now to her that she had added house to house, and joined field to field, when there was none to occupy? She says it is his soul alone that she thinks about, nothing else; yet did this poor woman set her child a life-long example of Sabbath-breaking and church-slighting.

Thus are scoffers made to be preachers in their turn! At first she soothed her conscience by resolving never again to sell on Sundays, to attend regularly at church, "*and* the means of grace" (being in the phrase of our country quite a distinct thing); but all would not do, so the goods that blocked up the window so long were removed and sold, and replaced by a huge vine in an enormous flower-pot, being the only creditable vestige of the unhappy boy. He had planted the seed of a raisin, and, strange to say, it had sprouted into a living vine. Possibly, the poor mother derives comfort from the symbol.

The first time I took courage to call, I said, "You have given up your shop, Mrs. Peters; have you done well?" "I was obliged to," she said; "I should have given away all I had." This short sentence, all she seemed disposed to utter, spoke volumes. That one so thrifty by nature and habit should suddenly become wholly regardless of personal interest; the lately worshipped idol ground to dust and scattered to the winds—what was this but the hand of a jealous God?

I should have had my fears for poor Betsey's wits—so sad, so silent, so self-imprisoned—had I not glanced at the canary's cage, and seen that the little bright pet had been duly fed and tended. And since then I had the satisfaction to hear from a cantankerous gossip that lives opposite, that she had no great opinion of Betsey's grief, for she had remarked her through the window, stirring about, and going up and down the house quite bright.

1838.

WALK XLIII.

How to keep out the cold. Anne King.

" HAPPY new year to you and yours," dear Maria.

You see we continue to walk, although the snow comes down, and our wash-jugs and cream-pans are coated with ice.

I think I have made one good discovery, of which you shall have the benefit. Warm well your shawl, cloak, and other wraps, especially your neckerchief and shoes, before you venture your nose out of doors, for vainly shall you put on "that over that, and over that again," as Betty Blackberry enumerates the finery she intends to wear when she is a lady ; in spite of all you can heap on, the cold and damp of unaired draperies will communicate itself to your system, and send you forth chilled and comfortless, with clothes enough on your back, apparently, to defend you against a Hudson's Bay winter.

On you go, starving amid plenty, when one quarter of the clothing (the blood being previously thawed) would be warmer as well as lighter.

But I preach in vain about temperance of clothing to my dear, naughty Kate ; she carries the frosty Caucasus on her shoulders, and wonders she cannot keep up with me.

I was glad to have Coombe on my side. You have read his physiology, and perhaps his phrenology, also, but that I know nothing about ; only I thought it very sensible of him to agree with me in opinion, and to send his readers to a roasting fire before exposing themselves to the influence of a "bitter sky."

What a painful thought links on here—that many go into this biting air, without fire to warm their looped and windowed garments, to return to an empty grate. I wish this may not be the case of poor Anne King, now Gilbert. Pity she had not kept her maiden name, settled so comfortably as she was with Jenny and Aunt Peggy, who, having neither chick nor child of their own, thought a great deal of their pretty Anne. I am afraid I was proud of her, too. She was a picturesque appendage to my flower-beds, which she kept in order, since she was no bigger than a sweet-pea stake.

A garden-girl should be slight and pretty, and have drop-curls (natural ones), like poor Anne, if only to afford occasion for the quotation old Mr. Whitaker applied to his daughter, "Herself the fairest flower."

You remember Miss W———? good and sensible, but singularly plain. Anne's occupations out of hours were not less in character with her beauty. She was charged by kind Aunt Peggy to weed the bit of garden, to milk the goats, and, above all and everything, to be kind to 'Un Margaret, the blind annuitant. Besides this, to please herself, she used, between the lights, to pluck "griglins" (*English* —twigs of heath) out of the broom, make them into crayons by burning the tips, and then draw cocks, and horses, and pigs, like anything—anything, *i.e.*, than the animals they were meant to represent. I have preserved a few specimens in my scrap-book.

But oh! what is genius? what is prettiness?

We found poor Anne, this bitter day, with a fireless grate and a littered house, trying to pacify two cross children, and exhibiting an appearance so lanky, that I suspect she had robbed her own wardrobe to eke out theirs.

"Her husband would continue to work 'on tribute,'" she said, "and not on 'owner's account' (you know something of mine phraseology, from your long residence in Cuddra), so that she never knew what she had to spend."

Ruinous as the system is, I can imagine its temptation to one who has a turn for gambling. I had almost said, who has not? at least, among miners; the labouring for regular wages is a dictate of prudence, generally, not an impulse of preference; I must confess it would be that with me, but I am truly sorry for poor Anne, whose honest, orderly habits must needs make such uncertain gains a cross and an inconvenience.

WALK XLIV.

The two twains.   A final farewell.

I AM glad, dear Maria, that you take an interest in poor Anne James and her adopted children, for I can give you the conclusion of their history, and that is what we can rarely do in real life.

We continued our occasional visits, though I may not have recorded them, to the widower's cottage, and were always welcomed by Anne with a smile, but it was such a one as made her woe-begone countenance seem more dejected.

No wonder; there she sat the livelong day, alone, and immediately under the chamber where her sister died. Then the infants' faces, instead of the dimpling and crowing graces, which could not fail to have communicated a gleam of joy to hers, bore the suffering, attenuated look of age; little pale atoms of being, sons of sorrow from their birth, and ever ailing. One of them, the strongest, too, laboured under a complaint rare, I should think, in one so young, a decided case —I speak to the learned—of hernia.

Driving over the green, one day last autumn, Kate and I remarked a man and woman trudging along the sea side of us, each carrying a baby. Kate suggested that they could be no other than Thomas and the good Anne, taking the twins in to the Penzance Dispensary, and proposed that the latter should mount with her burden into the carriage.

This saved the traveller some fatigue, but nothing had power to brighten her sad countenance.

"She seemed as one with misery content,"

and happy for her it was so, since her cup was not yet full to the brim.

The doctor thought very ill of his puny patient, and could only inflict present torture with a doubtful promise of future relief, provided the prescribed remedies were persevered in, but the steel—denying the poor body one moment's relief from suffering—might be said to have entered into the soul of the pitying aunt, so she laid it aside, and wisely abandoned her charge to nature.

In the meantime, the weaker infant died of inflammation of the lungs, and, in happy time, the other was laid beside it. I was from home at the time of their death, but learnt on my return that the kind aunt, her occupation being gone, proposed to return to her former home.

By the merest accident, I met her, passing along our little avenue, on the way thither. She wore nearly the same dejected look as before, yet she seemed some-what care-lightened, and was beautifully nice in her dress, which, of late, like Shakespeare's lover, had betrayed an appearance of careless desolation. We conversed a while on her duplicate sorrow; I attempted some commonplace consolation, about the babes being better cared for, and so forth. "Yes, ma'am, I know they are better off than with me, but "—her sad eyes filled with tears as she added—"they came very near."

We took leave, poor Anne and I, and went our different ways, no more to meet, probably, on earth; but I never expect to witness a more heroic instance of self-devotion.

WALK XLV.

Superstition.   Family pride.   An important secret.   Jenny Priske.

HO would credit it of the nineteenth century! but seeing is be-lieving.

I saw with my own eyes the little black flag attached to our churchwoman's bit of mignonette, which she assured me had begun to quail away since the poor child, her grandson, was burnt to death, and had revived after she put on it a bit of mourning. It was not, she added, seeing me smile, that she put much upon it *herself*, but, I might depend upon it, her daughter in Penzance had two-and-twenty plants, that the ladies used to stop at

Y

the windows and admire, which began with one accord to droop from the time
that the accident happened, and would certainly have died if she had not given
them a suit of black apiece. "And perhaps a little water, Anne," I might have
rejoined ; but I should like to be quite sure the figment is morally wrong, before
I disturb any one's faith in a point which affords such evident satisfaction ; and,
indeed, shall not a poor pew-cleaner be pardoned for a weakness which moved a
President of the Royal Society, on the occasion of his mother's death, to order, by
letter, that his bees in the country should be invested with crape, lest they should
die ?

I fell in with Jane Roberts on her way to "put abroad" some clothes, and we
had a little parley, which glided from present to past times, for Jane is on the
shady side, as it is jocosely called, of sixty, I suppose. She adverted to her first
going into service with old Mrs. Jenkins of the churchtown. "Dear soul, she had
a poor temper, and she knew it well. She used to say to me, 'I was young and
healthy then, so what right had I to be-poor tempered ? Jane,' says she, 'thou
may bless God for thy good temper; thou wilt go forth into the world, child, without a burden on thy back!'" This was philosophy worthy of the President
himself.

I went home by the moor-lane road to Goldsithney, for I always like to avoid a
bit of turnpike, not but that the lane was as dirty; it was dirtier than Lanteran
Hill, and then there were abundance of ruts, deep and miry; but these were not
the work of the incessant cars and vans, and other like vehicles, which ply on
public roads "from morn till dewy eve." They were made by our own rustic
ploughs and carts, and I knew the water that filled them would nourish the primroses that are ready to burst forth on either side of the way. It will not do for
them to shew their noses yet ; the snow still stands in high piles under the north
hedge, cut by the passing wheels into smooth, druidical-like fragments.

I wanted an expounder at my elbow, to tell me why these remainder heaps differ
from the new-fallen snow in their component particles, which, in place of the usual
flaky, feathery appearance, present an infinitude of crystal globules, reminding one
of that anti-climax to the sublime, a tapioca pudding.

I was proud, and my poor Asylum Kitty more so, that I could supply myself, at
her shop, with the two yards of twopenny ribbon that I was on my way to purchase
at Mrs. Gundry's, the Howell and James of Goldsithney.

To-day's walk was rather fertile of adventure. *Rather*, do I say ? when I met the granddaughter of a lord, selling tapes and needles; Lord C—— she claimed for a relation on the mother's side, besides many big-wigs on the father's; among the rest, two Irish *Danes.* This little person, who accosted me in a high-toned tragedy speech, appeared to have *hauteur* enough to supply the many distinguished houses to which she professed to be related. Of this she was fully aware; like another great personage, King Nebuchadnezzar—(I wonder she had not claimed him for a relation, too)—her pride had caused her downfall; but, she added, it was her "equals" that she despised only; wherefore, I suppose, three months after her return from a boarding-school, she eloped with one of low degree. Her father offered to take her back, on her making oath that she was forcibly carried off, but this she told him in the first place she could not do, for that she married him with her full consent, and in the next place she would not, for she loved him. "Yes," spouted she, "although he has deceased this two-and-twenty year, and many is the bitter dreg of sorrow that I have drained since then, and although I lived ten years with a second husband, by whom I had three children, two girls and one boy, yet, believe me, madam"—(I once before played the part of confidante to a heroine—it was Cleora, in "Tom Thumb," by the way, one of five characters which, under a scarcity of *dramatis personæ,* I had to sustain—and instantly recalled Princess Hunkabunka's confession of love to her father:—'Alas, my lord, I value not myself that once I ate two fowls and half a pig, but oh!'— and then comes her love for Tom Thumb). So, as I was saying, Mrs. Whaley, declining to accept the conditions of restoration to her family's favour, has been left to starvation and itinerancy; yet she has a home at the Mount, from which she sallies forth daily, to carry the basket of odd ware nine miles round the welkin. A son and daughter reside with her, dependent upon their mother's scanty resources, for the boy will not work, and the girl cannot, having, in child-bed, what they call "shot out her spine," and thus become a helpless cripple.

There is something fine, too, in the old lady's bearing under such distressing circumstances. Mrs. Townsend once offered to introduce her to a lady from Ireland, who happened to know Captain Henry, of something Grove; knew, also, that he had a daughter who "married unequal." "But no, madam," says this little dignified body; "I would rather choose to walk ten mile o' ground to earn one honest penny, than receive a guinea from the hand of charity."

I forgot she told me, *à propos* to what, I don't know, that she was a "*rare* secret-keeper," adding, in proof of her temptation to divulge one which she had preserved for eleven years, that she might, if she chose, have hung her second spouse over and over again, for that she discovered he had a wife and four children in England. I wish this mirror of conjugal forbearance could have persuaded the poor, ignorant thing in whose cottage I met her, to make her home more comfortable to her husband (my quondam Ariel, you may remember), who has lately returned from Devonshire, with a know-nothing young wife and two children.

> "If sylphs and sylphesses could live now,
> Under the blossom that hangs on the bough,"

it would not signify; but here are these four people lighting down on our poor old friend, Jenny Priske, whom I have so often brought before you, that she has the right to consider herself an old acquaintance.

It is certainly very hard upon her, to have all the party in her one room, and the daughter-in-law such a slattern, too; extremely provoking. Yet I cannot ever prevail upon myself to believe what they say,—that she once jumped out of bed on her animal leg, and broke her vegetable one (her crutch, I mean) in three parts, about the uncapped head of her unfortunate daughter-in-law.

No doubt, she foments the disagreements of the young couple, in spite of the edifying things she whines out about living in peace. "Charity, ma'am, charity; that's what I always tell them: 'charity suffereth long and is kind;' charity"—"'Is not puffed up,' Jenny," says I (Kate tittered); but Jenny as usual assented, and pocketed the compliment. Say what you will, Jenny is sure to assent, and, really, every other word in her mouth is "to be sure," and "so it is," or "exactly so;" and whatever you happen to advance is just what she "was going to say," and she knows it all before you can tell her, and so one is brought up at once. It is running a tilt with a feather bed.

A ludicrous illustration of this vain warfare just occurs to my memory. My dear father, you may remember, was very provoking in one respect (he could afford to be)—he never would set things to rights about the place. We had been at him a long while about trimming up the trees that overhung and spoiled our road to St. Columb, they made it so miry. One evening, when he returned from a Justice Meeting at that place, we opened at him again. He was long silent, till one said, "I thought I should have been drenched with the dripping of the boughs." "Drenched," repeated he, "but I, who was riding, thought my neck would have been twisted off." We laughed, and gave up the point.

WALK XLVI.

Grace Ellis.   A peaceful end.

N a parish that radiates from its central Vicarage at least two to three miles, and that contains some 3,000 inhabitants, the relation of our visits must needs seem desultory and disjointed and, I fear, perplexing to you, dear Maria.

At all events, you will remember Grace, our domestic factotum for nearly twenty years, and will be glad to hear that she has attained that grand desideratum among miners, a house of her own. It yet wants many of the concomitants of comfort; the plaister needs to have a finishing coat, and the planking must be new laid, that one may not cross it at the peril of a sprained ancle, and the stairs must have a side-railing. But "Rome was not built in a day." Every penny that the most thrifty housekeeping can spare, is devoted to masons and carpenters; but, to the credit of this honest couple be it spoken, they do not advance one step further than they can pay their way.

The trade of miner is—and that is one reason why I would rather be the tinker who lived in his own tea-kettle, and kept his own hours—in every way unfavourable to regularity. The miner neither eats, drinks, sleeps, or goes to church, with his family, insomuch that the wife finds it as hard to regulate the disposition of time as of money. Oftentimes, when she has set in for a job, she is suddenly interrupted —Grace, for instance, was in the midst of whitewashing her walls to-day, when word is brought that Tom has "changed cour," and she must instantly "fit dinner" for him. Away go the tubs and lime-brushes, higgledy-piggledy, and the bellows are plied to get up a fire for the potatoes, the stew, or the fish.

Passing her house, I was glad of the excuse to call on *Mrs.* Gilbert, so titled by virtue of a small rack-rent estate, but assuming nothing thereupon above her landless neighbours. One claim to pre-eminence she might truly plead, but she does not. She seems to think she has done nothing uncommon in affording an asylum, for sixteen years, to a sick, peevish sister, who demanded as much attendance as if

z

she had a rich inheritance to bequeath. *That*, in truth, she had, as I told Mrs. Gilbert ; the blessing of the poor destitute. But at length she is gone, and now the kind survivor can talk of nothing else but the happy end her sister made ; "at peace with God, herself, and all around her ; her evidence brightening more and more," her very sufferings helping her forward—*upwards*, rather, for she illustrated them by a ladder, hard to mount, but of which every succeeding stave brought her nearer to Heaven.

How strikingly this conversation would contrast with what one can imagine would pass in genteel society under similar circumstances. Mrs. Mary, for example, dies, and leaves Mrs. Grace in sole possession of the establishment and funds. Mrs. Mary dead ! How old was she ? When did she die ? How rich was she ? When will she be buried ? What did she leave ? Who will have it ? Any small legacies to her friends ? Funeral public or private ? Inside or outside the church ? In wood or lead ? Hearse or hand ? But not one syllable all this while about the ladder and its staves.

WALK XLVII.

·

Betsey Pengelly and her devoted daughter.

REALLY, it is a charity to call on poor old Betsey Pengelly, who lies, drawing every breath in pain and loneliness, from morning's light till her excellent daughter comes back, in the evening, from bal. She is meek and uncomplaining as a saint ; and patience on a hard sick-bed, let me tell Shakespeare, is better than patience on a monument.

The crum o' breakfast which is to serve till supper-time, and the well-cared-for fan to keep off faintness, are duly laid alongside the poor woman, by the most affectionate daughter in the world ; and when Mary returns from the labour which supports them both, she calls "mother" before she ventures upstairs, lest she should find her parent a corpse.

This devotion of all her time and all her strength to filial duty, is no common merit in one surrounded by evil example—a companion-at-work of boys and girls who, on the slightest provocation, threaten to leave, and frequently *do* leave, the paternal roof, and go "to quarters."

Few are the advantages which the poor have over the rich, but there are some latent ones, which one is glad to detect, in order to "right the scales a bit." For one, the child of poor parents is able to give some tangible proof of affection, and to requite in kind the benefits received from them; she can, in return, make those sacrifices of self which, above all things, cement affection; whereas, except in some rare and favoured instances, what can the children of the rich do? I mean, what can they appear to do? Among a family of six or eight daughters, how shall we distinguish the dutiful, the self-denying, from the careless and self-engrossed; what sacrifices can the daughter of affluence make, which shall entitle her to the almost reverential admiration we feel for my poor dear Mary? I'll be bound to say, she loves her mother more fondly for being dependent on her for everything.

In short, I hope I have proved—though the thing never entered her head—that no young lady in the land, do what she would, could appear so truly a heroine as poor Mary Pengelly.

WALK XLVIII.

The cradle and the grave. An unnatural mother.

NLY a few days ago, I was speaking to you of our former pretty garden-girl, with her two little boys; and this morning we found the younger in his cradle a corpse,—the father, mother, and a visitor or two, in the same room, all looking very sorrowful, of course; but I was glad to find poor Anne herself employed in washing.

It is one great advantage which the poor have during these seasons of sorrow—they do not add the pains of idleness to other pains; "the cradle must be rocked, though the babe has only been an hour motherless." I mean the womenkind poor; our men seem to think it proper to hold holyday till after the burying, which, on that account, is often indecently hastened. The dead must be put out of sight, that the living may eat; yet, to do them justice, house-room is the only thing they grudge the deceased. They will suffer privation for a year, to bestow on their dead a fine coffin; and Anne, though she knows not when she may be rich enough to buy another, has decorated the little creature, so soon to be laid in the damp earth, in the best christening robe, and cap, too, as if in derision of its little death-cold head. She was expecting the coffin every minute, she said. What a terrible illustration of the oft-repeated truth, that there is but a step from the cradle to the tomb!

Passing near the Workhouse, we could not help expressing our sympathy in poor Mrs. ———'s peck of new troubles; the worst of it was the breaking out of a new disease in the house, a thing without a name, which made it needful to wash everybody and everything, to the very skin and mattress. Then the sow had brought forth ten little pigs, and over-laid seven of them, an "uncultivated cratur." Yet this very sow might read a lesson on maternal instinct to some of the establishment. The loathesome disease above alluded to, was communicated by a wretch who brought hither her infant, and then abandoned it to the mercy of strangers.

Who is it says a woman is like a nonpareil?—the best of her tribe, if good, and the worst, if bad.

WALK XLIX.

Friend Mary. An apology.

WALK to Marazion is generally so barren of events, except the twenty-eight intervening stiles, that you would have heard nothing about it, had we not chanced to meet your favourite, Mary, returning from thence with a well-filled basket. I love to look on her honest face, so I invited a little parley.

"You have been shopping, it seems, Mary; buying something for yourself at the new shop, I suppose?" "Why yes, ma'am, I have been shopping, though I can't say I have bought anything for myself like, but the little 'Lizabeth wanted a crum o' cloak to put upon the tender limbs of her this cold weather. It have been slight with John, you may depend, lately; and I having counted, you see, and no great occasion for anything for myself like"—and thus she went on apologising for what most people would have thought highly meritorious, namely, the purchase of the pretty blue stuff, with a "small matter of lining," &c., for the child.

WALK L.

A conversion.   The Hepatica.   Uncle Edward.

E had once more occasion to pass near the dwelling of my armless patient, and again we called in, for curious was I to hear the particulars of his sudden conversion, and anxious to be assured of its stability.

Nobody at home this time but the cock and hen, and Anne the mother, who looked more cheerful than usual, and far more diligent. She was " working her knuckles to the bones " on John's dirty bal clothes, and it seemed quite a pleasure to her to be employed in his service. On my enquiring for John, Anne looked most significantly pleased ; but you should know Anne, she is like nothing anybody ever saw. It was the happiest of *aliases*, whoever gave her the nickname of the "prowler." She has all the attributes of a nocturnal animal. "John is a very fine young man to *me*, Miss Pascoe, you may depend ; a very fine young man, if it do last." She went on to recount, at my request, the particulars of this blessed change, which were as follows.

"After the worst of his illness had passed away, he was one day reading a godly book, lent by one who had visited him when he lay ill. Suddenly, the tears began to gush ; then he prayed, and then he sang. Afterwards, he asked pardon for his behaviour to me," said Anne ; "and, for sartain, it is a bitter thing for a son to strike a mother. 'Yes, my son,' says I, 'I do freely forgive thee ;' and now he do talk to our youngsters, and tell them how 'tis never too soon. When he goes off to work, 'tis 'God bless thee, mother!' and a shake of—hands he've none, poor lamb, but his stump like ; and when I ask what I shall fit for him at night, so timid (meaning teazy) as he used to be, it is now ' fit what you will, why do you ask me ?' and then 'tis pretty to see how he begs us to leave our sins, and agree to go on pilgrimage together."

Whoever else was so disposed, a wild, prettiesh-looking bal-girl, who sat, playing hidey-mopsey, behind the door, did not seem likely to join the Zionward group. This was the girl who told John he might spare his prayers, for " there never yet was a Priske saved." Extraordinary levity this, to confront and scoff at eternal perdition. It far outsteps the common thoughtlessness of youth ; it was a pitch of hardness that no damsel who did not work at a bal could well arrive at.

We called a moment with some flowers to strew over the little lifeless tenant of the cradle ; possibly, the roots from which they sprang were of its mother's plant-ing. " An hepatica," said she, placing it on the child's breast, while a gleam of pleasure for a moment visited her face, to think her baby was deemed worthy of the best in the garden, and, may be (who knows ?), pleased to display her floral learning to her admiring husband.

They had told me Uncle Edward Briant had been removed from the roof of his kind granddaughter, so thither we stretched our walk to see how matters stood. It was all true that the Parish of St. Erth had refused to add to the shilling a week, which was deemed by Joanna's husband insufficient to repay him for the old man's support ; but, happily, his former master gave in aid a stipendiary sixpence, and " Gaffer " can keep the children when summer comes, and the mother goes out to work ; so altogether his living would be made up. How glad I am ! the removal would have been a heart-breaking affair, besides that we have hardly so due a churchman as Uncle Ed was so long as he could " fetch " the church.

WALK LI.

An invalid. A faithful cat. Mine accident.

I HAVE many times wished to pick acquaintance with John King, of whose meekly-borne sufferings Mr. Pascoe spoke with cordial commendation.

By making a small detour on the Helston turnpike road, this object was easily accomplished.

The poor man was pale and languid, though not a professed invalid ; in fact, he had just come in from building a gap in the hedge, to keep out the sheep from the "taties ;" but his wife was obliged to bear the more laborious part of rolling in the stones from the surrounding burrows, and even with her help it was "busy all" his strength to complete the little jobs. He leaned his breast against the table at which he sat, as if requiring such support, his faithful cat bearing him company, and testifying much affectionate concern by walking up and down before him, at every turn sweeping his face from chin to forehead with her erected tail. He was sensibly gratified by our remarking her attachment to his person, and assured us "she frequently held up her paw to invite him to shake hands, when he was never looking for no such thing." Kate was tickled, and begged we might see him perform ; but it never answers to show off prodigies ; instead of seizing the proffered hand, pussy only "snuffed at it" like any common cat, and followed it with puzzled eyes.

To make up for this disappointment, I suppose, the poor man mentioned a wonderful fall he once had ; not to be paralleled, I should think, even in the record of mining casualties, dreadful and strange as they often are. He fell from a ladder, "two steeples outright," that is, a sheer perpendicular depth of two church spires. Seeing one just outside the dining-room window as I write, and trying to fancy another stuck on the top of it, I can better conceive than describe the tumble. Now only hear the state in which he was picked up, and yet survived to tell the tale.

At which end of the poor creature shall I begin ? His head was fractured, his collar-bone broken ; on each side, three ribs were knocked in ; something, I forget particularly what, happened to one of his shoulders ; his nose was laid flat on his face, and his two ankles "shot out."

I promised not to treat you often, dear Maria, with such a chapter of raw head and bloody bones, for it is quite out of your way ; but how the opium-eater would like this specimen of a dreadful accident, so perfectly good of its kind !

A more fatal accident befel the club to which this poor fellow had subscribed for many years. It broke, and with it vanished all his hopes of an independent provision for age and sickness. I know nothing more deplorable (for this misfortune can only befall the industrious and provident, who are thus, as it were, betrayed into pauperism) than the case of this poor fellow, who cannot now subsist without parochial assistance.

WALK LII.

Town and country.   The heath walk.   A summons.

I DO not believe there ever was house, hut, or hovel, such a hole for living soul to inhabit, as that which her three brothers have run up for the widow, Grace Stevens, and her five children. Yet it was exceedingly kind of the poor men, who all had families of their own, to make this effort to rescue that of their sister from the ignoble destiny of a Workhouse. I wonder if I can bring the poor woman to your recollection as the widow who "couldn't never" chastise her children, for thinking of their father, till her "temper was up, and then she gave it to them bitter."

I sincerely disclaim any shadow of merit in visiting the poor as we do in the course of a refreshing country walk. In a town, I might be tempted to feel set up, "that I was not as other men," resorting to the temples of fashion and amusement, but threading my distasteful way through dirty streets and infected alleys, to find myself, too probably, the dupe of low cunning and vulgar extortion.

It is our favoured lot to walk through primrose meadows, and over downs redolent of wild thyme and furze-blossom. I sometimes parody the sailor's pæan, and sing "the heath, the heath, the open heath," while my companion, in the exuberance of her gladness, goes out of her way to bound over a pool; for even our downs, generally the driest walks on earth, are, at this most unseasonable season of ours, saturated with rain.

Tell it not in Gath, but I never, my own venerable self, see a detached furze-bush, without an almost irresistible desire to jump over it, "for auld lang syne;" but this is a populous country, and I do not pass for being over canny, as it is, reading aloud to myself, with a fine, theatrical intonation, sometimes.

"I value a young man more than a gosling." This is one of Miss Mitford's lively sallies, and, just as I pronounced it, I came plump across John Roberts, who looked, poor fellow, quite in character.

But, if I had wandered from my path as I do from my subject, I should never have reached my poor little Anne's, at Woodstock, where I was this morning summoned, in the manner I am going to relate.

A nice notable little girl met Mr. Pascoe at the Vicarage gate, and, without waiting for the usual "who are you?" announced herself and her business abruptly and distinctly, after the manner of Southey's Glendoveer.

"I am Mary Anne Vasker; mother was called Annie Hoskin, now she is called Annie Vasker, she lives to Woodstock, and she *must* speak to Mrs. Pascoe, please, and she *must* come directly, for mother is very bad in bed."

Poor thing! I immediately recollected the good little body and her wicked sister, who, in connection, always reminded me of the pitcher story, which the wise and witty still cite for its allegorical beauty.

Betsey H——— was a bold, sullen, ill-favoured girl, and with the very mouth for expectorating toads and spiders, and subject to such fits of insane rage, that, I remember—it was just after I came into the parish—she flung a knife at her brother's head. The missile penetrated so deep as to put his life in peril, and, one good thing, keep the creature in such a panic respecting her own, that she behaved somewhat quieter thenceforth.

No doubt, Tom Eddy (that was the name of the poor fellow whom she found to marry her) fared the better for this hearty fright.

Good little Annie, being well rid of such a turbulent comrade, continued to tend and cherish her queer old father and queerer old mother to their last. It was a frightful last to the poor old man—"the coiner," he was called through the parish—but my memory here admonishes me that I have before introduced this disciple of Bamfylde Moore Carew to your acquaintance, and told you of his hapless end. He rose from his bed one winter's night, and, whether in or out of sleep they know not, threw himself into "the plump, right afore the door." What Crabbe would have made of him!

It was edifying to hear Annie's tender, patient care of her old mother; and she was rewarded. For a long time, she met in class that likely young man, Thomas Varkis, and they talked "diamonds and pearls" together, till it ended in a match. But I had no notion they had settled down within walking distance.

WALK LIII.

_____

Parson Vawdry.   Horned cattle.   A bit of true love.

A stuffed pet.   " The master."

"THIS is a day for the Cove," is an observation that a fine day is sure
to call forth from one or other of our little party. The opinion was
unanimous, but uncle was forced to ride to see his poor old brother
clergyman at Gwinear, who had nominated him one of the trustees
to a will, the seal of which will probably be soon broken, and who wished to give
him a few farewell instructions concerning it.

To anyone who has the gift of tracing characters, Parson Vawdrey would afford
a beautiful subject, only that its reality would be doubted, on account of its rare
simplicity; but I have *not* this gift, and will therefore try what I can do, dearest
M———, to communicate to you my sense of the glad feelings called forth by this
fine weather, and the valley, and the station, and—that climax of grandeur and
beauty—the sea. Long, however, before we caught a glimpse of its gracious face,
we observed those marks of animal enjoyment, above, below, and round about,
which are symptoms of a bright spring day. The voice of mirth was heard on all
sides; even where mirth was not, poor Mary Warne (invalid as she is) carolled
through the open door of her house, and Frankey whistled loud from his solitary
perch on the cobbler's stool, in that most unjocund state of his. Even Mr.
Richards, the perpetual overseer, a terror to evil-doers and parish paupers, seemed
to have " relaxed his brow severe," and stood in friendly sympathy with a few poor
men, one or two of whom had long been weights on the parish funds.

Human face or voice there were none along the little quiet valley which opens
so sweetly and vista-wise on the ocean; and for that, among other reasons, I love
it. There were traces of children returning from school, in scattered patches of

pebbles and primroses, which they had scud* (a genuine Cornishism) along the narrow foot-worn path.

Oh! the delight of sweeping round that noble battery, with all the world of waters before us, a hundred gallant little barks, as bright as the birds that sunned themselves on the Enys. The beach was also populous with little people from the Preventive Station; not "dancing their ringlets to the whistling wind," but gathering *perriwrinkles* and limpets. *A propos*, I fell to parodying Shakespeare, who is always in one's head, near the sea, substituting "all" for "half-way down stoop some who gather limpets—pleasant trade;" though not, I should imagine, very pleasant eating. *Chaqu'un à son gout*; but it strikes me shockingly fee-fa-fumish to see a supper-party pick these creatures out with a pin, and gobble them down, scholar's hats and all. On "Goody Friday" (an old Roman Catholic vestige, I suppose), all our bal-boys and girls bring them home by the basket-full, on mules, in carts, or any way, in short; relishing the scramble, I suspect, more than the fish.

To-day, even Captain Will was amongst the wrinkle hunters, having a mind, as he facetiously observed, "to some horned cattle for supper." Buffalo hunting, methought, would have suited him better. It was a rare act of condescension in one who, in his time, had held commerce with rocks and breakers on other scent than that of gathering shell-fish for an evening's frolic. I only observed himself and "Happy Harry," of the group; Carter and Cornish were, I found, more profitably employed in sawing timber for the mines. The latter, I suppose, is feathering his nest, preparatory to catching his bird, for you are to know that all our rocking, and spratting, and boating, during the past summer, above all, our shoe-polishing and knife-cleaning in the workshop, where the young seamen spend so much of their shore leisure, has ended in a bit of true love. "Why does Dolly always wait till the boat comes in, to clean her knives? I should think it very unpleasant with the young men about." I could not, for my life, satisfy the discreet Kate—now the murder is out.

You are not to picture me, dear M———, planted before our little parlour casement, looking unutterable things at the sea, without turning my chair. The truth is, I may not premeditatedly look upon it a dozen times while I remain, but I can enjoy the consciousness of its proximity, as one does, you know, "the silence

---

* Note by Miss W. *Scud* is to spill, in Cornwall, so that, if anyone talked to us of a "scudding sail," we should think of nothing better than a "leaky vessel."

of a mind." It is sufficient that the freshness of its breezes, and the rippling sound of its waters, come o'er two of my bodily senses, while a third is occupied with a book, or a fourth (wretch that I am) with a mutton pie.

A predetermination to enjoy never answers; it is grasping the butterfly that has looked so bright on the wing; its vivid, volant graces are no more; only a little dust remains to soil our rash fingers; or, if you will have a grander simile, it is storming a fair city, only to find its provisions exhausted and its beauties defaced.

But whether I go to the Cove with a resolution to enjoy it or not, Mrs. Richards, *i.e.*, Mrs. Captain Will, would consent to live on one meal for six days, to have a sight of the Vicarage folk on the seventh. It is meat and drink to her, especially Miss Kate's young face, not forgetting her gown and bonnet, for, seeming to her, we have the prettiest fancies in prints and ribbons; but she sees us and ours through Claude Lorraine spectacles. Harry and she were sorry, sure enough, to hear of the fate of Miss Kate's squirrel. Harry has undertaken to stuff it, having tried his hand very successfully a short time ago, on an otter, which came into the Cove, followed by her young one, whom she was teaching to swim. He described quite graphically how the little animal had, seemingly, been turned adrift, to follow the mother how it could, and how, when it shrieked for help, she seized it by the ear, and towed it on a bit, till, in her wisdom, she again abandoned it to its resources. How Harry could summon courage to shoot her, we cannot imagine, but I suppose his education of pegging lobsters and crushing crabs has hardened his heart; yet he is a mighty petter of animals, can hardly be persuaded to let one of Dido's many kittens be destroyed, and withal he kept the young otter running about the kitchen, going daily to the pool to catch "miller's thumbs" for its dinner, till the odd creature died of "the distemper," a good sweeping phrase, by the way, standing in the place of "nerves" to the human subject. I expect the inflated squirrel will be set up, beside the mamma otter, beneath our sitting-room window, and thus prove as consolatory to Miss Kate's feelings, as did the stuffed poodle to those of a lady I knew, who had the effigy of her pet placed at one end of her sofa,

"For ever silent, and for ever sad."

The wise woman I speak of was a Mrs. Pearce, a daughter of our liege lord, Sir J. St. Aubyn, who, having no one to pay her a similar compliment, slumbers, I believe, in the family vault.

I never beheld the new officer till this morning, when we encountered him just under the station. He is charming (I mean, as a feature of the place); a perfect corsair, pirate, giaour, of a man, hardly distinguishable, by his dress, from his own boatmen, but illustrious, by the elevation of his look and step. On his appearing, the Preventive children seemed to stop their play and quail before him. After he had well passed, I asked a little girl who that was. She replied, in a quivering tone, "The master, ma'am; that is our master."

It is remarkable how mist and mystery set off greatness. Our Godolphin looks like nothing under a bright sun, and our lieutenant, among the other thirty Lieutenant Smiths (which I once counted in a navy list), might look like another man; but here in this solitude, the only gentleman, and with a post of command, he seems something, especially as nobody, not even the sagacious Mrs. Ladner, can *think* where he comes from, or why his maid-servant, whom he brought with him, should look, and dress, and be treated, so like a lady; why her linen, the best that could be bought for money, should be marked A. F., and she not tell her name, unless it be meant to signify "a fable," and she should be really, as some surmise, his sister or his daughter; for there is, as everyone can see, a great family likeness, &c., &c. This is the substance of a flood of gossip poured out upon Kate and me, when we paid our last visits to the station.

Buonaparte at Elba was not more an object of general interest, than Lieutenant Smith at Prussia Cove.

Maria, I have often thought a thought, which the last observation has again called up: if I could but bring it out, how cleverly you would wrap it up for me; but how shall you do this without knowing my meaning, which I must try to convey by illustration. A giant builds a castle, a wonderful great castle, in order to be admired by the pigmies; yet this building would be compounded of such stone and mortar as is employed by the pigmies themselves, only he can accumulate more; but then the beholders, by reason of their shortness, can only behold it partially. He would have admiration in proportion to the magnitude of his work, but finds that, however he may rule over matter, the enlargement of the human capacity is beyond his control; so he must even occupy his castle, and be content with the applause of the pigmies, who would bestow an equal portion of it on a meaner fabric, all of which they could see. Now for my part I would not give a pin to be a giant, unless I had a world of giants to admire me; and I feel no greater envy at Buonaparte's elevation among men, than that of Lieutenant Smith. But

I have so ill-expressed my meaning, and written so much nonsense, that if I had not so notably numbered my pages, I would tear out the leaf.

Just this word or two more "*pour finir son affaire.*" It is now concluded that A. F. is a natural daughter of the master. She goes, along the row, by the name of "daughter Jane." Let them take care her assumed papa does not hear them, with that dark look and long scimitar of his!

WALK LIV.

MARCH, 1838.

Miss Mitford.   A tale of a tub.

WHEN I set out for St. Erth yesternoon, I said to myself (I had no one else to say it to, for my poor Kate had rubbed the skin of her heel, and could limp no further than the garden), "Maria," says I, "has heard enough of my auld world loves and regrets. I will not tell her one word about my walk to-day, though the weather is bright and gladsome enough to make the very fishes talk out of the abundance of their hearts."

To assure my good behaviour, I took a book—Miss Mitford's "Village," of all things. How came it that I never heard of it before, to show me how Shakespeare and I have happened to think of the same thing, he having only the trifling advantage of thinking of it first and better. Accordingly, the expedient of the book failed its object, for it set me fancying how Miss M—— would have described the various little passages of my walk. The parody amused me; would you like to hear it?

Books there may be more learned, but there are few wiser, if we would attend to its covert meaning, than one, the delight of my nursery days, now, I fear, out of print, entitled, "The world turned upside down," wherein our lecturing wives, dictatorial sons, and ranting demagogues, might view their own portraits in those of the nag carrying down the groom, the cock brandishing the dripping ladle over the spitted cook, the baby dandling the nurse, the doll the girl, with other diverting topsy-turvyisms. I do not recollect among them the doughty young damsel chaperoning the timid old lady, and if there should be a reprint of the work, as I hope, I and my trusty little Jennefer will deserve a place in it.

In so far as my taste is concerned, I like nothing so well as a *cum sola* ramble—always excepting my dear Katie's company—but the law has gone forth, that I shall not take a distant walk without somebody. This law, then, I obey *to the letter,* transgressing its *spirit* by choosing for my protector the smallest and most inefficient person in the establishment, little Jennefer. No such bad guardian, either, one would think, for, till she became our garden-girl, her business was to lead about her blind father, Peter, to the surrounding mines, where he collected, you may remember, his monthly dole from the charity of his old comrades. The girl told me she had walked as much as twenty-three miles in one day on this errand. Now her younger sister takes her office, which has cost me one of the tidiest little goodies in the school.

Anyone might know that Jennefer's early education had been to lead the blind, for, in the first place, she sets out stoutly in front of me, and, when sent behind, dogs my steps so closely, that I cannot diverge one inch this way or that, without her following me. Luckily, our fine weather is too recent to have made the roads dusty, so I do not, like other testy folk, quarrel with my shadow.

Who could credit that I had so lately given the miller's boy sixpence, to place stepping-stones across the stream that divided the mill from the marsh ? The stones remained to prove how well he had earned his wages, but I needed them not ; all the country was as dry as a biscuit, except the marsh itself, in which stood two voluptuous rogues of horses, up to their knees in water, while they supinely cropped the tender tops of grass that covered its surface and grew almost into their mouths, thus eating and drinking at a bite. No need to envy their brethren of the prairies ; I should have told them so, had I known the horsinian language.

I do rejoice in the enjoyment—when it happens—of that most respectable and oppressed of quadrupeds. But truly this was a day for all breathing things to be happy in. Our winter sorrows seem to have passed away, and given place to the glad influences of spring, no one knows when or how. Everything rejoices and flourishes in its own particular line. The very scolds of the village (let alone the cocks and hens) screamed louder and shriller than if it had been a dull day. One, a shrew *par excellence*, was railing at a man with a cobbler's apron, for not having paid the rent due for his house, while he angrily demanded the restoration of a tub to which she had helped herself in part payment. How they did rail at one another, the woman, as usual in a war of lungs, having the best of it, like a fiddle at a concert, the shrillest, if not the loudest, instrument.

One continuous scream did she maintain, at the top of her "scrannel-pipe,"* from the commencement of her harangue, till long after her own door had closed upon her. "Well," thinks I, "how times are changed; in my days, neither did tenants withhold their rent, nor good wives call names, with other sounds that are misery to hear.

Everyone was happy in those days; wonderful what alteration forty years make in any place. Then, too, I think children went to school against their will, and here was a bit of an urchin crying and struggling out of the arms of a great girl, who was endeavouring to lead her to school. She suffered herself to be dragged along, yelping all the way. "She don't like to go to school, ma'am," said the girl, in answer to my enquiring look; "she is always so." The silly mother, no doubt, had sometimes given way, permitted the child to be conscious of its power over her feelings, and then it is sure to be "always so."

There were several bigger scholars, belonging to a more quality school, not yet called in. A string of these, in red, blue, and green frocks, gay and variegated as their samplers, were running up and down a few stone steps, or sliding down the one-sided balustrades.

I was wondering what o'clock it was, and their countenances told as plainly that it had not struck two, as if I had brought the old chased watch I was just before regretting. Blessed buoyancy of youth! their jailer might the next moment shew his face, yet they seemed to exult in their freedom, as the lark that carolled, oh! how rapturously, over their silly heads.

That dear old way-field, which, more than any other spot on earth, reminds me of bygone plays, and pleasures, and persons—I cannot, even at this advanced stage of my earthly pilgrimage, recall them without a stinging at the heart, but I feel none of the pangs when I glance towards the final resting-place of some of the dearest among them; the churchyard harmonises better with my feelings than the playground, and no wonder.

* See Milton's *Lycidas*.

What a fantastic thing is an English March! The other day, snow was weighing down the very hedges which now teem with primroses, and such primroses! I fancy I can distinguish a St. Erth primrose among a million. Those consequential burgesses, the rooks, too, caw, certainly, more musically than other rooks.

The sun is almost hot enough to hatch the four rare eggs which Jennefer carried in her basket, a present for my pretty young neighbour. But oh! the uncertainty of this world. She and her sister, Miss Sutton, and her, everyone's, "sweet Johnnie," had driven away to call at Phillack Rectory, over among those arid mounds of land, that, viewed in connection with the scenery round and about the Trencroven hills, with their rich velvety bloom, the windings of Hayle river, Trevethow woods, park, mansion, and untold beauties, suggest the idea (in a small way, to be sure) of Arabias, Happy and Desert.

So much for St. Erth, which I was going to say nothing about. As to Miss Mitford, I lost sight of my parody the moment I set foot on the glebe meadow, and saw the oak of other days.

It is a pity I missed the sight of Mr. Punnett's smile of "beautiful happiness." That is a pretty expression of Miss Mitford's; don't you think so?

WALK LV.

Maiden aunt.   Cabbages and pine-apples.   A Colossus of all works.

"ANOTHER borrowed day." One can fancy how strange this idiom of ours must sound to foreign ears. M. Nollet, who still attends Kate for the guitar, improved his simper to a smile, when he replied, "Ha, indeed! borrow from where; Italie, perhaps?" This was very well for a Frenchman, unless, indeed, he did not wish to lend his own goods, and so proffered those of a neighbour. Whoever claims the patent, it was a *beau soleil* that gilded our path over the downs, to the cottage of the burnt child—scalded, I mean. He drank out of a fresh-filled tea-pot. I found it, on my return, sound asleep in our kitchen, just relieved from great agony by Kate's nostrum (probably, a spoonful of linseed oil), herself not a little proud of her success.

To-day, we were forced to enquire the way to James Sampson's, through that labyrinth of shafts and rubbish which renders the new-built down cottages so hard to reach, though you may nearly command them all by a glance of the eye. I should not on any account have applied for a guide at the old man Sampson's, if I had guessed that his wicked Delilah of a wife had returned from her disgraceful wanderings, or that he could have been so weak as to re-admit her among his girls.

I never beheld such an instance of the withering, fading influence of sin. The creature, once a lively, comely person, had become so odious, so squalid, bloated, and sinister-looking, that we could hardly bear to receive her directions, standing with our backs towards her. The child was "come charming," as might be inferred from our finding the mother bonnetted and shawled, to attend the Goldsithney market.

Lady Carrington has done what she could to atone for the grievous wrong of bringing—she could hardly have done worse by *springing*—a mine, here in the heart of her nice, new-built cottages. She has, I say, offered an *amende pittoresque*, by planting trees of all sorts among the surrounding heaps. It is only amazing how they keep their ground. They must have a charmed life to escape such amateurs in mischief as our bal-boys and girls. I am told the charm is to "spale," *i.e.*, to keep back a portion of their pay, if they are caught meddling with a single twig.

A pathway, the only good thing I ever knew of a mine, led us, with a short cut, into the Helston turnpike-road, on some part of which, we were told, resided the blind child we were in search of. What think you of three blind children on this road, so near that they might almost grope their way to each other? It is strange, since small-pox is out of fashion.

We were directed to a row of cottages recessed from the main road, and left to hit upon the right one, but that was not the first into which I popped my enquiring nose, glad enough to get it out again. The occupant must have been an out-and-out slattern. No *tester* for her in the dirty shoe which I spied on the table, among unwashed basins and spoons and slops. In my heart I love a regular Saturday stirrage, an inside-out, upside-down affair, without a clear inch to sit down upon; it betokens a clean Sunday's *ménage*. The tempest of good housekeeping, like other hurricanes, clears the atmosphere, but your sloven and all around her, is in a state of stagnant repose. Utensils remain where they were casually dropped, dust "creams and mantles" wherever it alights, fixtures become litters, and litters settle down into fixtures.

> "The sight's enough, no need to smell a beau,"* &c.,

so I hastily withdrew from this dirty cabin, to enter that of her neighbour, where a pleasant surprise awaited us. The smiling, clean young woman, bearing in her arms a baby, as smiling and clean as herself, proved to be an old servant of our emigrant friends, and she, it appears, was the identical damsel who presented the tenth little Crisp at the font, when Mr. Pascoe bestowed the name upon it, for bye the christening dinner. This young woman had once a mind, she said, to accompany her poor mistress out, but 'twas a "whished" distance from home, and her heart failed her. She was sorry to hear of their difficulties, and most appropriately shocked to find they could no longer afford to keep a servant.

In the next cottage, and, as usual, the last, we found what we were in search of. The mother, indeed, had gone to visit her friends, but there was one to care for her sightless one, "mother and mair." She was one of that class in whose favour might be parodied those lines, "To a friend," which are in every young lady's album :—

> "Hast thou a maiden aunt ? Thou hast indeed,
>   A large and rich supply;
> A store to serve thy every need,
>   Well managed, till you die."

How graceful are the ways of childhood, even through its infirmities!

The sightless babe grasped my finger, then shrank intuitively from a stranger's hand, into the good aunt's bosom, anon raised her innocent head, and seemed to ask, with her still bright blue innocent eyes, what it all meant, and again suffered me to retain the little pale hand. The scene was really touching.

For a long time, we have been wishing to call on our former acquaintance, Martha James that was, but she lived far off, and was healthy and well-to-do; in

* Cowper.

short, did not need us; but I felt sorry I had neglected her so long; her lively joy on seeing us was quite a reproach. " Here again is a mistress who has lived in service," said I, stepping into a spruce little parlour; "I was saying, Martha, you may always know the dwelling of an old gentleman's servant by its neatness."

" Why sure, ma'am," replied the brisk Martha, "it would be hard, after putting so much labour upon other folks' housen, one should not make one's own decent."

I have surely told you Martha's history before; if so, as dear old Scott said of his Calvanism, you can skip it, madam.

Martha was cook to those ill-starred gentlewomen who kept a school at Penzance about a dozen years ago, and failed because, I was told then, they brought pine-apples instead of cabbages to a country market. Poor sweet Caroline used to complain piteously that, whereas she had paid a guinea-and-half each lesson of dancing, the mammas thought it much to pay her half-a-crown. Emily, the poetess (and there was poetry in her verses), went to India, married, and died, and these three events occupied less than a year of her sad life. Her history out-steps romance, but be easy, dear Maria, I am going back to Martha, who took from her well-polished table in the best bedroom, where it was reverently placed, the prayer-book she had from her own dear hands. Martha, in truth, was that kind of spirity, stir-a-coose servant (you have no such words), that it breaks one's heart to lose; a culinary Atlas, a Colossus of all works. She was like those notable hens in a poultry-yard, who find time to fuss and push for other fowls' chickens, as well as their own, and, scarcely giving themselves time to lay a single egg, will hatch and rear brood after brood. This last-named talent of Martha's, unluckily for her mistress, won the hearts of two widowers in succession; the first suitor, Peter James, was the father of five boys, whom he just lived long enough to bequeath to Martha's care, bidding her, with his dying breath, to follow him, "like Christiana with her five boys," which charge, she assured me, weeping, she was resolved to observe; and surely none had a right to blame her, if, having watched and coddled and laboured for them, till they were able to "shifty" for themselves, she bestowed her hand and services on another "widow-man."

But I must walk walks, as well as write them. Kate waits for me to accompany her to Marazion, with the intention to call on the bride, whom we attended to church only last Wednesday. I leave you, therefore, to figure to yourself how busy and happy Martha must be, having now to "scratch for ten."

EE

WALK LVI.

A pet canary.   Bed-liers.   Armless.

RIGHT "miscellaneous" walk, the detail of which will, I fear, only puzzle your dear aching head.

We sometimes are obliged to make a kind of muster call on our favourite cottagers, just to keep ourselves in their minds, and to shew them that they are not out of ours. We did some good, too. Mary Symons really believes her canary would have died, if Miss Kate had not, with her naturalist eyes, spied a minute bladder under the left wing. Before this discovery, Mary "couldn't never think what ailed the poor thing; quite off his meat; wouldn't be without it for nothing;" with such a large brood of her own, nevertheless, of all ages, from the girls plaiting straw in the window-seat, down to the infant of days, who hardly filled the doll's cradle Miss Kate had lent for its accommodation; for, as poor Mary touchingly said, she had had so many, that the old cradle was fairly "rocked to bits, and she was looking to have another child, but God knows what is best for us." In the matter of the canary, saffron-water and puncturation have proved effectual; the pet is convalescent.

Another lucky hit this day, was a peep at old Susannah Cornish, whom we found in "racks of pain;" nobody to hand her a cup of water, far less to run for the doctor, for the promised powder. The poor maid must go to bal, to get "a crum o' meat" to put in her own mouth.

It was not many days ago, that I was exhorting this very Susannah to call in, upon a time, on Betsey Pengelly, who lay weary and lonely the livelong day. I told you all about her and heroine Mary; close by, too. She replied, she ought to visit her friends more frequent, but I might depend it was busy all her strength, when she came home from work, to right away her little chars, and fit a bit o' meat for herself and the *chield*, a strapping wench, who would cut up into three of her little meek, travail-worn mother. Well, now the two worthy bed-liers are within twenty yards of each other, abandoned to pain, and to that sore trial to the poor, solitude;

yet never indulging one repining thought, that such should be the meed of a laborious, blameless life. Ah! they know better; "their all is not laid here." This resigned spirit is the more commendable, that they never read Thomson's excellent "Castle of Indolence," to learn how.

> "Without it (toil) would come a heavier bale,
> Loose life, unruly passions, and diseases pale."

Yes, yes, the fulfilment, in our eyes, of the prophecy, "In the sweat of thy brow," &c., is an evidence of many thousand years in favour of revealed religion. Sweat we must (it would be more polite to say perspire, only that would enfeeble the image); sweat we must, if we would eat, *i.e.*, relish our bread, for our own, for other's good; or else suffer from remorse at having done nothing towards procuring either.

A propos, I cannot make up my mind to pass my hopeful disciple and patient, Armless. Nothing can be more encouraging than Anne's present bulletin,—"Not a respectful word from his lips, and the best of destructions to the children." This sentence is verbatim, and, in speaking it, a gladsome smile lighted up her smutty features. I cannot affirm that she hadn't a clean inch about her, since the arms were plunged to the elbows in soapsuds. At any rate, I hope her habits are improving, for she shewed considerable concern, that Miss Kate was obliged to retreat to the door, during our parley, owing to the intolerable effluvia from an uncleaned drain at the entrance.

There are many excuses for poor Anne's sluttishness. She came into the world a good-humoured slattern, had a bad education, a drunken husband, and many years' itinerancy with her armless boy, whom she is said to have exhibited, as an extempore show, at all the fairs, markets, and "throngs of men," this side London.

WALK LVII.

New cure for a pig. Brushing. Old eyes. Generosity of the poor.

ENNY TREDREA was, as usual, in a world of trouble. How shall I bring back Jenny to your remembrance? Will you recall her under the amiable designation of the bitterest scold in the parish, with the most shrewish of bantam cocks, who has been recorded to have out-cackled his mistress; or can you identify her as the unfortunate householder, who was obliged to go into lodgings during that memorable gale that carried away a moiety of her dwelling? It is now rebuilt and re-tenanted, and very wisely contracted to half its original size, which was large for a cottage; but, nobody being willing to "live in a wide house with a brawling woman," the room, still unoccupied, could never obtain a lodger.

Jenny's present grievance is a sick pig, which she was coaxing to eat when we arrived, and which, disturbed at our approach, upset his tub, and almost ourselves to boot. No wonder, poor wretch! Jenny had been doctoring him after her own head. I wonder was *she* ever subjected to this course of medicine? First she "guv un brimstone—that was no use, then bold almanac,"* and now she is trying "gunpowder hetted over the coals."

"Why, your frying-pan will blow up, Jenny," said Miss Kate. This was the first time I had seen Jenny smile, during the best part of twenty years. It might be truly called a successful sally.

We met your favourite Mary (Mary the friend) at the little corner plantation, and called up the

"Orient blush of quick surprise"

into her honest cheeks. What a beautiful feature is a blush! When Milton declares

---

* Bol Ammoniac.

of his Eve, that no thought infirm altered her cheek, I hope and trust he did not mean to say she did not change colour; if so, she would have been a sad, insipid beauty, which I by no means believe of her. I daresay she reddened when she was dismissed from the bower on Raphael's visit; I do not mean, like any of your "working-day" misses, with indignation, but from a pardonable struggle between her conjugal inferiority and the "conscience of her worth."*

A gentleman once said prettily of this come and go complexion which I am admiring, that its effect was like breathing on a polished mirror.

Mary assured me they should have sent the "little 'Lizbeth to school, but for fearing of her behaviour."

Have I never introduced you to 'Un Molly? If I have not, it must be because she is so distant—the other side of that weary Relubbas—and so unimportunate, that she slips out of mind. I do not think that 'Un Molly Gilbert ever asked me anything towards sup or bite, cure or cover, since I have known her. I once reproached her with this, and she told me it would be no better than a sin, to beg for what she did not want. Neither did she ever apply for parish aid, so I concluded she was—wherever the means came from—well provided for. Finding her in the act of patching a pillow-slip (which she smilingly told me was forty years old), just for a change, I began to doubt her "well-to-doness."

"Why do you work without spectacles, 'Un Molly?"

"Mine, ma'am, are grown too young for me, I'm thinking. I can see better, seeming to me, without 'em, but the sewing is nothing particular."

"Capital for one of your age. Now, what *is* your age?"

"I'll tell ye, mistress, if you please, the answer my mother gave to me, when I asked her that same question. 'How old are ye, chield,' says she; 'how shouldn't ye know how old ye be? Anybody can tell you that you was born the year after the new style.' When that was, I can't say, but, from what I can learn about it, I'm thinking I must be eighty-six, more or less."

"Astonishing! I am going to make a bargain with you, 'Un Molly; when I bring you the new pillow-case, I must have the old one."

'Un Molly quite entered into the joke, and helped me to search for the primitive portion of this curious piece of embroidery. She then told me a veracious story of one Kate Pope, the pedigree and piecing of whose bolster-cloth wholly eclipsed

---

* *Paradise Lost.*—Book viii., line 502.

hers, for, when 'Un Kate came to sell it to the ragman, it weighed—how much do you think?—eight pounds and an ounce. 'Un Molly had it from her own lips, and the poor never think of suspecting each other of exaggeration (I am afraid that *is* rather the snare of the wealthy). Their punctuality is sometimes quite edifying, though it helps to spin out their narratives.

'Un Molly never had any children, though he whom she and her husband had adopted—a stranger to their blood, and an orphan—seemed unto them as their own. The old man, at his death, left him heir to his small savings, with a charge to take care of 'Un Molly, which he has duly observed, she said, ever since, poor labouring man as he is, with a heavy family. 'Un Molly said that, thanks to him and a good providence, she had never been without a "meal's meat."

All this while, it never entered into her head to admire her own generosity in this transaction, to be thus grateful for a small share of that which some would have thought should have been all their own.

The tale was honourable to both parties, and sorely "shames those rich-left heirs" who grudge, and will litigate for, the smallest portion of their ample inheritance. Alas! there are more rich men than "'Un Mollys" in the world.

I think I shall be as pathetic as Burns, if I happen to survive my auld Molly; whether as poetical, is another matter.

At parting with Miss Kate, she wished her, with all due solemnity, a good husband. Nothing could be further from the vulgar levity with which this is usually said. 'Un Molly had herself been blessed with a good husband, and could think of no greater blessing. By the bye, I saw Kate slipping a shilling into her hand. I hope, for both their sakes, this took place before the parting benediction.

Long may it be before I have occasion to take up the bard's lament, and say,

> "I've lost a frien' and naebor dear;
> 'Un Molly's dead."

WALK LVIII.

Spectacles.   True wisdom.   Jenny Priske.

WALK by proxy, and therefore a short one, for it is not easy to see, far less to describe, from another's eyes.

A propos, it was to carry the promised spectacles to Molly, that Kate was induced to leave me in bed with a cold.   Out of three pairs, the dear old soul chose the worst, because, she said, they fitted her nose best; the others were very well for seeing, but they kept slipping down.   The rejected ones were a fine stray waif for 'Un Polly Lukey, who had just before, she told Kate, "knocked out her two eyes," but little thought, when she saw they were out, she should have the good luck to knock them in again immediately.   Our dear little 'Un Polly, too, is wondrous wise, but hers is not the wisdom one is apt to ascribe to the three sages of Thessaly, and other sages of this cast.   Hers is the wisdom which its gracious Author saw fit to "reveal unto babes"—wisdom which her native simpleness throws out in bolder relief; this "wisdom from above," in which she exercises herself day and night.   Every breath, one may say, is with her a thanksgiving, every gesture, a prayer.   She might truly say, that, by her inability to read, she had lost her company.   Did I say that 'Un Molly is enchanted to find, on the authority of a printed book, that she is eighty-seven, a year older than she had supposed?   The poor are exceedingly ambitious to be thought old and sick; this is their little vanity.

Harriet Priske, Kate found ironing her new cap, a great stride towards reformation.   We shall really have hopes of her, when she covers her raven locks with a matron's cap.

Old Jenny was full of dolor and complaint, as usual.   Complaining is her elixir of life and beauty.   It *is* so with some people.   I never trouble myself to dispute the point with Jenny, but let her go on lauding and bewailing herself by turns.   But is it not strange, and one of our human anomalies, that she never alludes to her real misfortunes—the loss of her husband and her leg?   Yet she cannot fail to value those only genuine claims to sympathy and toleration.

WALK LIX.

A finale.

I HAVE been quill-driving all yesterday and to-day, dearest M———, in order to make up and pack off this bundle of stuff, before my departure for Carnanton, and before Mrs. Scott's for town. I shall think myself lucky enough, if I can achieve both; how far you will think yourself so, remains to be proved. Before I send you any more, I ought by rights to have had my cue. Tell me, dear, where did I break off last? yet, what matter? are you not saying with Tommy Tudor, on occasion of a dry preacher, "Shut your book, shut your book—enough of the sort;" or like poor little Mosey, Mrs. Neynoe's lap-dog, when the worthy alluded to came to "conclude;" ready to spring off your cushion with delight.

As we may probably exchange some letters before this reaches you, I do not see the use of spinning it out longer than will suffice to take an affectionate leave.

Yours ever and anon, C. C. P.

Will Benjamin now say, "What! no more?" It is more likely he will leave out the *no*. "What! *more*?"

WALK LX.

A slattern's household.   Great Eliza.   'Un Sally.

RASHLY pronounced Anne Prowle to be the queen of slatterns—but no such thing; we were told of a family upon the downs, suffering the extreme of poverty, but whatever we had heard or imagined, was outdone in the reality.   Dirt and destitution could no further go.   And yet there was no sickness; the father was in regular and profitable employ as a mine-mason, and, with small deduction for "a pint o' beer at a time," brought in his wages for the maintenance of his family.   He never had been a sot; that master-key to domestic neglect and misery was not here to solve the puzzle, but there was one which answered the purpose as well—a sluttish wife.   Never did my eyes behold such a loose, slammerkin, smiling, snuff-taking slattern as Mary Anne Hoskings, with her red hair streaming down under her tattered cap, her snuffy nose and chin, her light chintz gown "all in squads," with her ultra-fashionable sleeves dipping every now and then into the washing-tub she was loitering over, her handkerchief —but I will pursue the search no further.   Reverting to her approaching confinement, and the dilapidated state of the premises, I asked, "What will you do with those open beams? you will catch your death."   "Yes, I suppose I shall.   John was saying it *oft* to be boarded—dangerous, too, for anyone slipping their foot— I was nearly down through, yesterday."

"Is this your only chamber?"

"Oh yes, fie! and a clever chamber it will be, when we have got a winder to let in some light, and a bit of stairs to get up by.   John was saying—"

As I advanced further into the room, I caught sight of a girl blowing the fire (for *that* the lazy will do, whatever they leave undone).   She was—squalid-looking thing, about eight years old, pale as ashes, and marked with the small-pox—one of those poor creatures that shrink from the light, and blink when they get into it.   But she had an additional motive now for trying to keep out of sight—her clothing was simply and solely, without hyperbole, nothing but her shift. You are incredulous! Stay a moment till I describe my next visit, when I found the mother washing that shift. After some preliminary talk, and great abuse of the great idle maid, her eldest daughter, who refused to work at the bal, I enquired for "the little girl who blew the fire." The woman still grinned, but looked more sheepish, as she made reply, "I won't tell ye no lies; the maid Lavinia is up in bed, while I'm washing her shift to put up to her." "And the others?" I enquired. "Be there, too." At this moment, one of the bed-liers cried out in a peevish tone, "Mother, do speak to Lavinja; she will keep getting out on the *plancheon*,* leving me in the cold." The woman repeated her impotent commands to "lie quiet," again and again, observing truly that "she might as well argay with the winds."

"I'll try," exclaimed I, in a thrill of indignation. "Fury lends arms"—and supplies legs also, or I should hardly have ventured on the ladder, in the rickety condition of its staves. It reclined against the floor of the upper room, as one has seen in a stable-loft, so that, by the time I had mounted half-way, I could peer in and make my observations. On the two beds—steads, I should say—that confronted me (for drapery there was none, except what the spiders had made, to give them a claim to the title), the square, naked frame, to the sight, seemed all alive with small heads, which popped up for an instant, and, in terror at the sight of me, then clustered together in the centre, like pilchards' heads in that paragon of Cornish dishes, a "star-gazing pie."

Apart from these wild bed-ouins, squatted the fugitive Lavinia, in that sort of "hight a-guinea cock" attitude, which is not the most graceful, even with the accompaniments of frock and sash, but, without them, and in profile, put me in mind of a flesh-colour grasshopper. I expected to see her hop off in character at sight of me; but no! there she stuck, staring at me over her elevated shoulder, never heeding, and scarcely seeming to hear, persuasions or threats, till I thought of offering a bribe. At the first hint of a new frock, she was "off like a lamp-lighter," an image, dear Maria, whose obsoleteness I regret, and for the sake of which I was sorry for the introduction of gas. I forget whether there were lamplighters in your Truro days. One of these I shall never forget, and yet he is the earliest thing I can remember, with his ladder and his smutty face, from which he had not time to wipe away the clouds through which his bright eyes

---

* Floor.

gleamed, like the sun through a smoked glass. On he dashed from post to post, with his pot of oil to fill the lamp, and his torch to kindle it, and his ladder to get up to it ; then down again, and up again in the twinkling of an eye, or rather, before any twinkling had time to take place. I have never in my riper years seen that human being who so completely came up to my notions of despatch in business.

Mais pour revenir à nos—coches. Mr. P—— could not endure the thought of the poor soul's going through her approaching confinement with that hollow floor under her, and so offered to lend John a few pounds to planch it, which, let me here record, the trusty John returned more promptly and thankfully than many so called his betters do. The exertions of the lazy, on the one or two occasions of their lives when they *do* exert themselves, are preternatural. The flooring was bought at Marazion, and, that the mason might not lose his day's wages, the females brought it home those two miles on their backs. The eldest—"the big Eliza," who is the terror of all the country—sustained Caliban's part of bearing and grumbling, though as much pleased at heart as that worthy on his introduction to Stephano's bottle. It was the first occasion, I believe, on which she had gone to labour without a previous *leathering*; yet Eliza is "no vulgar—boy," I might say —there is little need to alter the text for her—she looks so like a great hulking bal-boy, who has put on his mother's petticoats for a frolic. She has her good qualities ; there is no shuffle, no vulgar prevarication, in her wickedness. When she lies, she looks you in the face ; and when convicted, laughs. You then begin to preach, but she "knows it all as well as you do," and audaciously pronounces judgment on herself, "if so be she don't mend her ways," which, however, she tells me she thinks she shall do "some day or other." This makes the neighbours pronounce her to be past shame, and induces me to doubt whether she ever had any.

Boldness in vice doesn't always infer that true hardihood of nature inseparably connected with the highest efforts, whether it be of the martyr at the stake, the soldier in the field, or, alas, the felon at the gallows—which last (if her fortune be truly told by her neighbours) is most likely to be my heroine's destiny. Her felonious exploits have been chiefly confined to her father's house. "Why do you not keep her without her meals," says I, "if nothing else will do ?" "We are afraid, if she should be a hungered, she should bring shame upon us ; better she should rob *we* than do that." Accordingly, this said *we* Eliza considers as lawful game, and she can hardly be called a thief, for whatever she sees, or anything that comes within her reach, she confidently appropriates—hat, frock, or handkerchief, though the owners should go without any, which is often the case ; when I meet the other members of this accomplished family bonnetless on the downs, I am told, as a matter of course, that the great Eliza took it. Well ! she has her moral uses, like adversity—she serves, if not for an example, yet for a warning, to the little ones.

I have said very little of 'Un Sally lately, although my visits are duly continued, because, dear Maria, I fancy you have a doubt, if not of the sincerity of her piety, at least of its *reality* ; and, indeed, her sentiments are so much above the flight of ordinary minds, that I can fancy, to one who only reads about her, she may have a dramatic air. I have aided that impression, perhaps, by saying she is what Mrs. Siddons might be amid age, sickness, and solitude, and in a thatched cottage. I can imagine how her high-soaring visions and sentiments may tell lamely on paper ; that you might at first sight think they were assumed ; but it is not by these I judge 'Un Sally's genuineness.

I have made two or three happy hits in my life, by reading character from minute traits ; the portals may appear well defended, whilst a chink in the wall may betray the carelessness of the garrison.

My ancient heroine might work herself up to a state of unnatural elevation—that's what *you* think—from a consciousness that it pleases me ; but she would not take her shillings and think no more of them ; she would enquire who had sent those shillings, instead of her thoughts for ever running on those who have happened to drop a word of comfort—and so on.*

* Although 'Un Sally lived for some years after this Walk was written, and her name occurs once again, this seems a fitting place to add a letter on the subject of her death, from the pen of a valued friend of the author's, whose opinion of her character is worth recording.—M. R.

Letter from Mr. Robert Hichens on the death of 'Un Sally.

LONDON, February 5, 1844.

My dear Mrs. Pascoe,

I am greatly obliged by your kind letter of the 22nd ult., informing me that our poor old friend has cast off that earthly tabernacle which weighed down the immortal soul ; all her bright visions are now more than realized. Faith, for her, is swallowed up in sight. Her quiet departure

WALK LXI.

Clerk and sexton.   Respect for superiors.

S you are interested in my history of one of our church functionaries, I am disposed to introduce you to another, in the person of our clerk and hind, honest Tom Bray, and relate a joint anecdote of both. How I wish you could hear it, as I did, from Kate, who tells it *con amore !*

Now our dear old bailiff, Tom Bray, has, I believe, a sincere regard for his master, and would, I really think, have been sorry to have seen him murdered by the ruffians; but Tom had served three, and survived two, vicars, and these things,

is what one could have wished for her, had one been permitted to choose, for those about her would not have appreciated her transports, and might, perhaps, have cumbered and clogged, in some degree, with earthly cares, the parting spirit. I was sincerely attached to her, and feel I have one friend, who pleaded for me with God, less in the world. I recollect now her saying to me, " Maybe you will live to bless God that you knew old Sally Fox ;" and I hope I do. I never shall forget her giving her blessing, at my request, to my two sons, and I trust it will rest upon them. Did I ever tell you one of her bursts, like the roll of an organ, when she asked me what day I was born ? " If anybody had told me then, in my days of sin and folly, ' Sally Fox, there's a man-child born into the world to-day, who will be a friend to you fifty years hence,' I should have laughed at them ; but so it is come to pass." I then said to her that it was marvellous to consider how the threads of human life, crossed and twisted in with each other, as it were, all arranged from the beginning by the divine will. This set her marvellous imagination to work, and next day she told me of a splendid vision. When I recollect how little I did for her, and how great was her gratitude and her love, I cannot but reflect how few, even of those who have learnt the *duty* of Christian almsgiving, appear to have realized the *privileges* of it. With the mite that is left, do what you please. It cannot be better appropriated than as you propose.

 * * * * *   With kindest regards to Mr. Pascoe,

I am, my dear Mrs. Pascoe,

Very sincerely your friend,

RT. HICHENS.

HH

as the eel-skinner said, were not much when you are used to them ; besides, if the rioters did not reverence the parson, how should they take account of the sexton or the clerk ? So, during the affray, argued these two casuists, and, if all the truth must be told, Tom and Dick were observed skulking behind the church, whilst a horrid tumult was raging in front of it.

"Tom," quoth Dick, "'tis a pity, if you plaise, we can't see a little of what's going on out there."

"'*Tis* a pity," said Tom ; "but what's the use of running our noses into danger?"

"Now you see," resumed the first speaker, "if I could climb that ash-tree yonder, like Zaccheus—for I too am small of stature—"

"How should *you* climb a tree, uncle Dick, with your rheumatics ? besides, 'twer'n't no ash, 'twere a sycamore-tree that Zaccheus got up into," interposed the higher authority.

"I ask your pardon," resumed Dick, "it *was* a sycamine, sure 'nough ; but howsomedever, ash, or sycamine, or what you will—"

And thus these two faithful adherents of the vicar (Kate declares, how ever she learnt the story!) went on discussing matters behind, whilst tumult and sacrilege were going on before ; but poor Tom, in justice I must add, has every virtue under the sun but courage.

Whilst on the subject of the church, I will tell you what a stubborn old Methodist told me the other day,—that "he was hindered attending it, by seeing the Sunday-school rise and curtsey as I passed." Now he was never more mistaken in his life, if he thought it fed my pride, but there is nothing I know of prettier than a village maid's smiling curtsey. It is an action which from an equal would be of good-will, but to a superior is a devout recognition of *His* laws who has decreed difference of rank and degree, and, if I know my own joints, they would not refuse to bend to anyone of higher degree than my own, and I *do* love to be curtsied to after this fashion. And I do love, as I listen on my homeward way, to hear from the lip of childhood such texts as "God is Love," and a pious mason instructing an attentive youth at the bottom of the ladder (I caught the words from his eminence),—"he shall then know the height and depth of it." But, alas! the bright millenial vision fled when I passed a public-house, the sight, the fumes, and din of which, shewed too plainly that the principle of evil still held rule on our earth.

WALK LXII.

The parish re-visited.   Warm welcome to an old friend.
Little 'Un Polly.

 DO not know, dearest Maria, whether our Walks must be rigorously restricted to walking; for it is hard, writing to you, to keep back the bits of philosophy and gossip which they now and then suggest. At all events, I may tell you of Cousin C———'s late visit to the Vicarage, leading, as it has done, to the very cream of cottage visiting.

Cousin C———, you know, was born in our squire's house of Tregembo, of whose haunted chambers she is fond to enthusiasm.* She speaks, even now, with affectionate unction, of the old forest that had seen its best days before she was born, and is now reduced to a few unsightly trunks, bearing somewhat the same relation to their high-sounding name, that the bleached bones of a malefactor do to the living hero, who kept all the neighbourhood *in terrorum.*

It was very touching, and I did not feel a bit jealous, to see the rapturous reception which C——— met from her—I should say her parents'—old protegées; for the little missie was too young to be a patroness. Great, however, was the love, and fervent the admiration, she even then attracted by her fair skin and golden curls, which made one old woman liken her to "a little *Sant* in glory," and this sentiment was kept alive by her "angel visits" from the neighbouring Vicarage (then served by my uncle) of Breage.

On the present occasion, I had every reason to anticipate the warmth of welcome which met us at every cottage door, especially at dear old Polly Luke's, for she had told me, in the plenitude of her love for "Miss Shearlotte," that she would "travel

---

miles and miles upon her tippy-toes, only to kiss the dear fingers' ends of her." At sight of her, however, love got the better of veneration, and the old woman snatched her again and again to her bosom, as their talk of old times and departed friends aroused her grateful feelings. "There's Mrs. Pascoe a-laughing," said she, between whiles (for it was impossible I should not); "but I don't care, my tender, dear Miss Shearlotte!" and then another hug.

One has heard of the "penalties of popularity." One honest soul, with her hands in the wash-tub, stood curtseying, and colouring, and dimpling, and asking for old friends, and adverting to old times, till, seized with a sudden spasm of tender recollection, she flung her unwipen hands round C——'s neck, crying out, "my tender, dear Miss Shearlotte, you're so naatural I couldn't help it."

We used to call Cousin C—— the Lady in Comus, but, whoever gave her this name (you or I), it is quite misapplied. Her goodness is the very reverse of the milk-and-water purity and didactic virtue of that heroine. The sprinkle of pickle which glanced from her towards Louisa and me, while she sat with her hand locked in 'Un Polly's, would have given Comus better hopes of her; but he would have been mistaken, for all the while her looks seemed to be asking the old woman's pardon for the disposition to fun she could not restrain.

I never saw anyone (except, indeed, those she went to visit) so delighted as C—— was with the adventures of her ten days' sojourn amongst us. Her mind is of that tender, plaintive, perhaps rare, class, which loves the past better than the present or the future; loves it, not like some, boastfully or complainingly, but out of purest, warmest devotion to persons and things gone by; as somebody sweetly said,

> "Forms familiar gather fast,
>   Fondly loved and early known,
> While the spectre of the past
>   O'er the present reigns alone."

Not quite alone, either, in her case, for she brims up and runs over with present tenderness even to her neighbour's cat, else she would not deserve all the hugs and tender squeezes I have recorded.

I do not remember ever telling you anything of this dear little 'Un Polly of ours; if I have not, it must be on the true love principle, that she lies too near my heart to be talked about. Long before I wrote Walks, she had been my prime favourite, from her fervent piety, wakeful charity, and strong, inconceivable energy, which it is a wonder has not long ago worn out the most pigmy of bodies. Nor is this all; she has had to fret over a worthless husband, who abandoned her and her children before I came to the parish; so how she contrived to "*fouchy* away," so as to keep herself from being chargeable to it, I cannot say. She was first brought to my notice by dear Miss L. Grenfell (to whom she often refers as "Miss Liddy in Heaven"), and was, I dare to say, greatly assisted by her; for within these five years I have myself been made the channel, by Mrs. Hitchins (the "Emma" of Henry Martyn), of sending gowns and *shimmies* for the dear old grateful creature, and my aunt (another of that sisterhood) was her life-long benefactress. You will not wonder, then, at her rapturous reception of C—— C——. The house of Grenfell are not all the memories Aunt Polly has helped to embalm. I was saying to one still more dear to memory*—I know not whether it was during her last visit here—"There is a little good old woman in this parish, Lucy, to whom I always repair when my spirit is heavy—her cheerful piety is sure to restore its elasticity." I was not aware that she marked my random words. Some days after, when I stood beneath our ivy porch to see that dear one drive from it, and she was near enough to observe the tears that somehow would flow, as if foreboding what was so soon to come, she presented her lovely, pitying face at the carriage window, and said earnestly (but it is nothing, unless you knew her half-playful, half-plaintive manner of saying these things), "Go to Aunt Polly; go to Aunt Polly!"

Two favourite phrases are ever on 'Un Polly's lips, and ever linked together—"Well, my dear," and "Bless the Lord"—and their abiding expression on her countenance is heightened by the glad twinkle of her little loving eyes. She enquires in her own primitive fashion for all my friends and relations, beginning the catalogue with "How is sister? how is cousin?" and if she were to hear they were all dying, she would exclaim, "Well, my dear," and "Bless the Lord." It was in this tone she spoke of her daughter Kitty dying of consumption, and leaving a kind husband and helpless family.

But there was one cross which, lying in her path daily aud hourly, Polly could *not* so limberly get over. This is the habitual drunkenness of Reynolds, her last remaining child, whose housekeeper she is, being, as he would describe himself,

---

* Mrs. Marsh, *née* Napleton, who died May 5, 1836.

young for marriage. I sometimes find her sadly cast down with this, though, in relating the tale, she does not spare one of her favourite mollifyings.

"Home again drunk last night; pity, isn't it? Well, my dear, we must pray for them, and we *shall* prevail, bless the Lord." But now Reynolds Luky is "'listed for a teetotal," and brings home all his gettings, and civil words with them, and he never swears, or but seldom. Of course, Polly's "well, my dears" and blessings are redoubled; she is better fed and clothed, and she can attend "the means of grace," and be herself that means to any sick neighbour.

But perfect bliss is not for man,—not even for the sunshiny bosom of 'Un Polly. Some days since, she met me at the door, and told me, with uplifted hands, that she was "come to a great misfortin—a great misfortin, sure enough," wasn't it? and she would tell me how it was. "Reynolds's two canaries, my dear, and he so good now, bless the Lord! after I carried them up into his chamber, too, to keep them from the cat." "Who eat them up after all, 'Un Polly?" "No, my dear Miss Pascoe, 'twas all the *auld* fool's doing—no blame to the cat. I must needs be paddling about the cage, thinking to right up a bit of nest for them, and bent the wires a crum, I reckon, for the little hen—but you shall hear all. In comes Alice Trethewy. ''Un Polly,' says she, 'I have a mind to see your two birds.' 'Yes, my dear,' says I, 'and welcome; they are up in the chamber.' 'Be they?' says she—and up we went. My dear Miss Pascoe, I looked to the cage, and what did I see but both my birds gone! I don't know what fashion I was. Alice looked up and said, 'Don't ye go for to fainty, 'Un Polly; here is one of the birds in my hand, and likely we may find another before Reynolds comes home.' That was all I thought about, my *dear* Miss Pascoe; I was afraid he would swear, and he a teetotaller, bless the Lord! So home he comes. 'Reynolds, my dear child,' says I, 'mother has done a bad job by ye; but oh! my son, my dear son, dontee swear! be angry and sin not. Mother will get another canary, if she do travel all the way to Penzance for one, only don't ye swear; be vexed with mother, if you will (I deserve you should), only, my dear son, remember what is said, 'Swear not at all." And, bless the Lord, he refrained his tongue in a measure. How thankful I *oft* to be, my dear, shouldn't we? He neither cursed nor swore, bless the Lord!"

'Un Polly* seemed overwhelmed with admiration at her son's placability, and

* When Polly was on her death-bed, and the doctor, who was visiting a child ill of fever, called in to offer his services, she said in reply, "Do me good, my dear man? no one on earth can do me good now, bless the Lord!" The doctor said he had never been so moved before, as by the good old woman's energetic exhortation. She expired while trying to pronounce the last words of the Doxology.

now, but for the one drawback, that Reynolds will, for all she can say, go on telling his prayers in bed, 'Un Polly's would be (as my own little canary used to say as plain as bill could speak)

"Joy without alloy."

WALK LXIII.

NOVEMBER 29, 1838.

A gale. Tom Rapson, the cobbler.

IT must surely be a sympton of growing old (what else can it be?), that I, who used to exult and flap my wings, like any other curlew, in a storm, should have shrunk from accompanying Kate and uncle to the Cove this day. They drove up (walking was out of the question) to behold the fine ground-swell of which yesterday's outrageous wind was a sure promise. Harry himself declared he had never but once witnessed such a toss of the waves. Three or four in succession passed sheer over Great and Little Cudden Head, their faces well washed up to the grass top. They could talk of nothing else, all the rest of the day, but the wonders of that great deep, and made me almost feel guilty in not having gone to view them. But I had enough to do to breast the gale as far as Tom Rapson's, in Relubbas Lane. They told me he and his wife were in a perishing state—ill, and wanting everything. You have heard of Tom Rapson before, though you may not know it.

My magic lantern turns up its shadowy figures with such shadowy rapidity, that even *your* memory must fail to retain the fugitive impression; yet I think it would hardly have lost the grotesque outline of Tom, had he ever presented himself before you in his cobbler's niche, seated, or rather "scrumped up," before a low window, five of whose nine panes are blocked up by old rags and hats, and the other four obscured by the dust of ages;

> "Tom in his straw,
> While free from law,"

like his namesake of Bedlam, "in his thoughts as great as a king." "Free from the law" he has, it seems, always shaken himself—first, of the law of sobriety, having drank up I don't know how many "housen." This was before we came to the parish, for I can remember him sitting tapping at that identical window, in the "stall which serves him for parlour, kitchen, and hall."

Never was there so ill-matched a pair as he and his wife, unless I except his own pair of legs, one being considerably shorter than the other. Kattern's every third word is a petition for some gratuity, whilst Tom takes pains to prove he wants for nought. The only boon I ever knew him catch at, was the professional gratuity of a pair of high boots, for which I had vainly tortured my inventive faculties to find a use. They were too small, I found, for those arrived at boot age, and too inflexible for old women afflicted with corns—in a word, hating waste as I do, I was delighted, and so was Tom, who wore them to morning service, in consequence, three Sundays following, besides being mounted on high weekly occasions. One of these was a visit to the mistress of the Workhouse, then supposed to be dying. I found Tom at the bottom of the stairs, laboriously pulling on his boot, in which he stumped up to prove his grateful remembrance for one who had shown him much friendship.

WALK LXIV.

Garden-girl's death. Blind Peter.

MOST melancholy walk, truly. It was to condole with the disconsolate mother of my poor little Jennefer, for so many years our garden-girl, errand-goer, letter-carrier, and, as I told you before, my companion in need, when Katey happened to be otherways engaged, or unequal to a long walk. But she is gone! the poor little humble-mannered, ready creature, and so suddenly!

Mary, the mother, worked hard about getting up the potatoes (for blind Peter can do nothing in helping forward these necessary matters), and so caught a desperate cold, that exhibited itself in the form of quinsey; but I suppose it was something of a more malignant character, for the baby first, and afterwards Jennefer, took the infection. We heard the poor child was ill, but they said "the fever had turned;" so, though it was borne on my heart all yesterday, that I must go to see her, I yielded to the arguments and entreaties poured upon me from parlour and kitchen (Mem. Never resist a good impulse). "You could not stand it up there on the downs," says one; "you would be blown away," cried another; "or drowned," adds a third, "the showers are so sudden and heavy." The skies, in short, were more than forbidding, they were appalling. Then I should catch the disorder, and—the acme of evils—infect the whole household!

I went on with my tent-stitch, with an occasional qualm of conscience, till about six in the afternoon, when little Mary came in weeping, to say "Jennefer had passed half-an-hour ago." It was very strange and shocking, but we could gain no further distinct information from the poor little frightened girl, as to the manner of her sister's death; so this morning I went to the house, only waiting for Kate to plait up a cap, lest the mother, in the plenitude of her affection, should deck the little death-cold head in her very best. It was a considerate thought, and as I glanced at the dejected countenance of the worker, and the blush-satin strings, and thought of the object of all this finery, I was irresistibly reminded of Flora MacIvor, and the white favours, and the shroud.*

It is a proof of Scott's fidelity to nature, that one never meets an affecting trait or scene, but it suggests to the memory something from his writings. Steeny Muckleback's funeral was also in my head, as I sat opposite the grieving mother, making abortive attempts at consolation, and turning out the contents of my basket.†

What an elevation grief bestows! In general, Mary is the humblest, civilest, most thoughtful of human beings. Now I could fancy she looked with scorn on my gifts, as if there was an impertinence in an attempt to divert or mollify her sorrow; and I positively felt ashamed, as I looked for some one to receive the offerings which her sorrow seemed to disdain. But when the cap came forth, and the mother heard it was Miss Kate's own work, she clasped her hands in an ecstasy of sorrow, indeed, but it was evident this was the first ray of comfort which had reached her heart,

> "To see her bairn respectit."

The basket of flowers, the culling of the whole garden, was a less fortunate stroke. They had been *her* care, and seemed to realize her loss. The poor mother turned from them in an agony. "No more flowers now," she said; "no more—this was the time when she might be looking for her return from work, but now she might be looking long enough—never, never more. What was all the world to her?" &c. But she was mistaken, for when I remarked on the appearance of the babe she was pressing close to her bosom, and rocking to and fro in her grief, she turned her feverish eyes full on me, and patiently listened to some directions about dosing it. "Would I please to look upon *her*?" she asked, as I rose to go. I was pained to refuse, but I had half promised Kate to keep from the infected chamber, and owed her this concession, since she had forborne visiting it herself, at my earnest request; but I was quite sorry I said anything about infection—it was a new stab to the festering heart. "There was no infection with *her*," she said, so I thought I would just follow the old nurse up the few stairs, as she went to fetch the basket that conveyed the melancholy garland—but oh, what a sight it was! On their one

---

* *Waverley*, Chap. 68.
† *Antiquary*, Chap. 31.

uncurtained bed, covered over with a scanty coarse rug, I could trace the little skeleton form, before I drew from the face the homely coverlet; it was yellow, and dark, and wasted. I should not have recognised it, but the look was not revolting, as I had been led to expect. I only remained while I could hold my breath, but that moment's glance served to prove the truth of what the poor little mother had just said—"It is a dismal thing when death comes to naked walls; but oh!" she added, "I didn't care for the nakedness, if *she* was here."

I think the bereaved soul was soothed at my visit to the chamber of death. Her manner was less wild when, in reply to my offers of assistance, she said, though with a fresh burst of sorrow, "I suppose, ma'am, we shall be still looking to you?" She did not mean for any gratuity; her delicate reserve in making known her wants, has been truly surprising, considering their urgency. I do not think she ever asked, or even *spelt*, for a thing, in all the years I have visited her cottage. Who amongst us, that hasn't known want of food and raiment, can estimate this fine quality?

But all this while, I hope, dear M———, you recognise as old acquaintances poor blind Peter and his little faithful Mary, who *would* keep her faith with him, in defiance of friends and prudence, after his eyes were blown out at the mine.

1839 to 1846.

WALK LXV.

JANUARY 22, 1839.

The garden-girl's mother.

T will be eight weeks next Wednesday since our poor little Jennefer died, and for that time I have been so taken up with guests, coming one after another, for a day or two, a few days, and a week, that, what with bowing out and bowing in, preparing and setting to rights, I have not had till to-day a moment to call again on the poor sorrowing parents. I have a notion that my visit of condolence there, was the last I recorded, before this phantasma of visitors confused my brain. At least, so I thought as I ambled along the downs, flattering myself that I should find the poor folk in better cheer, for in their line of life, thought I, the hurry and exigencies of life, anticipating the office of time, give a healthy tone to the wound, before it has time to skin over. But I reasoned as one who never had a child. Mary was paler and sadder than at my first visit. I do not remember that she raised her eyes or head while we stayed, except once, on a sudden burst of grateful feeling to "Miss Kate," whom she should never, never forget, she said, for that *cap*,—nor Peter either. They would walk on hands and knees to do her good; they were saying so, only the evening before; but oh! when those evenings came, and no Jennefer, nobody knew—they might think they did—nobody could ever know what it was! They were wishing for morning before they laid their heads on the pillow; sometimes they might wink their eyes before daybreak, but that made waking worse. Once she dreamed about her, "and oh!" said Mary, "how beautiful, seeming to me, she looked. I spoke to her, and she told me she was in happiness, but not yet in full joy."

Poor Mary loves Kate better, for that cap, than she does her more prudent aunt, for the blankets, sheets, and bed-gowns, which warmed their poor bodies in spite of themselves.

"How like the baby grows to her poor sister," I remarked, and indeed the resemblance was quite striking; for a moment she looked gladdened, then, with a bitter shake of the head, added, "but 'tisn't she."

WALK LXVI.

Marazion. The two spinsters. Study for Crabbe.

WALK to Marazion promises little interest, real or fanciful, or, as it is the fashion to say, moral or physical; the only incident coming fairly under the latter head, on the present occasion, is the filling up of one of the twenty-eight stiles; and, for the moral, what can I hope to cull out of the two or three shops, and two or three old ladies, on whom I daily call?

There is Miss A———, the Ninon of the village, with the tint of eighteen, instead of eighty, on her well-formed cheek, sitting erect, like a lady in wax-work, and she has around her, plants, &c., as bright as a new penny. *Miss A———* —for, whether in consciousness of her remnant bloom, or her dislike of innovation, she chooses to be called Miss—is a sort of person who makes me mind my p's and q's; wherefore I am much better pleased to call on her opposite neighbour, Mrs. K—— C———. Opposite, indeed! for, instead of the righteous rigidity of her *vis-à-vis*, she is the most indulgent of spinsters; and yet I am ashamed to think how much shorter my half-hour's visit seems with her, than that spent with her more discreet townswoman. The truth is, when I look on her mellow countenance, and see her reclining on her layer of cushions, I feel sure that she is neither criticising my ways nor my dress, nor censuring my sentiments. She has a ready, genuine laugh to greet all you say, and her voice is as round as her person.

I can't help thinking what different popes these old ladies would have made. If Miss C——— had filled the papal chair, there would have been carnival all the year round; had her slimmer neighbour—I will not say filled—but sat upright in it, Christendom might have looked to it!

Marazion has, no doubt, its human gems and curiosities, if one had time to delve for them, but if I walk thither, it is in my best bonnet and shawl, and I am restricted in regard to time, and it requires, even in our intercourse with the poor, some courage to break the ice of first acquaintance. Then I fancy one gets more stared at, when intruding on the inhabitants of a town. So, for one reason and another, my charitable visits are restricted to a call on my old cook, Kattern Phillips, and poor Mrs. Gurney, whose "o'erfraught heart" seems lightened by a two minutes' talk about the virtues and graces of her lost daughter.

There are two or three eccentric characters that my friend Crabbe would have rejoiced in. I can call to mind three who are worthy to sit to

> "Nature's sternest painter, but the best."

Had he been alive, Crabbe would have rejoiced in "Happy Harry," so named by my aunt, from the at once benign and merry cast of his countenance. If you meet him ten times a day, he nods, and asks you how you do, with the smile of gratulation you would welcome a friend just returned from a long voyage.

WALK LXVII.

A good son.   Sunday walk.   Hobble-de-hoys.   Uncle Dick.

FOR a novelty, a Sunday walk! When I joined the Sunday-school this morning, and cast my eyes round on the classes, I mentally exclaimed with the disappointed Pyramus,

> "But what see I? No Thisbe do I see."

James Bettens' office of teacher to the second class of boys, was supplied by a scholar from the first. He had sprained his wrist (*Cornish*—wrested his arm), and now what was to be done? I do not mean in reference to the school; his place, poor fellow, might be easily supplied here; for, though the best of good lads, I cannot say he is particularly smart as a teacher, who ought to have three pair of hands, with a rod in each, besides eyes in the back of his head. No, it was of the poor widowed mother and her six orphans I thought. Within the last year, poor Bettens, the father, died of miners' slow but sure consumption, and James, though but a lad, and not with "full gettings," undertook their care and maintenance, without seeming to think he had done anything very meritorious, either.

We could better have spared any arm in the parish, that's a *sure* thing, and so is my "sprain ointment." Luckily, I found some ready-made, but the glory of the cure, if it be one, must be shared with Betsey Peters, who had just charmed it. I think I must have mentioned to you this good boy, whom I found with his arm in a sling, looking dolefully at the bit of fire, which must be supplied by his labour alone.

How I enjoyed my walk back! Such a sense of rest, especially rest from man. The very animals looked as if aware of their Sunday privilege. I fancied I could read in their eyes what Lord Byron calls the "rapture of repose." At that moment, the sound of the church bell, borne on the gentlest of spring zephyrs, saluted my ear; yet, ah me! to how many a deaf ear does the charmer make his appeal.

However, we are bound to admit that things are a fine deal better than when Mr. P——— took possession of the living. Then there was nought on all sides but ill manners and rude merriment. The few church-goers were shocked and obstructed by gangs of saucy, idle (I can neither call them men or boys, so will borrow a term from old Mrs. Laity) "great men-fellows;" but whatever you may call them, they are the most unmanageable of human beings, unless they happen to be good, and useful, and compliable, like my friend James Bettens.

The church bell ceased as I entered the churchyard gate, and by this means I missed my usual Sunday parley with "Uncle Dick," which was a loss to him, as well as to me, and probably to you, also, for he is a Bayley's dictionary of quaint phrases. I never converse with him without culling an odd word or two, and he, I can see, rejoices in these opportunities of displaying his exuberant politeness, and profound reverence for his betters. Uncle Dick Briant is a short old man, who makes himself shorter by his habitual courtesy, and, if it is not a calumny, by a habit he got into during the late war, of stooping, in order to bring his stature within the militia standard. I sometimes feel a misgiving whether Uncle Dick is not the "sly old shaver" he is generally designated in the parish. I should be sorry to think it, but there is a look in the little wizened face, strongly at variance with the solemnity of his manner, and crying tone of his voice.

Allowances should be made for what they call a "swivel eye," which is apt to communicate a dash of pickledom to the most innocent of countenances. It reminds me of that which lurks in the submission of a schoolboy, listening to a jobation from his master. You are never sure, in the midst of his profound attention, that he will not sputter out into a sudden fit of laughter. Uncle Dick would be horrified to hear me say so, for, with his hat in mid-air, as if it partook its wearer's reverence for his betters, he stands assenting to all you say, and interlarding his discourse with his pet phrase, "If you do plaise." In fact, all that happens throughout the world—the births, the buryings; the hour of the day, the state of the weather, or his own rheumatism; the number of his children, or grandchildren—is all as I please, or anybody pleases, with whom Uncle Dick has any dealings.

It is to be questioned whether he so much as lowers a coffin without this civility, or would displace the bones of the "leastest" little still-born babe without asking leave of the small proprietor; though, let me recollect, he is reported not to be always so courteous towards the dead; there is a general complaint that he is sparing of his pains in tolling for them (Kate avers that she has counted as few as five premonitory tolls), and in other respects he is charged with being slack and superficial in his mortuary labours, though he stoutly denies the charge. "Don't ye tell me," said our cross cook, when he happened one day to enter her kitchen, and accost her with his usual politeness, "please me this, and please me the other! Why don't ye have the good manners to dole longer and dig deeper? that is what would please me; not that you shall ever have the burying of me, if I can help it."

I cannot enter into the indignation which many besides the cook express towards our poor sexton.

Humility is with me a universal mollifier, and particularly engaging in a profession inclining its followers to a sort of saucy philosophy, from Hamlet's grave-digger down to George Harris, who preceded Uncle Dick in this department.

The grave on which I surprised him at our next interview, up to his ears in the newly turned-up soil (if I had no objection), was decreed for John Gilbert, who (if I pleased) was to be buried on Monday. "Master liked a deep grave," he said, "seven feet at least," and so, hoping no offence, as he, John Gilbert, was to be buried on Monday, he had thought it well to make a bit of a start, and begin on the Saturday, "just to get things afore the night; and truly one may say, here is the night," added the orator, accompanying the action to the words, by planting his spade vigorously into the hollow ground, and then detaching it, in order to act his next piece of philosophy, he wagged it to and fro, observing that "it would not do for a man to be wavering, like to a door upon its hinges, now looking to one world and now to another."

I was on my way to the singing gallery, and, announcing my intention to Uncle Dick, he launched forth into praises of the new choir. "It was mighty pretty music," if I had no objection; he approved of it, his wife approved of it, Miss Hoare down to the shop approved of it, and "who should know if Miss Hoare didn't, who had a piany of her own ?"

WALK LXVIII.

THE COVE.

Lame boy.   An attached servant and kind mother.

Truro Infirmary.

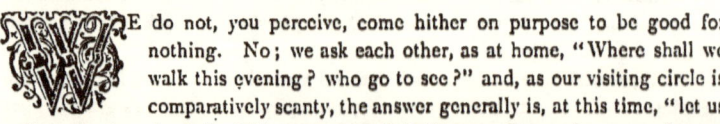E do not, you perceive, come hither on purpose to be good for nothing. No; we ask each other, as at home, "Where shall we walk this evening? who go to see?" and, as our visiting circle is comparatively scanty, the answer generally is, at this time, "let us walk to the lame boy's." This same poor lad, Thomas Drewe by name, has an inveterate wound of the most dangerous character. What with weakness and pain, he can seldom prosecute his business of journeyman tailor, though he can occasionally earn a few pence by fetching sand or coal with the donkey. The sea air does him good, though, as to ultimate recovery, he is almost out of hope. Now he has a mind to make use of the County Infirmary, and we are accordingly looking about us, to procure him an early recommendation, only the fond mother has unluckily "heard tell that the living there is no great things."

In the estimation of the poor, short commons, whether it be that there is "no stomach to the meat, or no meat to the stomach," is the worst of symptoms, and the heaviest of grievances.

His devoted mother, Peggy Drewe, deserves a page to herself, for her indomitable kind-heartedness, her surprising energy of action, the last growing out of the first, and the circumstance of her having been in her youth a servant at St. Hilary Vicarage.

She loves to tell and I to listen to the tale of those days; how the old parson was a free-spoken, merry-spirited man, kind to the poor after his way, neither grudging them meat, clothes, nor smuggled brandy; but how he came to be cruel cast down with the unhappy marriage of his only daughter; and Mr. ———, whom she married, was "a hard man, sure enough," continued the pitying Peggy. "I went to live with him after he married with Miss Josepha; it was the old gentleman's desire, judging I should be kind and feel for his daughter, poor soul! He used to take me by his side in his one-horse chay (primitive times those), and say, 'Peggy, you must be kind to your mistress; there is good need.' I did all I could," said Peggy; "that wasn't much—but poor dear missus was not the only sufferer. There was a poor 'prentice maid who, if she did not feed his dogs to his mind, or, indeed, if she did, seeing his temper was otherwise disturbed, he would beat her. I don't like to think upon it even now, though I have put much trouble over my own head since whiles. The poor maid would drop on her two knees and beseech me to stand her friend. Many's the time I have gone without my own victuals, to see her used in that fashion. At last," said the compassionate cook, "I could bear it no longer, and I wrote (being I was brought up to brave scholarship), I wrote a letter to the overseers of Probus. I thought no harm could come of it, if no good, but thanks be to the Almighty, good did come, and that speedily; the maid was fetched away. I have often wished I could hear what became of her. I used to think the poor maid might have sent me word (but maybe nobody came our way), or write me a line (but then she didn't know a letter in the book);" and so Peggy went on neutralizing, as they arose, those little acerbities arising from offended love, generated by the ungrateful conduct of her *protégée*.

From this sketch, I leave you to infer what an indulgent mother she is likely to prove to an afflicted, ailing son. She has often walked three or four miles after night-fall, on her return from fetching Hayle sand, because Tommy happened to express a wish for a roasted apple, and her bodily fatigue being the least unpleasant part of her day's work. So insurmountable is her repugnance to begging that I seldom can make her take a thing beyond the express object of her application. "No," says she, "that is what I came for, and that, so please you, I will have, and no more."

It will be supposed that, with an unfortunate little grandson, cross, distempered, and blind, her sick Tommy, and nine persons to cater, carve, and patch for, Peggy has no time to spare; accordingly, when we are gossiping of old times, she often doubles up her tall form on a low, three-legged stool, takes from her pocket, first, her spectacles (toil and scant fare are sad eye-dimmers), then unfolds her well-used housewife, and stitches away with the same vigour as she does everything else.

＊　＊　＊　＊　＊　＊　To continue the story of Peggy, I must tell you what has happened since writing the above. We walked to the turnpike one day, to hear her adventures at the Truro Infirmary, whither she had conducted her poor lame son. Tommy set out on his walk in tolerable spirits, she told us, but "he was cruel taken down when she came to go away;" and no wonder. The doctors had examined his poor leg, and pronounced it, in his hearing, "a bad look out." These few words fell like icicles on a mother's heart. "I sat down in a hedge," said she, "for I knew no one to ask me inside their door, and when I fetched a mile this side of Truro, I hid my head in the hedge, and wept for better than an hour, to think of those hard words. Still, there was one of the gentlemen there of a kinder make; he came forward, looking pitifully, methought, upon Tom, while the old doctor cried out, 'Look! here's a pretty business they've brought me.' 'Poor fellow,' said he, 'it must give him a deal of pain; 'tis a pity for one so young.'" "A word spoken in season, how good is it!"

WALK LXIX.

Dr. Bull and his Persian cats.

OMPANY at home has prevented either walking or writing for some time. I now resume my history of the poor lame boy, whose cottage Kate and I visited last evening, and found him returned from the Infirmary. Although somewhat frightened at his first introduction to the head doctor, with a Persian cat on each shoulder, yet he had found his mother's indulgent inference true, that one so kind to dumb animals could not but be the same to one of his own sort.

And now I cannot refrain from relating a little history of the said cats. Kate, who has ever been sighing for a Persian cat (the only breed patronised by the aforesaid gentleman, who is extremely chary over his kittens), communicated her wishes to her friend Georgina T———, and she engaged a friend to speak to another friend, to ask Miss B——— to obtain from Dr. Bull a kitten of the right sort.

Nothing could be more gracious than the manner in which the suit was received. He knew Miss T———, knew that she was a great belle, and very fond of cats, kept them in the parlour; in short, a most beautiful, long-haired, large-tailed, full-ruffed kitten was despatched to Miss T———, with certain conditions, as here detailed. She was never to be touched by a child; to be fed with meat, not raw but underdressed; and, above all, she was never to put her foot inside the kitchen. Now I must here explain that this exclusive gift, intended, as the doctor fondly thought, for the fair Georgina, was given by her to her (I will not say *equally* fair, for who is ?) but still her fair friend Kate, and found its way to St. Hilary Vicarage, where Lilla met a most enthusiastic welcome, and lived a happy life. Mr. T———, who, in his frequent visits to the Truro Infirmary, often met, and was duly catechised by, the doctor, about pussey's health, was too well schooled to "let the cat out of the bag," and confined himself to a simple bulletin. She was quite well, growing handsome, a prodigious favourite. All went right until one day the doctor was so

NN

charmed with Mr. T——'s report, that he exclaimed, "I will call at the Rectory soon, and judge for myself."

We were spared the panic that seized the whole family, for, all along, Kate and I had imagined the doctor had known and acceded to the transfer. But "murder will out," and I was the innocent blower-up of the plot. Thinking to ingratiate the poor lame boy into favour, I bade his mother seize the first opportunity of telling the doctor what a big beauty his kitten had become. She had not to wait for an *à propos*, for, on the arrival of the simple pair at the Infirmary gate, they were met by the doctor, with one cat on each shoulder, and several at his heels. Peggy told me the doctor looked queer, but said nothing; however, like the parrot, he "thought the more."

The deception had been discovered, and a dignified letter demanding an explanation was despatched to Mr. T——, who takes his revenge by rallying Kate on her inability to keep a secret. One sentence a little twinged my conscience, and mollified my vexation, namely, "Had Charlotte W—— asked me for a kitten," &c., &c.

I am sorry I cannot give my story what Junius used to call "a sharp point," were it only that all the ten cats were let loose on the offender, with their twenty times ten claws; but I believe here the affair rests and will rest, only we can never hope for another cat from Dr. Bull.

WALK LXX.

THE COVE.

B. Bettens and her brother.   Wesley.

ERE, dear Maria, is a "Walk" that I slap-dashed down on my return to the house; read it or leave it at your pleasure.

I suppose there was hardly ever a thinking being who, in his own conceit, had not something or other to pique himself upon; some reminiscence, personal or relative, whereby to tickle his self-love. Whether it was that he had seen one of the royal family, caught one of the largest trout, had been at the bottom of a mine, or at the top of a mountain, had seen (or else his father had) Garrick in Abel Dragger, or remembered the coming in of the new style.

I, for my part, am proud to have it to say, that I have seen a fish's nest, and been bitten by a large, curly, black dog, belonging, by-the-bye, to the Preventive-men, and who, while I was conversing with "the mistress" (a generic title for the officer's wife), walked deliberately round to my side, and seized my leg. Not having "brought the blood," I have no right to dilate to you on my adventure; still, I can enjoy the hydrophobic horror which the faces of the listeners express.

For once, however, I am not going to be the heroine of my tale, but an old woman whom I visited to-day, who has grown almost double by means of age, disease, and privation, and has withal so grotesque a set of features, that she truly described herself as "a wicked-looking old body." Her glorying is that she was kissed by Mr. Wesley, on occasion of a visit he made to her father's cottage, accompanied by Squire Brackenbury. I hasten to say that the damsel thus favoured was a mere child, only nine years of age; but she shall "never forget it," and will take care that those around her shall not, either,—that her children's children shall record, "My granny was kissed by the famous John Wesley," whose traditional kisses becoming scarcer by distance of time, will doubtless rise in value with each succeeding generation. But till this comes to pass, posterity, I grieve to say, is not likely to do much towards the maintenance of poor old Betty Bettens, who, at this time, just keeps life and soul together by the one shilling she receives weekly from the iron hand of a relieving officer, occasionally eked out by what she can gain in the way of knitting for hire. What can she gain, alas! at the age of four score, with only one, and that a very dim, eye, and her head nearly touching a chest that heaves frightfully from asthma?

Betty's brother, seventy-seven years of age, and a cripple during the greater part of them, resides with her; but as *he* cannot knit, his weekly shilling seldom supplies more than one meal a day. "But sometimes, ma'am," said he, with a cheerfulness of tone that brought my heart up into my throat, "*sometimes* I have two" (oh that I could make our relieving officers and guardians of the poor swallow the "physic" Shakespeare decrees for "Pomp"). "But your clothes," enquired I, sitting between this impotent couple, who would have furnished good subjects for the Pool of Bethesda. "We never look for any," they meekly replied, fearful, no doubt, of being dragged away into a Union for their audacity, and thus forfeit the all-compensating comforts of native air, place, and kindred. The old man confessed to having worn his one whole shirt three months without washing. "And when it *was* washed, what did you do ? Did you lie abed ?" I was going to ask, but amended the phrase for very shame, and promised to send him another.

How sore a reproach to the rich is the disproportioned gratitude of the poor! If I, and others with my means, bestowed as we ought, we should not be sent to Heaven for the donation of some yards of fourpenny calico.

Betty is somewhat in 'Un Sally's line—a person of reflection and sentiment, and one who repeats poetry. How is it we never meet this spontaneous philosophy—at least, *I* never do—among people of education, and yet it is by no means uncommon among the aged poor. I sounded Betty about her comparatively wealthy relations. "Do not they come to see you ?" "Seldom, if ever, ma'am. If we had hoards to leave, perhaps they might." She will never seek *them*, for I can see it is with evident reluctance that she receives the willing gratuity ; and though her feelings are deeply grateful for sympathy or assistance, she soothes her wounded dignity by continually adverting to the scores of hungry "bowels" her father relieved, when he was a farmer, and she his eldest daughter and housekeeper.

I have promised the mistress to introduce her to this worthy couple, and I am glad to bespeak for them so kind a friend, when winter shall shut us out from our Cove neighbours.

Mrs. Drewe is an estimable person, with sufficient intelligence to save her from being a tiresome companion, and withal is kindness itself; only she wants nursery polish. I do not mean lacquer, as you may suppose, when I tell you she was a pupil of Miss Nancy Warren, whom you may have met at Mr. T. John's. Her name was Leverton of *Tre*-something (of course), in the vicinage of Truro, so that is another bond of amity.

WALK LXXI.

___

Jemmy Buzzo and the Dunstanville Charity.

 VISIT of congratulation! You are to know that we once had a great neighbour, entitled Lord de Dunstanville, the least of whose praise was his descent from the hero of the following couplet :—

> "I, John of Gaunt, do give and grant
> All my estate in fee,
> From me and mine to thee and thine,
> Bassett of Umberie." .

He was every inch a nobleman, and it was from such as he that we are to suppose the designation was framed. When he died, as if to relieve the sense of grateful sorrow that pervaded every heart, from the land-holder to the land-labourer (for all had in some sort tasted his princely spirit), a subscription was opened, with a view to raise a monument to his memory, among the druidical vestiges on his own Carn Brea. A large sum was subscribed (from £2,000 to £3,000), and, after much contrariety of counsel, it was resolved that the building should neither be so large as to put the hill to shame (as some suggested), nor so small as to disparage the public spirit of Cornwall (as others feared); a third party, meanwhile, having the gratification of riding their hobby also, by seeing the overplus applied to the excellent purpose of pensioning off some superannuated miners.

The first meeting in order to award these same pensions, took place at Truro the other day, and, upon the "nothing venture," &c., principle, Mr. Pascoe resolved to put in a word for our neighbour, Jemmy Buzzo. Jemmy married Peggy, and Peggy was niece to the old blind Margaret, who, thanks to the Admiral, enjoyed the Hetherington Charity for many years, and who used, to her dying day, to tell about how she saw Miss Kate for the first time with a doll in her arms, and how I smoothed the little girl's head, as she was shewing it off to the old woman, saying,

oo

"This is *my* doll, 'Un Margaret." You would think there was never such a witticism uttered before. I used to stand like Sully simpering at his own memoirs, as the *bon mot* was duly repeated. Poor 'Un Margaret! the scene was almost the last she ever witnessed. No wonder, then, that it clung to her memory; it was as the glimpse of his native land to the condemned exile.

And now, to cut my story short, the good Peggy is rewarded for her filial cares towards her old aunt to the day of her death, and the repetition of those patient ministrations to the crossest-grained husband that ever poor woman was afflicted with.

While Jemmy was able to work, he thought so much of himself and his performances, that he never opened his mouth but to take in the best of everything that their joint labour could procure, and to let out all manner of vituperation against the much-enduring Peggy. She is a singularly clean, industrious, and courteous-mannered person, and when there was nothing else to find fault with, he would quarrel about the manner of her hanging up the bellows, though I could never learn, any more than Peggy, that there was more than one way of performing that feat of housewifery.

At length the disposition to palsy which, perhaps, was some apology for Jemmy's bad temper, took a decided form, and he was forced (in miner's phrase) to "knack," *i.e.*, abstain wholly from labour, while his poor wife worked the harder.

'Un Margaret's pension stopped with her breath, and young Anne, our garden-girl (the griglin genius, you remember), could not do more than milk the goats and maintain herself; besides, her pretty face soon gained her a husband, and Peggy was left to her Penelope labours of turning over heaps of often-turned rubbish during the day, and breaking in upon her much-needed rest, to keep the house such a pink as it always was ; to weed potatoes, fetch water, mend her own and Jemmy's clothes, and even to "right up the crum o' gar'en."

Poor dear Peggy's spirit sustained all this bravely, even the payment of a shilling once a month or so to a death club, which had already engulphed enough money to have given to themselves a good living to the end of their days ; but here was her grief, as it was poor Jemmy's,—though she did toil night and day, his bread she could not win. To give her husband those comforts which, as she said, his poor body frame looked for, she was forced to go in debt, and the deeds of the pretty cottage to be lodged with Betsey Peters at the shop.

While things were at this low ebb, many an exhortation did Peggy receive, in favour of throwing herself upon the parish. "I never wouldn't," and "Would I starve to please anybody?" and "The parish is bound to help they that want, and I'm sure you want bad enough, and why shouldn't you have it, if you want it, as well as another," with other such persuasive corollaries. But Peggy remained staunch; there were still the two reversionary resources for paying her debts—the death club and the cottage; and as for herself, and how she was to be maintained, there was time enough to think of that when the time came.

And now, well has poor Peggy been repaid for her simple acquiescence in the Divine precept, "Take no thought for thy life, wherewithal thou shalt," &c. Jemmy has been chosen one of seven annuitants on the Dunstanville Fund, to the tune of ten pounds a year for his life, which could not have been if he had ever received so much as a farthing of parish pay.

Does not your kind heart dance to this tune, dear Maria, as ours did? They say there was never any hesitation about Jemmy's election, from the moment the committee read Mr. Pascoe's paper. Kate and I envied him the good tidings he was the bearer of, and eagerly catechised him on his return, about what was said. Peggy exclaimed, "Bless God and you, sir; now I can pay my debts." Jemmy wished he might kneel down and return thanks.

WALK LXXII.

Young Harry's kind acts.   A patient.

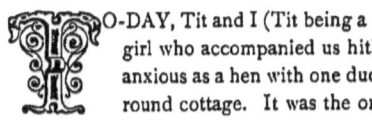O-DAY, Tit and I (Tit being a loving diminutive for Susan Jago, a little girl who accompanied us hither, and keeps Cousin Kate as busy and anxious as a hen with one duckling), Tit and I carried a fish up to the round cottage. It was the only one our young Harry (himself an odd

fish, you remember) had caught for the day, and he was sorely puzzled how to get it up to poor Betsey Hocking. " Harry always remembers the sick and the poor," his mother-in-law observed, as soon as he left the room, and well did he deserve this praise for having declined beforehand to let me, who would have paid for it, have this very fish, and sending it so beautifully packed with fresh leaves in a fair basket, fit for a queen, to the poor sick and, by-the-bye, homely-looking girl. She was very glad to have it, and so would be the poor mother, who was gone to a neighbour's house to have an amateur operation performed on her eye, because the invalid could not bear to witness her anguish—anguish indeed it seemed to be. I met the good old creature groping her way home, with her head enveloped in a cloak, and right proud was Tit to bear a hand in helping her over the stile, and to assist in transferring the fish from the basket to a dish. So here was another day provided for—the hand of Providence as apparent as if the old ravens, occupying Great Cudden Point beyond the memory of man, had brought flesh and bread in their beaks.

After making a few purchases at the village shop, a little sugar, and a pot of treacle, and placing the basket on the arm of my red-ridinghood, we entered a farmyard at the brow of the hamlet, to enquire for chicken. No chicken there, but a patient or two. On we went, and, passing through a gate into a mowstead, we perceived a *grand seigneur* of a cock, with a bevy of feathered beauties following at his heels. This promised more success, but, while peering about for the chicken which ought to be there, we discovered a party of ducks, with their bills plunged into a pile of freshly winnowed wheat, and gobbling it down with all their might, which was no joke ; so, while a little boy from an opposite field ran to call the gude-wife, Tit and I kept the marauders at bay.

Mrs. Vellanoweth came quickly, and proved to be a frank-tempered, plain farmer's wife, with manners as primitive as her name. She thanked us, and wished she *had* chicken, for our sakes. She had tried to procure one, but in vain, for her sick daughter. So here was another patient, and, as the case was a very simple one, I expect to be thanked again when I call next. Severe and ever-recurring, spirit-consuming heart-burn would be intolerable, were it not for its ready remedy ; blessings on the chemist, I say, who invented carbonate of soda. Years of suffering has he spared me, wherefore may his crucibles never crack, nor his glass retorts burst, and be all his experiments crowned with success !

There is one thing, however, better than carbonate of soda, and that is the drug which, if properly administered, would render the virtues of the latter remedy needless (at least, so I have found it), and I wish, dear Maria, that your complaint was one of the stomach instead of the head, that I might have the pleasure of curing you with a mixture of calumbo root and magnesia.

A LETTER.

GARDEN SHED, APRIL 28, 1840.

Dearest Maria,

I HAVE literally bade Betty "take my desk beneath the garden shed." Not *the* garden shed, either, but one of two new ones with which the pastor has surprised us—"make pretend" surprise, that is, such as you practise on little Clarissa, for Kate and I had taken a sly peep behind the scenes, before we were formally conducted into the plantation at the bottom of the garden, to see what our carpenter had done for us. It is quite a dome, and the upright split firs of which it is formed are, I hear, to be made more weather-tight by a rustic lining; it is also to be furnished with a circular table and bench, and other appliances, to aid the picturesque; then it full-faces the bay, and commands such a view of the Mount as you get of a beautiful face in an opposite opera box. For my part, I would compound for less beauty, in either case, for a touch of the more retiring graces, and so I am writing, by preference, in an angle of wall over which "behoves no more than" a cover of thatch and four posts, to make a retreat that you and I would not exchange for Windsor Castle.

You remember the garden avenue, and the little orchard at its head, and "Miss Josepha's garden," namely, an oval of flowers, of which Miss Kate is the present incumbent, since it goes with the living to the young ladies of the family.

The orchard is reduced to a tree or two, that form accidental porticos, and look pretty between me and the amphitheatre of green. What fine words! Porticos, amphitheatres! This comes of my philosophy, I suppose. Certainly I do feel, dear M———, as if, let me alone, I would ask for nothing on earth but this. I envy none but Milton's Adam, who could talk with Him as he walked, without this depressing sense of unmeetness and unworthiness. Not but that there is something in a measure purifying and ennobling in the grateful sense, the devout consciousness, that *He* is the Fountain of all we admire, the Spring of all benefit, the Source of all beauty. Wonderful! that He should pervade, animate, beautify all we behold; that the giant, delighting to run his prodigious course above me in the heavens, should call Him Master, while yet He thinks no scorn to make glad the hearts of that pair of robins who, having, as I guess, a nest hereabouts, are continually flitting and coquetting among the rosebuds in front of me.

This is weather when, if alone, my heart is always ejaculating with 'Un Polly, "Bless the Lord."

WALK LXXIII.

Little Betsey's death.   Plaintive reading.

O poor little Betsey is, I find, gone to her long home. What a sweet sound that has when the home, as in Betsey's case, is likely to be a happy one! but home is a magical word that in all languages implies happiness, even, strange to say, where the home is not a happy one.

I knew it would please old Anne that I should look upon her daughter, although Kate, who had seen the body, prepared me to feel shocked. It was thought better that Miss Tit, being a nervous damsel, should not accompany us, but the poor little soul followed, to beg, in a whisper, that I would give her "love to the dead." We smile, but it is a fact that our learned countryman, Whitaker, sent a similar message to *his* daughter Betsey, by a poor dying woman whom he clerically attended.

Poor Betsey Hocking was, indeed, woefully changed. Her features had, at the best, been commonplace, except her eyes, to which consumption had superadded the rich gem-like lustre that outvies the brightness of youth and joy. These were now closed, and how do you think? No wonder that Kate looked mysterious, and Tit horror-stricken. A leaden tea-spoon had been laid on each, the concave side uppermost. I was checked, by the presence of the mother, from uttering, like poor Kate, a hasty exclamation on the withdrawal of the face-cloth, but Mrs. Saunders (Betsey's aunt), on perceiving my emotion, removed the tea-spoons, observing that, now her poor eyes were effectually closed, they were no longer needed. I was glad she did not also displace the small bible, whose contents had so often spoken peace to the breast on which it now rested. I can well recall C—— C——'s reading from it one of those plaintive psalms that suited so well with her sweet, low voice. One has often heard of singing like an angel (oftener than is true), but C—— C—— may be positively said to read like one. Her tones seem to reach the soul, without needing the gross medium of bodily organs. They are the whispered admonition of the "sister spirit" to "come away." I can remember how poor Betsey's eyes followed the motions of the reader, their sparkling lustre quenched in unutterable tenderness—they were playmates in early childhood, when my uncle and aunt took under their especial protection the widow and her two orphans.

From C—— C—— I have gleaned these particulars of old Anne's former history. Anne's relations, and no wonder, watched anxiously how she might bear this incomparable sorrow, the loss of an only daughter. I was glad to observe that her large, rolling eyes, which turned ever and anon towards the bed of death, or the white coverlet, retained the customary expression of meek resignation, and only for a single moment betrayed that her thoughts could be diverted from it. It was when one of the condoling neighbours mentioned that a poor labourer had, that very morning, his arm torn off at the shoulder-joint by that engine of calamity, a thrashing machine.

A similar accident happened at Carnanton before my father came there. I rejoice to recollect that he had no such Juggernautish appendage to his farm.

Agriculture, we see, claims its victims, no less than mining. Kate tells me she shall know no rest till we have visited the victim in question. It will be a painful visit.

WALK LXXIV.

Living or posthumous celebrity.   Miss Seward.   Old Anne's dream.

FTEN have I said to myself, "I would not live in a world without poor," and I said it again to-day, when I was considering who and who I should be able to call upon, now that we are removed to the Cove, and a mile or two out of our usual walking track.   I do not think these things aloud, because it would be considered a vaunt, but now nobody hears me except you, dear, *and if it is decreed that my simple rambles shall ever invite the attention of others, it will be when this ear is passed being soothed by flattery or stung · by censure.*

I do not know, after all, why it should be thought ostentatious to profess pleasure in relieving sufferings which it is pain to behold, or why any thinking being should arrogate to itself merit for obeying such a mere human impulse.   As well might he be vain of seeing with his eyes, and hearing with his ears; as well might that noble sea, which I glance at while I write, be proud that it does not overflow the bounds appointed to it by its maker.   To be kind, and courteous, and bountiful, against our native bias, that indeed is praiseworthy.   Let me not seem to under-value benevolent instincts; their loveliness I admit, while I dispute their merit; and I am free to confess that, admirable as it is to keep down a bad temper, it is more agreeable to have to deal with a temper that needs no keeping down.

I am going to make another confession, which I do with some hesitation, because I daresay the avowal would be considered a base one by most people.   I fancy I should prefer *living* to *posthumous* celebrity.   I can imagine much gratification in finding myself the object of admiring and kindly feelings, in seeing myself re-cognized, as I passed along, for the one whose writings had conveyed pleasure, instruction, or had even harmlessly beguiled a heavy hour; but for that "secondary existence" which Hannah More's biographer so happily describes, I have no long-ing.   Connected with it comes a ghostly thought or two, that drinks up all my joy in its contemplation of it—chiefly this, that *there must be an end*, and another thing is its want of identity. One man embodies Shakespeare to his fancy in one form, another in another, so that your Shakespeare and mine are not the same person—we are both idolizing a phantom. I know you can upset my argument with a brush from your pen, but shall therefore resume my first plea.

To one who sometimes dares to hope that after this flesh has perished he may see and live for ever with the author of all wisdom, all beauty, and all intellect, how indescribably poor and perishable seem the praises of man, whose breath is in his nostrils; for oh! what is he to be (comparatively) accounted of? Would that I knew the word Lord Byron wanted, but never found—the word that should have been lightning to express his thought with a force and brevity corresponding to my sense of its truth!

"Do you call this walking?" you ask.

This morning the pastor and his dame went home to the Vicarage to the church service, to represent, as usual on a week-day, the parson and congregation in their several persons. On reaching the brow of the turfy ascent which is the land barrier to our happy valley, I turned round to "cull a view," quoting Miss Seward, and to bless my stars that the farewell I then took of my "Stormy Lannow" was but for a few hours.

"You never sing that song now," said my companion; "the words are beautiful. Lord Byron admired them." So did Scott, who was nevertheless thrown into horrors on hearing that Miss S—— had bequeathed him her voluminous MSS., with which she meant he should enchant the world—strange mistake—while they are all probably condemned to the appropriate use of making paper kites. This one little effusion of feeling is fondly remembered; the truth is that for one happy moment Miss S—— forgot herself, forgot to be clever and fascinating, in the warm interest she felt for that ill-starred hero of real life, Major André. He was, I believe, the lover of Miss Seward, afterwards Miss Edgeworth's mother, or mother-in-law, the scornful nymph of the song.

For a quality not downright vice, affectation is the worst anybody can be charged with. It finds no apology in any breast, for it is a perfect non-conductor to the affections; even admitting an affected person sometimes succeeds in obtaining admiration, the affections instinctively arm themselves against their claims, while, on the other hand, you shall see a person of vicious habits pitied, and pardoned, and vindicated, for the sake of the one merit, that they make no claim to admiration, while the converse shews us one with every moral and kindly quality, disliked, laughed at, loathed, avoided, because she is artificial. Vaulting ambition is not the only folly that o'erleaps its object, and whose capers are apt to terminate in a fall "on t'other side."

I hope you do not think I made all this long-winded speech to Mr. P——; they are but the thoughts our little opening dialogue suggested. I thought thus to myself as we plodded homewards.

At Tresiholles, I was pursued for some way by a bonnetless, breathless mother, to beg some medicine for a sick child, which I promised to bring back, and changed my ring, not to forget it.

At the little sugar-loaf cottage, I had other commissions, but I fear alleviation of pain is all that can be done there. Poor old Anne, for as weak and broken-hearted as she looks, will probably have to follow to the grave her only daughter and sole companion. The poor girl had long helped to maintain her mother, just such another meek, pleasing old woman as Susannah, of Union memory, and they did not even ask the dole of sixpence a week. By dint of the most unremitting diligence, they earned their bread, and duly paid the rent of that little dove-cot of which they are such appropriate tenants, till poor Betsey got sick—"overworked, and never of the strongest," a neighbour told me; then the best resource failed; it was little old Anne could earn, even when she could be spared from her poor girl's side, and edifying it was to see how they both committed themselves, without apparent solicitude, or one repining word, to the care of Him who providently caters for his still more lonely creatures. In virtue of this confidence, they have never, she frequently assures me, known want. The Lord raises up help, as sure as they need. She says one neighbour or another comes in and drops his mite, of which I had an instant proof in a handsome young woman, who, abashed at seeing me, hung back, and after a few awkward and ineffectual efforts to speak, drew from her pocket two oranges, which she placed, without comment, by the sick girl, and left the cottage, or the room, which is the same thing. The comical little building consists of one apartment, partially divided by a dresser, set off with good store of crockery-ware on the entrance side, and supplying a back to the bed on the other.

If I did not know 'Un Anne to be truth itself, I would not record the following circumstance. On enquiring after her health one day, she told me her face was beginning to trouble her again, but no matter, she knew what would cure it without fail. I am always glad to pick up an infallible nostrum, and as her complaint, from her report, appeared to be what is called an evil (which had, at an earlier period of her life, tormented her for five years, and incapacitated her from attending to her family), I caught at the present opportunity of enriching my receipt-book. It was communicated, she said, in a dream, dreamed three times following in one night, so it must be true. She "saw a voice," which distinctly dictated to her this recipe. Three herbs which she named were to be fried in cream, and applied hot. She woke her husband, and got well scolded, slept and dreamed again and again, with this emendation, that if cream could not be procured, lard was to be employed as its substitute. Poor Anne was no great captain, so, instead of turning away in a rage, she went in search of the simples, fried them, applied them, and she was made whole—from that *hour*, I must not say, but so speedily that it was only less than a miracle.

These are unaccountable occurrences, and doctors and sceptics may try to get over the difficulty they cannot remove, by talking of the doctrine of chances, &c., &c.

I can believe that mind has much to do with the regulation of our bodily feelings; why else did I experience a greater sense of fatigue when I took my parting look from that hill-top, than when, after a five or six mile walk, I again stood, my eye exulting in a line of sea and a circle of coast, with its little graceful indents, fringed by the foam that, rising high over opposing rocks, the moment after subsides, and peacefully embraces their feet, like some generous tempers who relent in their purpose while in the very act of avenging themselves?

WALK LXXV.

THE COVE, JULY 14, 1840.

C—— C—— and the coast.   Miss Willyams and Silvio Pellico.

OW often have I recorded my Walks hither, and always with undiminished delight! *pleasure* was on the tip of my pen, but it is too cold a word.

I have a new companion at present. She who added to the enjoyment of our late sojourn here, was C—— C——, and she, you know, is already the heroine of one Walk, but she made herself too interesting as a talker at our workings and walkings, to give me leisure to make her the subject of another. During the week or more that she spent here (the heart of her early associations), you may imagine how we feasted upon recollections, her quick, tenacious affections kindling at the least touch of the past, and grateful at finding a ready listener in me. My sympathy was repaid by auld world stories of my favourite cottagers, and lessons on the geography of the coast, with which she was long familiar.

Day by day I rehearsed my lesson as we turned and fondly lingered on our hillside. I was a shocking dull scholar. It would be worth any phrenologist's while to examine my skull, only to see how utterly deficient it is in the bump of locality. The little fringed bay, the detached rock, the interlineation of bright, clear sand, the range of hilly cliff, darker, bleaker, and higher than its neighbours, the far-stretching sweep of coast, with another sweep behind it, bolder, but almost too faint for the naked eye to detect all these beauties, I can trace and gloat over with an insatiable delight, but it was not till after many a patient lesson, that poor C—— could beat into me that the first point (I mean after that bold, projecting heap which defines our little Bessy's Cove to the east, seeming just under my nose while I write), *that* point, why or wherefore, C—— C—— could not inform me, is called the Hoe. After that is Praa Sands; the next point, if I recollect right, is Rinsey Head, with the Wolf Rock in the van; the gloomy or bloomy (which you will), fine line of cliff is Halzephron. Would it not be worth while to write a poem, only to introduce that name? The strongly-contrasted white rock in front is, C—— thought, the famous soap rock. After boasting of the poetry of our names, how shall I confess that the last point is called Polpradanack, so provokingly like Poll parrot?

My present companion is also brimful of glowing pictures and romantic legends, and must needs look on our baby wonders with disdain. It is Louisa, fresh from Italy, and who spent months of last summer in the Chateau de Chillon, being admitted *en pension* by the governor and his charming wife. I have an anecdote relating to the spot, which will interest you, and while I think of it I will write it down. One day a pale, interesting-looking stranger came to view the chateau. On descending with him to the vaults of the dungeon, immortalized by Bonnivard's pillar, Madame Valeton perceived the countenance of her companion materially change, and though she had been accustomed to conjured-up emotions of all degrees and descriptions on these occasions—had even seen four ladies fall simultaneously into hysterics, on mistaking a family mangle for the rack on which B—— suffered—yet there was something so real, she said, and so touching in the stranger's manner, that she enquired if he were ill. He smiled as he replied, "I am like a child who is always looking out for the phantom of which he is afraid; wherever I go, I enquire out all the dungeons in the neighbourhood, and visit them, but Bonnivard's dungeon is a palace to mine. I am Silvio Pellico."

I am thankful to be thus relieved of the impression I had received, that this captive Phœnix had degenerated into a nervous devotee, and finally that he was dead. How it would rejoice me to be assured that I should meet and know this beautiful spirit here or in Heaven!

WALK LXXVI.

Flowers and sermons.

ENT about to distribute the remaining Cottage Horticultural tickets of admission, not so easy a work as I expected. The labouring classes have rarely an hour to give to pleasure-seeking, at least not in such hard times as the present.

Among the happy possessors of those which I had bestowed earlier in the day, were three holiday folk, a father, daughter, and niece, in all their braveries, and smiling from ear to ear. Not so poor Kitty Crebo and her daughter Susan, both labouring under mental dejection, which I vainly assured them a sight of the gay flowers would tend to dissipate. Mary Stribley would have liked nothing better, but for her baby, who might take cold ; and her neighbour, that most precise of beaux and bachelors, Nickey Roberts, said it would take too long to get ready. Worthy, courteous old Barnard G——— I should never have thought of inviting into a scene of even harmless dissipation, if I had not happened to meet him, with my last undisposed-of ticket in my hand, as he was cheering his half-palsied frame by a stroll in the sunshine. " Thank ye, ma'am, all the same," said he, " but I would go further to hear a good sarment than to see the finest flowers the earth doth yield." I should have told him how it was possible to extract the best of sermons out of these sweet monitors, citing the first of human authorities, and, I speak in reverence, the first of Divine authorities, also. I might have told him how the lilies of the field, or even the senseless stone, preach to the willing ear. I do so rejoice when I can detect our beloved Shakespeare drawing from the well-spring of Scripture, and that really is not seldom the case.

My other tickets were severally offered to a thrifty old market gardener (a due churchman), an amateur Sunday-school teacher, and the young printer's assistant who printed so carefully and so meekly the perpetual inaccuracies he had to correct for the author of the " Singer's Friend."

The poor young widow, Jennefer Curtis, went to the show with cheerful feet, wearing the first smile that has lighted up her woe-begone face since the death of her husband. No wonder; she carried in her hand a paper from Mr. Pascoe, containing the sum of seven shillings and sixpence; he was truly glad to exercise his privilege of subscriber by recommending hers as the best kept garden of the parish.

WALK LXXVII.

Frequent change of residence.   Further tidings of old friends.

ES, this *is* a changeful world! I make the remark just now in reference to this particular parish, and by no means intending to palm it on you as a new idea, for I doubt whether any rational being ever existed without having made a similar observation. Poets have adorned it with flowers of special rhetoric; moralists have availed themselves of it to point their appeals to the conscience of their hearers. Still, however varied are these changes produced from this simple peal of "This is a changeful world," bards and moralists and divines as ye are, ye know comparatively little of the matter, if you do not reside in a mining district, where the shifting and changing, at least of dwellings, is endless. "They are gone from there," is the general reply I get, when intending to pay a visit after an interval of a few months. You may as soon expect to find a cruizer at the port where you left her, as a Cornish miner's family in the house they occupied on a last visit.

A cottage which is called, and will be so called as long as it hangs together, Ivy Cottage (though a wretch of a mason has long ago stripped it of every leaf to which it owed its picturesque name), and my recollections, if I could stay to enumerate them, would furnish the names of half-a-dozen or more successive occupiers, some of them familiar to you, I trust. There lived Jenny Priske of one-legged memory, and there resided friend Mary, and there the great Betty watched her dying husband, and through that door abandoned the orphans he left to her care.

It was at this cottage my steps were, it may be a year ago, arrested by a small cart, containing some rickety furniture, which stood before it. The recognition was reciprocal, for its occupier dropped a curtsey, and followed me with the same pair of inflamed eyes upon which, some years ago, I had wasted so much skill and golden ointment. "Can that be Maria," asked I, "who was a servant at Captain Nickey's, and always so good a church-goer?" It was her very self, and I could fancy it no more than a year since I had, Sunday after Sunday, seen the self-same flowered gown in the identical low pew near the southern door. But to my mortification she had sought a new service. I fear I did not suppress as I ought my infinite surprise, at learning that poor Maria had found anybody to seek her in wedlock. "You married, Maria! you surprise me." "Yes, fie! but he (pointing to a great loon of a boy helping her to unpack), he was a son by my former husband."

Not many months after, a cart stood again before Ivy Cottage, but this time they were packing *in* moveables—the second husband had been killed underground, and poor Maria was again starting forth, like her illustrious namesake, with

> "The world before, where to choose her place of rest,
> And Providence her guide."

This little history of a Maria, somewhat differing from Sterne's, and still more from mine, we must allow is no otherwise memorable, than as the germ of a promise I, at that time, mentally made, that I would, the first moment of leisure, avail myself of the singularly fluctuating state of things, to write a conclusion to some of my histories. These are, I know, in their tiresome perplexity, vague and desultory, and the fault of a populous parish; therefore I mean, where I can, to bring them to a speedy conclusion.

Let me prepare my intended *dénouement* by imagining how different would have been the chronicles of an agricultural district; the labourer on the land, wearing himself and his cottage fairly out in the service of one master, who, if he have ample means and generous feelings, will spare his old servant the pang of quitting his house till, to use his own phrase, he is carried "foot afore" out of it. Thus you may call in, after an interval of many years, and find no change, but here and there a grey head, or may be the pleasant transformation of dirty brats into stout grown men and women, able to take the labouring oar in their turn. But how fares it, meanwhile, in a mining neighbourhood? You shall hear.

The widow Pearce, with whom my stories begin, that paragon of quaint diction, went to live in a cheap cottage down amongst the burrows, with that alphabet-hating son of hers whom I coaxed (Honor would say *slocked*) to school in vain, after wasting upon him more instruction than would have made his fortune, had it been bestowed upon his mother's pig. He took huff because he "hadn't no prize at the school feast," and sturdily refused to come back. I hope, though, poor fellow, that he did not spend his Sundays in so much evil as some of his comrades, for he continued to reside with his mother and sister, and to bring in his gettings to the common stock—at least, so she always told me, and continued to exhort him to "folly his church and his larning;" but learning, poor lad, was never his forte, nor a disposition to follow friendly counsel, and so, about six weeks ago, when his comrade bade him duck down his head, "for the kibble was coming foul of it," he kept it in the same position, and, shocking to relate, was killed on the spot, leaving his mother without a gleam of comfort or hope, except what she drew from his having said that morning, on departing to his work, "God bless thee, mother." This anecdote poor Honor duly repeated to each individual comforter who dropped in to gratify their benevolence or curiosity, or a compound emotion partaking of both, which is nourished in a neighbourhood for ever furnishing fresh fuel for pity and honour.

My next Walk, I believe, treated of the —— family, but they, being regrators of fish and oranges, and no miners, remain pretty much *in statu quo*, except that the husband is dying of asthma, and the old house has been replaced by another. Mills, the consumptive miner, of whom you remember the "cunning woman" at Redruth made a "perfect cure," died almost immediately after his walk thither to consult her. His widow was a great, if not my greatest, favourite in the parish; so clean, so sensible, so meek, yet so clever and industrious, and above all, such a pattern of discretion; but unluckily her sister died, and the widower (whatever possessed him) sent for Anne to keep his house and look after his orphans. Alas! when I heard what I feared how it would be (for I recollected the discreet Anne and the twains); sure enough, this was another register affair, and I have thereby lost two of my tidiest, most reverential little day scholars, and the cleanest *ménage* I ever put my nose into.

I am here antithetically reminded of that discreet bal-maiden, Mary Pengelly, who, after her mother's death, went to live with Betsey Peters, at the earnest request of the redoubtable dame herself, in whose heart I fear the world has resumed the influence it temporarily lost on the death of her only son, which, by the way, puts my prophecy out of countenance, for I remember to have described her as of the tribe of the "never smile again" mourners; but *that*, with all my unskilful hits, shall stand on record as bearing evidence against human consistency on the one hand, and my own particular penetration on the other. Yet I cannot believe that some thought Betsey induced poor Mary to take up her quarters with her, having an eye to paying up, by means of her services out of bal hours, the small remaining sum due for house-rent, until one day she detected, or fancied she saw, her ill-fated husband casting sheep's eyes towards the ironing-table, of which, if the charge *were* true, poor Mary was as innocent as the king the cat chooses to look at. The awful Betsey picked a quarrel with her lodger on the spot, and gave her notice to quit on the following day.

It was just about that time I met Mary carrying "a turn of water," and, though the dolefullest-looking of spinsters, she quite giggled at the idea of anyone being jealous of John Peters. But, as I said, the whole truth must be told, and even Mary is one of your rolling stones who will gather no moss. Next she went to reside with Mary Johns, the *beau idéal* of a pretty, modest widow, but there the three little boys cried, and romped, and "made a shape, and had their way," and off went Mary in search of quiet elsewhere. But nobody is perfect, and this locomotive propensity is all the harm I know of your favourite *protégée*, poor Mary.

Then there is 'Un Sally, whom I like and you do *not* like so much—at least, *her* sedentary habits (she being a bed-lier), you would say, must prevail, and she stoutly declared they never should take her from the house alive; but what could she do when that great Friar Tuck-looking Nickey Ford, her son, took her up from the bed of her affections, as one would take up an infant, and placed her in a cart destined to convey her to a new place of residence. She still speaks of her removal, as a queen might of her dethronement, in a strain of indignant eloquence, and I must say I share her regret, for it has become quite a labour to visit her at that distance.

You must now hear another humbling confession. My Diogenes (you remember the tall woman who included her height among her list of afflictions) turned out no philosopher after all, but a vulgar, rapacious mortal, who, having got herself well supplied, between Kate and me, with church-going clothes, never did go to church more than an afternoon or two, just as it appeared, to exhibit them. Yet let me not be too hard upon this poor untaught being, who, in strenuously working with her hands, instead of grumbling, Diogenes-like, over the bread of idleness, shews herself the greater philosopher of the two. Let me remember *I* shall be a better philosopher than either, if I cultivate that "more excellent way," to think no evil of my fellow-creatures.

Thus far, you must allow, I have stuck to my text, that this mortal life of ours is an ever-shifting scene. But oh! was there ever beneath the fickle moon, whom the poet represents as grieving to see herself outwitted by human life,—was there ever vicissitude equal to that which has befallen two of the establishments which cut such a figure in the Walks, and have now passed away, as if they had never been—I speak of the Preventive Station and the Poor-house.

WALK LXXVIII.

FEBRUARY, 1844.

Jenny Priske.   Edward Crebo.   The churchwoman.

RETTY little widow Johns, with her three small boys grouped around her—the youngest on her lap, the second having his arm coaxingly laid across it, the eldest hanging over her with an air of affectionate protection—seemed to be taking them all in at a glance of her loving, dove-like eyes. She looked like Charity in the picture, though there was little thought of the picturesque when, replying to my comment, she said, "Yes, ma'am, they *are* fond of me; they call me their dear little mother, and tell me I shall never work when they grow up to be men." The idea! such a trio of little fair, fragile things. The father (poor Ally) was for years my scholar, and is often cited by me to the present race of Sunday scholars.

Old Jenny Priske must for shame die now; "hyperbole can no further go." She told me to-day that she was in eternity, and when I offered to send her cocoa, pertinaciously replied that it was no use, for she was in eternity. Alas! one I know has entered that unfathomable gulf, in good earnest, within the course of a few hours this Saturday evening. I stepped into Thomas Carpenter's shop just now, to consult his foreman, Michael, as to whether there was time to take out and dry the action, as heretofore, of the church piano, which, like other grandees, is apt to be affected by "skiey influences." I did not give our musical Michael the pain of refusing me, for, spying a rough-hewn coffin cover near him, and being aware of the pious courtesy invariably observed towards the dead, I anticipated his reply. "I see you cannot, but who is this intended for?" It was very shocking to hear him name one whom I believed to be a breathing man. He, Edward Crebo, was the second of three brothers, who migrated from the land of my fathers when I did—they followed their eldest brother, who followed my cook. That was no great relationship, to be sure, but Edward was a regular church-goer, and he was a Mawgan man. My reason for liking his wife was even less substantial; she was the most ladylike, perfect beauty I ever beheld in humble life; as a poor woman once observed to me, "she was a lady to look upon, down to her finger nails." I have always esteemed her for looking so like a broken-down lily under a disgrace which our village brides, with few exceptions, regard as no disgrace at all. Some said Edward was a don of a husband, and was far from regarding his wife as his own (singularly ugly) body, according to the apostle's injunction. Certainly the poor fellow, after laying Mary's beautifully-sculptured form in the grave, used touchingly to exhort every married man who approached him to be tender over their wives, for that many a light word spoken while they were living would rush down their hearts like mill-streams after they were dead.

Returning to the Vicarage, I stepped into the churchwoman's room, "which serves her for parlour, and bedroom, and hall," and we discussed poor Edward's untimely fate and inexperienced family, and then mentioned 'Un Jenny's declaration to my solemn and supercilious auditor, for our churchwomen, let them be ever so lowly in their own eyes on entering into office, are sure to become oracular, and hold their ecclesiastical noses exceedingly high afterwards. Anne, too, has a slow and supercilious sniff, which adds great emphasis to what follows. After this preparatory grimace, Anne expressed her disapprobation of the light mode some had of dealing with solemn subjects. "I do not say," continued Anne, "that I am not myself sometimes caught off my watch, but then "—another pause and sniff —"observe, I back to my post, while these—I tell them my mind plainly, but I can never find such ones are very willing to close with me. Now this is what I say "— Seeing preparations for another sniff, and being late, I suddenly recollected that to-morrow is boiled beef day, and reminded her of the fact. To this she replied, "The broth comes handy on a Sunday, for it saves both meat and fire, too, while I am at church." When at church, Anne sits in the rear of four or five rows of Sunday scholars, having within her reach a white wand, long enough to tickle, if needful, the most undefended part of the most distant offender, which she effects so silently and adroitly, that the first intimation of punishment is a sudden and fearful outcry from the delinquent. After all, Anne is a good and conscientious woman, and, I really believe, has not much malicious gratification in the sufferings of her victim.

WALK LXXIX.

THE COVE, MAY 9, 1844.

Anne Green. Margaret Christopher. Child burned.

Pauper relief.

THE walk which recent occurrences have recalled to my recollection took place a long time ago, witness the companion of my walk, who had then no more thought of mating than the scarce-fledged lark who carolled over her young head, but has now a little fellow by her side beginning to call her "mamma."

At the door of a cottage stood a young—*so* young a person that we took her for a girl, and complimented her thereupon by the surprise we shewed at hearing she was the mother of a fine boy and girl. A day or two ago she was brought back to

TT

my recollection by the kind haste of her neighbours to interest me in the case of
"a poor dear soul lying in a piteous condition, sure enough, up by Higher
Kenegie." Anne Green, who has herself miseries enough to afford new lights to
a parish register (see Crabbe), if that could be, nevertheless related with compassionate unction the story of our young-looking matron. Her misfortunes began
years ago, with a—I will not say *what*, as the doctor did not ; however, it was, some
said, a very *ougly* wound in the loins, which was lanced, &c., the et cetera compre-
hending those minute particulars which I spare you, though I could not myself
escape from them. On the healing of this abscess, the poor creature went into
the fields to work, I fear prematurely ; but it is for only a small portion of the year
that field work is to be had, and the call for hands at these seasons of planting and
reaping makes the increased rate of wages a temptation to the thrifty housewife ;
the soil which fills our garners with corn and potatoes, is made to yield at the same
time a "crum o' trousers for the chield (meaning the boy), or a blanket for the
maad" (meaning the girl), or, for the mother, the inexpressible comfort of a
change of linen ; all of which might well be hoped for from the golden sovereign
which poor Margaret Christopher amassed last summer ; but soon after, the industrious creature told her mother-in-law she could not think "what fashion she felt
on the opposite side to the healed wound." In fact, and to shorten a sad tale, a
fresh abscess had begun to form, and the sovereign destined to clothe was hence-
forth now required to feed, for John's gettings, like those of all our miners for
some time past, had proved inadequate to provide sufficient of the meanest sub-
sistence. At length, poor fellow, he was obliged to have recourse to that fund, the
poor rate, to which his forefathers had long contributed in the more dignified form
of landowners, and to see himself written down "John Christopher, pauper !"
How all this must have chafed the spirit of his little active wife, now unable to
turn an inch in the bed, no less from the anguish of the fresh wound, than from
the breaking out of the old one.

Meanwhile, a little girl of seven (the age when a young lady tears her frocks for
others to mend, and makes litters for others to set to rights), this fine little girl
took upon her small self the multiplied cares of the family—looked to the children,
tended her sick mother, cleaned up the house, and "fitted dinner" for her father
to take to bal or to eat on his return. It was during this last operation that her
flimsey petticoat was set on fire, and, as usual, acted the part of tar to the barrel.
Shrieking fearfully, and in a sheet of flame, she flew upstairs, where the unfortunate

mother made some wild and futile attempts to subdue it, which, of course, produced . no other result than cruelly burning her own poor hands, and giving the fire time to consume the few garments which had hitherto guarded the little victim. Neighbours, as usual, flew to assist and condole, and during three weeks' suffering, as I would not you should hear described (though I was forced to), the dear little girl went to Heaven, by the universal assent of the most rigid among the gossips, who decided that "she had her chastisement here, dear lamb;" and so this dreadful casualty, which is happening in our cottages day by day, is reconciled and put aside, because the poor cannot, and the rich will not, provide these little unguarded victims with a few hundred yards of some less ignitable material. It might be procured for sixpence a yard, perhaps less, and thus save a dozen or so of precious lives, at a less expense than goes to invest the individual limbs of the squire's wife or daughter in folds of velvet or embossed satin. As it is, I have often thought the poor mother would have a right to upbraid the insinuating shopkeeper in the words of the antiquary's fish-wife,—"Ye are not selling twopenny pint jars, ye are selling our children's lives."

Can the fair reader—she who looks up from the daily newspaper, exclaiming, "Another child burnt to death; how very shocking!" or pauses to charge with neglect the overworked mother—can she be aware that a few pounds would effectually pinafore a whole district, or (to restore the more appropriate term) provide all the young children in two or three parishes with save-alls?"

A Parody.

"'Tis an old tale, and often told,
But did my wishes and finance agree,
No youthful, tender, fellow-mould
Should lack this canvas panoply."

How have I wandered from poor Margaret Christopher! They did not apply to the Union (I believe) till this additional calamity, and the expenses of burial, made it unavoidable; then, there being by good luck a humane chairman, an order was made out at the Helston Board for three shillings a week, and the attendance of the Union Doctor, yclept (you would say in sport) Mr. Caudle; but it was far from a joking matter to poor Margaret, when this amiable functionary called, redolent of rum, and, by virtue of his professional authority, insisted on cutting the tumour. The patient did not fancy it had .arrived at the stage proper for the lancet, and though, with the despair of helplessness, she submitted, it proved she was right ; no discharge resulted from the incision, and the subsequent pain became intolerable, though only in paroxysms, more resembling tic doloureux, which made me, in my ignorance, suspect that the operation might have injured a nerve—unintentionally, of course ; only the surgeon *could* have helped smelling of rum before, and repairing to the " Falmouth Packet " after, his unlucky performance.   In justice I must say for this boon doctor, that he shewed a fellow-feeling for his patient in one respect—he admonished the Board of the absolute necessity of supplying her with abundance of nourishment, especially in a liquid form.   It did not come at first in any form except the shape of a dawdle, who consented to leave her own two children in the Union, for the gratuity of one shilling per week, which, it seemed, poor John was to provide, in addition to the food of the imposed inmate.   John, being of a " contented make," acquiesced in all, and thought how he would bestow his sleeping hours " between cour and cour " in walking to Penzance and back (twelve miles), in order to lay out the allotted three shillings to the best advantage for the invalid.   It would go further, he rightly said, in porter than in wine, and in good juicy meat than the half-fed article sold in the villages.   But that matter was also settled for him ; he was informed, after walking hither and thither, and being handed over from one parish authority to another, like a shuttlecock, with nothing but a huff for his pains, that the three shillings was to be cut down to two shillings, the amount of which was to be supplied, not in money, but in material, to wit two pounds of beef and a half pint of wine.   Again poor Christopher meekly bowed, and again travelled hither and thither, to present the following documents, on two separate bits of paper, addressed to two officials.

My blood boiled, if the poor young man's did not, on reading these precious sentences.

" Deliver to pauper John Christopher two pounds of beef.

Deliver to pauper John C———— half pint of wine."

And just fancy ! this wretched supply, which was to repair the vital drain of the week, was not procurable till Saturday.   I drop the pen in sheer heart-sickness at this more than negro treatment.

Note by C. O. B. R.   The beloved writer whose heart was so tenderly moved by this *one* tale of suffering and endurance, has been mercifully spared the sight of the wide-spread calamities of 1877-8.   We wonder what would be the feelings of those who have been accustomed to see the smallest symptoms of distress met by turbulent outrage, could they behold the sad faces and shrunken limbs that cower among the ruined houses and fireless hearths of West Cornwall.   No strikes, no violence, only endurance, and reluctance to profit by public charity, would he find in the half-roofless villages which cover our once busy and populous hillsides.

WALK LXXX.

G. Jones' death. The apple stealer. Green geese. Want of courtesy.

O walk, but voices under my window, at the witching hour of twelve. I thought not of robbers, I thought not of ghosts; the spot was too simple, too canny, for either; but I did recollect the preventive men, whose dismal duty it is to perambulate these rocky, shafty heights all night long. But then, what could mean the woman's treble which intersected the deep bass tones? I soon learnt, through the casement Mr. Pascoe threw down, that Lizzie Richards, the fisherman's daughter, had been keeping Katherine Jones company, alongside the body of her lately deceased husband, at that little lone cottage on the western cliff. She came, she said, to ask Captain Will to help put the corpse into the coffin just brought by the carpenter, and urged, in excuse of this untimely visit, Mary's argument to our Lord, when opposing the disinterment of her dead. Captain Will, to his honour, though suffering from a cold, instantly rose, and went on his appalling errand.

The deceased, George Jones, was an awesome subject to deal with, living or dead; he certainly must have been a descendant of the Jones who drew on himself the hatred of the mildest of poets, Wordsworth.

> "I hate that Andrew Jones; his sons
>   Will all be trained to waste and pillage.
> I wish the drum
> With row-dow-dow would come,
>   And sweep them from the village."

Yet ruffian as he was, a bad father, a cruel husband, a swearer, a scoffer, and eke a desperate poacher, his heart was open to the all-powerful influence of conscience, as I learn by the boatman's wife whom I met this evening on the cliff. She volunteered the following narration. He was leaning his head upon his arms, at the end of the table. "George," says I, "do ye think you shall recover?" "I reckon," says he, "I never shall." "Then," says I, "my dear soul, call upon the

UU

Lord." "I would," says he, "if I knew how. How can I tell whether He will hark to me? He is one that won't be mocked." "Well," says I, "nobody else can do nothing for you; you must labour for your own soul; there is no giving one for another" (referring, I suppose, to the Divine atonement). "And so, poor fellow, he pitched to cry for mercy; he fairly sweated with earnestness, till he fell asleep from weakness; but Kattern, his wife, when she went out, charged us straitly not to leave him sleep a moment, so when she came in she poked him, and besought him to keep crying upon the Lord." "I do," said he, and passed his hand lovingly over her cheek. The narrator said she seemed to "vally" this slight loving gesture, perhaps the first indication of the heart of flesh Jones had ever shewn to his unhappy yoke-fellow. Yet some rough virtue appeared even on that stony soil. He was honest, bating poaching, his view of which was probably different from the richer lovers of sylvan sport. The instant he admitted a conviction that he might not recover, he sent for his landlord and said, "I'm thinking I shall never work no more, and its no use for you to be looking for the quarter's rent from those I leave behind me—they have nothing to give for it; but there is an old boat of mine down under, you can take that and pay yourself." And now, this Friday morning, the poor fellow is to be borne from his pretty cliff cottage, under such a torrent of rain as has drawn us continually to the window. Cataracts are streaming and gurgling down the opposite cliff roads, till, realizing Lady Macbeth's simile, they have "made the green sea red," or, to tell the sober truth, reddish brown, a good way out, and the poor pastor has to go home through these floods, to lay poor Jones's body in that churchyard which it seldom if ever crossed, but where, nevertheless, it must remain, till incorporated with the consecrated soil.

Friends are assembling round the widow, and we see one poor half-drowned relative after another scrambling down our back hill, of which, in fine weather, it needs all one's wits about one to get safe to the bottom. The last pilgrim to the house of mourning was a female, with her best black bonnet enveloped in a hand-kerchief, and the best gown caught-up a foot or two. Alas! for the white petticoat that appears under it!

It seems to me that the rancour of the poor never pursues its object beyond the grave, and they have readiness to believe in the sudden beatification of the habitual life-long sinner, which latitude of candour, however to be lamented in a religious view, argues placability of mind in them.

The boatman's tall wife sang this sort of placebo to-day over poor Jones, which

I felt myself in conscience bound to qualify by the successful little allegory (wherever I picked it up) of the boy who, feeling himself in the clutches of the master, and foreboding a severe punishment, calls vigorously for mercy, and fails not to promise he will never steal apples again. " Now who, Betsey," asked I, " will venture to assert that the same boy, when he again passes that orchard, will not get over the hedge, and fill his pocket with more apples ?" " Likely he might, ma'am," replies Betsey. " Give me, then," say I, " the good boy, who, seeing the apples look red on the bough, can hold on his honest way, thinking within himself, ' It is pleasant to eat apples, but it is more pleasant to have the favour of my kind, generous, and gracious Master, who has said, *Thou shalt not steal.'*" The lesson might be profitable to older and richer delinquents than " the apple-munching urchin," if we would but apply it.

I do think this is an honest neighbourhood. There is a woman taken up for stealing geese to the amount of twenty or more (I don't bring this in proof of my observation, you may suppose—but wait, you are coming to that). She appears to have perambulated the country, in particular the downs, with a large empty basket on her arm, and, watching her opportunity, has clapped the heedless wanderers into it, then offered them for sale, with this legend attached to lull suspicion. A brother had gone to America, and left her a legacy of an old goose, or an old gander, or a few goslings, according as her day's success had been. She came, among others, to our door at the Vicarage. I never *look* at poultry so proffered, however urgently invited, because I would not betray my profound ignorance of young and old, smooth or rough-legged, well-feathered or hairy-breasted, and other indications on which the knowing ones descant. I was contented to hear they were young, and to ask whether they could by any means be made fit for the table against the coming of expected guests. " Green geese would be such a variety." " Impossible ; they were no better than carrion," cook said ; " get as good out on the downs." Then came the story of the brother, and so, despite Anne's critical looks, I purchased the green geese at the nominated price, my cook, I could plainly see, thinking her mistress the greenest goose of the three, resisting the temptation to parody the old catch,—

> " Why shouldn't my goose
> Be ate as well as thy goose,
> Since I paid for my goose," &c.

We began, as soon as we heard of the woman's cunning, to enquire out an owner for the stolen property. Watty Curtis had lost two geese, exactly the number; he would know them among a flight, for their feet were punched. His claim was corroborated by dear old Tom's observation; he testified that one at least had undergone that barbarous operation, and Watty was invited down, in order that, if satisfied of his goose's identity, he might take it home; but the honest fellow came out of the poultry-yard without either—they were none of his.

Next we called on John Williams, a small farmer, of St. Perran, *so* small a farmer that the loss of six geese was to him a heavy calamity; but he and his wife said that, bating one old goose, blind of an eye, his were no better than goslings, so they were none of his, either.

At last our pains were rewarded by tidings thàt Waters, a still smaller farmer (of Rugeon), mourned the loss of two geese. I was quite charmed with my commission, to call and inform the good wife that her geese were likely to be restored to her, the better by a gallon or two of Mr. P——'s good oats, to which she responded with high glee; and one had a mark in the feet, too. "Were yours, ma'am, slit?" "No, punched." "Then," said she, with a fallen crest, "they are none of ours." There was not the demur of an instant in disclaiming the proffered good; no glance of thought whether it were not more profitable to be honest, more creditable to tell the truth; so, as I began my commendation of the poor for their honesty, I may conclude it with commendation of their truthfulness.

As I made an old woman, namely myself, laugh (Molière's well-known test of wit) at the following account, given in a letter to a friend, of a walk on the road to the Cove, I have a right to think it a laughable occurrence. Speaking of the lamentable want of courtesy (or bump of veneration) in Cornwall, I observed that I was on one occasion rather gratified by indications of its absence, in a little boy driving over the down some "wilfu' beasties," who, do what he would, persisted in going the wrong way. By shrouding my lordly person in a hedge, I prevented what he seemed to apprehend as an additional difficulty. "Haven't I helped you?" I said. He grinned his gratitude, and as I pursued my way, congratulating myself that I could yet be of some use in the world, I heard a shrill, imperative scream, "Dreave back them bullocks, will ye?" and turning, found on my hands some four or five young steers flying in all directions and attitudes.

WALK LXXXI.

Peggy Green.

'ON Peggy Green, then, is gone! the last of her generation in that smuggler group, among whom (if she held a less romantic vocation than her predecessor Betsey, to whom this indentation of the Cove owes its name, and, it is said, used to sell the winds to the mariners —"bottle them up," says somebody) she was no less useful a personage. Peggy's business was to carry about under her cloak the contraband article, supplying with it that class of the community who do not mind doing dishonest things within the pale of custom. Poor old Peggy was a tall, gaunt, strengthy female, with an expression gleaming from her eye that promised no less vigour of mind; you were sure, at a glance, that hot pincers would not have drawn from her the secret of her employers. Many were the lawless orgies, I venture to say, at which she has assisted in that cellar underneath, where Captain Will is now sawing up planks to make her coffin, conformably to a promise she extracted, some weeks before her death, from her old companion and co-offender in gone-by days. They say for the last few weeks of her life she permitted him no rest on this point.

WALK LXXXII.

Luxuries and privations of the poor.

NOW *do* the poor get on! how are they able to sustain their accumulated burthen of privation, cold, and sickness? How do they get on? Every one who habitually visits their dwellings will often ask himself this question, but if he chance to bring it on the tapis, I mean literally on a warm Brussels carpet, he will be sure to receive the plain answer, "They are used to it." This is a comfortable way of viewing the matter, but I believe it to be quite false, and question whether the nursery training in the most aristocratic quarters is not more calculated to enable its object to endure hardness in after life, than the system pursued in their ignorance and kindness, poor things! by the inmates of the hut. To begin, there is that passive luxury of giving them their own way, which the poor mother in the story book does, on the plea that she has nothing else to give them,* and then they are never tantalized; self-denial is never exercised, like the children of the rich, by seeing that before them of which they may not partake. The tiniest fingers are plunged at pleasure into the family dish, and if it contains one morsel more dainty than another, the greedy propensities are fostered by the mother's admonition, "lev she have it." Precisely the same principle prevails in regard to clothing. I have repeatedly seen the mother tear up her last maiden garment to make "a crum o' something for the youngest, tender lamb!" She must have it, whoever goes bare; and on that careful bosom the happy little creature nestles at night, lying as warm and soft as the son of a duke—warmer, by the way, unless the duchess happens to nurse her own children.

When the children are old enough to work, much solicitude is shewn that they shall have warm clothing and *food*, I am sure, for often have I known a miner's wife, after making her own miserable, hasty dinner on barley bread and stained water, rise and take a nice hot pasty from under the baker, and, no other child

---

* See *Guy Mannering.*

being at hand, walk a mile or two with it to the boy or the maiden at bal, on the plea which she forgets to advance for herself, that, working hard, they would "look for something comfortable."

Then, in regard to the third element of happiness, fire (and all children are salamanders, with the exception of the one out of twenty who are yearly burnt to death in every parish), who does not know that the young cottager basks within a few inches of the little grate, and comes and goes, and strokes the cat, and lights straws, at pleasure, no nursery-maid, or tall fender, or big school-fellow, bidding him stand back; and when the time arrives that these children cease to be thus humoured and petted, why then they can take their own part, and claim their own share, and elbow into their own place, unfettered by the strait jacket of public opinion, of good taste, and good breeding. Work being over, they do what they like, go where they like, dress as they like, spend Sunday as they like, and marry as they like, which last privilege varies according to the popular calling. In a mining parish it is on the average at seventeen or eighteen that the bal boy and girl, having kept company for a year or two, look about, and seldom prematurely, for a family dwelling, and it is from this point that they enter upon their task of compelled labour, care, ceaseless short commons, and, nine times out of ten, the heavier load of domestic strife, debt, and sickness. "Oh, but they are used to it," cries the gentleman who has exchanged the bare commons and tyrannical treatment of a public school, for a scamper at will on the back of a free-paced, showy horse; or a "yes, they are used to it," says the young lady from her soft couch, whereon she reposes the muscles to which the dancing master and governess once allowed no minute's rest. "They are used to it, my dear," replies the older gent, crackling his newspaper over the well-filled grate, or eclipsing with it the two candles; and his wife—but no, perhaps she does not respond, if she is a careful mother and mistress, thinking that no use can make care and suffering agreeable.

I know, dear Maria, you won't think I have brought the higher class into juxta-position with the bal boy or girl, in order to insinuate that the latter class are hardly dealt with. I know this to be untrue; nor is it by rote that I say there *is* an equalization of enjoyment throughout all ranks—but this text would lead to another tedious homily, which I shall spare you. All I want to establish is the falseness and cruelty of shutting up our sympathy and our purses against the poor, on the eel-skinning plea that they are used to it.

WALK LXXXIII.

Doctor Dick and his patients.

THIS pompous heading will apprize you that you are to expect a Character instead of a Walk. "Forewarned, forearmed." You can, if you like, skip, and go on to another Walk; but oh! what would not Doctor Dick be in the hand which has, alas! forgotten its matchless cunning. Feeble are now the fingers which presume to picture this exquisite wight, to set the seal of portraiture on him, to make the grotesque become durable, though it is shameful to parody what Southey said so sweetly of Kirke White.

Neither was Dick Bennetts "a vulgar boy," in that sense which implies conformity to rules and rudiments, though in no other that I know of did he resemble Beattie's Minstrel, for, if not vulgar, he was decidedly as desperate and idle a one as ever wore paper cap and made a drum of an old kettle (the origin, no doubt, of kettle-drums), or went about recruiting dunces and minchers, till he became as great a pest, in a small way, as an invading army, and the terror of peaceable householders.

Talent is sometimes hereditary, and when so, I have observed, mostly derived from the maternal side. "Old Nanny," the only name by which our hero's mother was known in the parish, was the veriest oddity and hardest worker I ever knew; she worked like any man, and smoked like one, too, having this advantage over masculine puffers, that she could whip her pipe into her skirt pocket as soon as master appeared. Mr. Pascoe hates the smell of tobacco, as Nanny knew to her cost, for, popping her lighted pipe one day hastily into a tindery pocket, while the ashes were on fire, she had very nearly made ashes of herself. She would, I doubt not, have proceeded to this extremity, such was her Cherokee hardihood, and her reverence for master, had he not spied the smoke curling out of her pocket, and helped her to extinguish it.

Nanny was left a widow with one boy and two girls, whom she maintained in idleness and snuff, insomuch that probably that embryo Esculapius of hers would never have turned his hand to earn an honest livelihood, if old Doctor Turner, the most corpulent and humorous of apothecaries, had not happened to want a lad to sweep his shop, and to regard Dick Bennetts, in virtue of his idleness and waggery, the very chap to serve his purpose. Here my narrator (for I was then new to the parish) lost sight of Dick, and it is left to fancy to pourtray how he pounded and compounded, and spread and spatulated, and broomed, inhaling science and dust, and dog-latin, till he became that mirror of M.D.s whom it was our good fortune to meet this morning, for the first time, at poor Susannah Cornish's—but let me not forestall.

Doctor Turner was in due time gathered to his—patients, a well worn out parish doctor, and (what great results from trifling causes spring!) bequeathed to Dick his medical books, instruments of surgical torture, and his buckskin inexpressibles.

There is no resisting destiny. Dick returned home with these insignia of office, hired a little shop, where he was bottled up as tight as his own elixir, and forthwith began to exercise his calling. His first essay in the healing art was to kill his affectionate, hard-working old mother, a fact I can assert on the authority of Doctor Turner's surviving partner, who assured me Dick Bennetts had applied to him for, and, as he afterwards learned, administered to old Nanny, a dose of hyoscyamus large enough to have killed all the old women in this and all the neighbouring parishes.

Shortly after, our hero committed another mortal blunder, and this time it was literally blood-shedding, for, having heard of a surgical operation in a case which medicine could not reach, our bold *debutant* made an incision into the liver side of a hapless patient, and the poor man actually died of this newly-discovered opening dose. These two bold strokes improved his popularity, and increased his practise, so I conclude; for now, instead of "that Dick Bennetts," I hear of "Doctor Dick" and "Doctor Bennetts," and sometimes "the doctor." As soon as he came so much into fashion that every one was calling him *in*, there appeared great danger of his being called *out* by some of the regular craft, who at first scorned him for an ignorant, low fellow, but, finding he ran away with their patients, now threatened to pull him up for practising without a license. Not so the parish officers; they, with a forbearance a little suspicious, left him unmolested to try his practise on all old women and chargeable children. But I hope this dabbler in drugs has left off killing; only this I have remembered, he has had three wives, two of them young and healthy when he married them.

Strange that Doctor Dick and I should have gone on so many years practising as brother quacks without ever meeting, like two parallel lines in geometry. You might have known how greatly I desired this *rencontre*, by Kate's rapturous exclamation, as we left Betty Pengelly's door, "Aunt, I declare there is Doctor Dick gone into Susannah Cornish's; now we shall see him at last." It was not, however, so easy a matter, for his pony, a wicked-looking black sprite of a creature, chose to occupy the whole road, with the air of meditating a kick, or, as Dick himself would have expressed it, "fetching a dab," at anyone who should attempt to pass him. We did, however, manage to slip by in whole skin, and learned from the maid Hannah that the doctor was with her mother in the adjoining room, a slip of a place. We kept her talking, in order to amuse ourselves with the oracular speeches we hoped to hear from thence, but our malice was disappointed; nothing was to be gathered from the unpretending tones of Doctor Dick, but that he took abundance of snuff. His prescriptions were no less unaffected. "My dear soul, take gruel, and keep up a gentle sweat." "Where am I to get gruel?" enquired the patient, while I, unable to resist the pitying instinct to set her heart at rest (as Kate reproached me), walked into the chamber, and broke the charm. There stood the doctor, wedged in between the bed and the wall—no escape; I had him like a moth under a tumbler, and could inspect his plumage at my pleasure. It was a rare specimen of the *sphinx atropos*, all head and drapery. He wore, I thought, moustachios, or, to keep up the metaphor, *antennæ* on his upper lip, but this turned out to be snuff, which, for the greater convenience of his nose, he keeps, they say, in the pocket of his waistcoat, while for the same reason, I suppose, that garment is so singularly short, that, with the long, flowing frock-coat, his figure reminded me of the times of short waists, when we belles were accused of tying our petticoats round our throats, and putting our arms through the pocket-holes. His face was as short as his waistcoat (I think I never saw any face so short, except my own, when I have caught its reflection in a silver spoon), and as merry as a mountebank's. In a moment all my pre-conceived notions of him were upset. Without waiting for me to accost him, he said he had been long meaning to ask me (a consultation, to be sure, thought I) whether I had "a few flower roots to bestow upon his bit of gar'n." I saw at once that he hadn't a spice of the scorn with which established dignitaries are too apt to treat intruders into their peculiar mysteries. A single glance at his *vis comica* sufficed to shew that he was the identical idle rogue, with the same turn for drumming and masquerading, as when he headed the little troop of ragamuffins, in a paper cap adorned with a cock's feather. In a minute we were the best of friends. I promised the roots, which he said he would call up for, bringing his wife's reticule to convey them home, while he in his turn invited us to call in and see his organ, which, employing a bold metaphor, he said he had "gone bare of back and belly" to purchase. Nobody has any right to accuse you of the former, thought I, as the doctor turned his back, and displayed the ample skirts of a coat, once, I suppose, the property of his old master, a ton of a man, but a world too wide for his slender shanks, and so comically contrasted with his rivulet of waistcoat, that they reminded me of the tall woman and the little man in the show. No doubt this antithetical style of dress is much in his favour with his employers; it is a set-off against the insignificance of his bodily presence, and the smirking expression of his short face—that face that, if he attended me in an illness, and if he did not kill me with anything else, would kill me with laughing. I am surprised the sick poor can tolerate him near their beds; he must look as if he were making a joke of their dolours and dumps, of which they are generally very tenacious, and he seems to take no pains to rein in his risibility. By-the-bye, Kate could by no means restrain hers, when she saw him vault on the back of the wicked little pony, whose hind quarters were so completely covered by the long and full skirts of his rider, that it seemed hard to pronounce, as they trotted off, whether the compound animal was biped or quadruped—or milleped. On it scudded, stopping for a minute at one door and another, just touching up the living, as Old Mortality did the dead, and, who knows? like that worthy, sometimes putting a finishing stroke. They would make admirable pendants, such as one sees hanging cheek by jowl against old-fashioned walls. "Before and After Marriage," "Summer and Winter," "Ancient and Modern Chivalry," &c.; and why not "Mortality and Vitality." I wish Emma would turn her mind to it.

Now of Doctor Dick more anon; for the present, you have had enough of him. His patients must furnish materials for future Walks, and I will begin, now my hand is in for the likeness, with the sick woman to whom I owe the honour of an introduction to him. Although you have heard of Susannah Cornish before, I must recall her to you as a thin, loving, humble being, shorter than me by half a head, with a much-enduring expression of face, and a voice kind and pitying as that with which one says "poo-or thing;" the phrase might well be applied to her own little self. Left a widow with five little children, and no provision for them, but that feeling of beautiful self-respect which shrinks from being beholden to charity, she worked more than her constitution would allow, to keep them off the parish. "It is what I am now suffering for," she would often say, glancing at her wasted arms, and hands deformed by labour and rheumatism. One child, a daughter, remained to her unmarried, or I believe her meek spirit would have bowed even to the refuge of the Union, and reconciled her to passing the remnant of her well-spent life in the society of the profligate and malignant; but the "little maid" (as she termed a bouncing lass of eighteen, who would have sliced down into two or three such little bodies as her mother), the little maid wanted a home; she was young and friendless, and giddy, and, moreover, not over wise to pilot herself; and so Susannah was willing, she said, "to struggle for her own bit of meat, and try to fetch the rent of the crum of house." Such a crum! nothing so small was ever inhabited, since the vinegar bottle in the nursery tale. Towards this her daughter would assist, out of her bal wages. At length Susannah herself got employed in a gentleman's garden, washing potatoes, feeding swine, and performing those "slaggery" jobs which the other hirelings of the establishment thought themselves too good to do. While these resources remained, we heard no complaints.

Our frequent peeps over the hutch, as we passed down Relubbus Lane, were gratefully welcomed, whenever its inmate happened to be at home. It was a pleasure then to look on her patient face, to hear the sweet minor tones of her voice, and glance round her beautifully clean cottage. On one such occasion, I was alarmed at receiving, in place of the usual gladsome welcome, a feeble answer from the inner room. There lay poor little Susannah on a comfortless, curtainless bed, groaning under the torture of rheumatic fever, yet spending the little breath that remained to her in prayer and thanksgiving. How admirable, how enviable it is to perceive the aspirations of the soul, as is the case with the devout poor, rising above the privations and sufferings of the body! This buoyant principle of Christianity was never more evident than in my poor little widow, who, however, after a long period of patient suffering, recovered her health, although her poor fingers were warped and crooked ever after.

How, then, was she to gain a livelihood? She thought that if the *Junion* would be pleased to allow her so little as sixpence a week, to help out the house-rent, she might pick up her "crum o' living, by going from house to house to hold the child," whilst the mother was otherwise employed. Her married children had great families and small gettings, and could do no more for her.

"Sixpence a week! well, that is easily got," said we, and accordingly Mr. Pascoe wrote to the Helston Board about it,—Susannah belonged to that district. The gentleman whom he tried to interest promised his aid, provided the applicant would attend their meetings. So, after all, it was no such light matter as we thought, but having packed up and packed in, to our own warm cart, the dear old soul, on a wretched bleak wintry day, we regarded the thing as done, and that she could not escape sixpence a week to the end of her days.

Those wretched farmers, who with us have quite o'ermastered all the benevolent and gentlemanly influences, bade the dear old creature "go to the place provided for her and such as her" (awful words these to have retorted on them), and the gentleman said *he* could do nothing; so home she came, with an accession of misery and rheumatism.

After this, we picked up acquaintance with the curate of Breage, and interested him in Susannah's story, and obtained through him the promise of a shilling weekly, until his return from a visit he was about to make to some distant friends. Mr. Perry told me he had small hope of prevailing to get the dole continued after that period; as it was, it could only be obtained by weekly application at the place of payment, a journey of six or seven miles. A neighbour going that way undertook to call for the promised shilling, but brought instead the intelligence that an order should be made out for the relieving officer of our division, and that to him Susannah must apply. Now her seeing this person was a mere contingency. She might have watched for a month together at her little casement, for the chance of seeing him go along, nor had she any means of sending to him. Thus was she thrown back, almost without resource, for a week or two.

Private charity, in a populous and poor parish, cannot do everything for everybody, and if it could, modest misery, rather than intrude, would suffer itself to slip out of remembrance. Nothing is so terrible to a delicate spirit as a rebuff. I have before now felt my own cheeks tingle, at sight of the burning blush that an impatient word has called up into the face of an ill-timed suitor, and apologised until I daresay the cook has said to herself, "What a poor creature my mistress is!"

A weary time it was before Maister Warren shewed his official face in Relubbus, and when he did, Susannah was told he had received no such order, and couldn't pay the money.

I have drawn out my tale to a tedious length, to what would be tedious to those who feel not the force of your lately-quoted maxim from Terence (I would he had been our relieving officer), that "nothing of human suffering can be indifferent to a human being."

Calling, as usual, to enquire after Susannah's health, and if the money had been paid, I found the dear old soul just returned from gathering a few sticks, like her sister widow of Zarephath, that she and her daughter might "eat and die." Not that the dear little simple body made any such sublime allusion; she only said that she had been about the lanes, seeing if could she "pick up a little fire-'ood, for coals were fine and dear;" and she spoke cheerfully, told me she was thinking (plase the Lord!) of coming up to church next day, and promised to "call in to Vicarage." Her concluding words were a wish that God might requite my kindness to her when she was in her grave.

Next day, when we assembled in the gallery, to rehearse the psalms of the day, one of the choir told me that poor old Susannah Cornish had been found that day dead in her bed! The touching particulars I had from her daughter's quivering lips. "Mother blacked her shoes as uyal agin church, and we said our prayers together; then mother said, 'Be a good maid, dear, and God will bless you when I am in my grave.' She seemed tired like, and so we did not say any more that night, but when I went to kiss her next morning, her face was as cold as a stone —mother was dead."

How terrified the relieving officer looked, when I told him of the catastrophe; he reminded me of Macbeth. "Dead! dead in her bed! That case did not belong to our Board; thou canst not say I did it; cold and hunger killed the old woman; I only withheld the means to live."

WALK LXXXIV.

Doctor Dick again.

SAID you should soon hear more of Doctor Dick, and as I think it is a fault of the "Walks," that they are too desultory for a stranger to preserve a personal interest in the individuals, of whose history and character they are composed, I will proceed with a few hints I threw down one day, after Kate and I had puzzled, had plodded, had scrambled and climbed our way to Doctor Dick's newly-built and self-planned house—for all these manœuvres were necessary, in order to attain it. Surely it may be ranked amongst the eccentricities of genius; it is a nondescript, like its master, wherefore I can only describe the situation, perched as it is on an abrupt and narrow rising ground, between Relubbus and the Godolphin Hills, and occupying, like Jack the Giant Killer's castle, the whole, or almost the whole, of the eminence on which it rests. But another point of resemblance is that, though visible to all men, it can be approached by few.

We saw no breathing thing, but an exceedingly woe-begone, owlish-looking boy, sprawling upon a hedge, who, in reply to our enquiry, told us he was Doctor Bennetts' boy, the son, probably, of a former wife, for the baby which lay in the arms of the present Mrs. B———, and the little girl that held by her apron, looked well fed and clothed, and it was plain to see, had not, any more than their mother, been practised upon. She was a buxom matron, well able to take her own and their part; besides, it was her happiness to have met with her spouse when patients had become more plenty. She spoke of him as "the doctor," and seemed to have much pride in shewing off his finery. First we were ushered into a square of flower garden, the beds being studded round with bullies (beach pebbles), and looking gay with annuals, all the doctor's planting, as neat as could be in itself, but strewn round and blocked up with rubbish and raw material. The house was after the same fashion; a roof, shapeless and dilapidated as the heir-apparent, covered rooms of science and specimens of the fine arts. On entering the parlour, into which we were reverentially ushered by Mrs. Doctor Dick, my eyes were at once treated with a sight of the aforenamed fine gilded barrel-organ, the possession of which had cost its owner so dear. "A beautiful instrument, and excellent," Mrs. B——— said, only that somehow it would not make any sound when played upon, and besides, it hadn't a good ground bass. These were its only faults, which I hinted were to be the less regretted, as the handle appeared to be wanting, but that, she observed, was only mislaid; so I could not but agree with her, the height, breadth, and gilding considered, that it *was* a fine instrument, though it could not, in its present mute condition, be strictly termed an instrument of music. The piano occupying the other side of the sanctum might be pronounced both, for Mrs. Doctor D——— assured us that it wanted nothing on earth but tuning, which it was soon to have from a young man of Relubbus, who played the clarionet "capital well," and he had undertaken to cure it of a way it had of sounding all the notes alike. I did not think of it at the time, but this explains the great gamut letters which I found the doctor had printed with his own hand on all the white keys, in order that the eye might supply the deficiencies of the ear. Why the notes would sound all alike, I am unable to explain, but can attest the fact on my own experience, for, beginning what I intended to be a tune, in order to avert attention from Kate's giggles, I was obliged to join in it, and make the best apology I could for both of us.

I have had adventures before now with old pianos. I remember going with Julia and Elizabeth Reynolds, to dine at Acton Castle. We were the only ladies, and when we adjourned to the drawing-room, felt an irresistible desire to try the old instrument, which I will be bound to say had not seen the light since the arrival in these parts of its eccentric owner. If you have ever heard of Captain, afterwards Admiral Praed, you will know he was not a man with whom you could take liberties, any more than Blue Beard. For a long time we hesitated and parleyed, after the manner of the heroine of that drama,—

> "Shall we venture? Yes or no?
> What can make us tremble so?
> Mischief is not———"

Now whether it was so or not, at the first application of poor Julia's fingers, off flew the ivories in all directions. She uttered a faint shriek, hastily shut the piano, the gentlemen came in, and I have never heard to this day, some twenty years having elapsed, what was the result—perhaps the piano has never been opened since. No doubt pianos have distinctive traits, as well as other things, and are no more alike than any two sheep's faces, and certainly my experience proved the truth of this remark.

WALK LXXXV.

Summary of parish events and changes.

"WHAT a world of change this is!" we go on exclaiming, as if we had dropped from some bright, stationary star, where leaves do not turn yellow, nor empires decay. I say so when I visit Truro, where I first opened my eyes more than half a century ago, and where, dear Maria, they first had the happiness to light upon you. I find old houses have toppled down, and been replaced by smart shops; young, laughing faces puckered up with care and age, out of all recognition; or if by chance I meet a countenance I fancy I know, it turns out to be a son or grandson of the man I took him for. Now this is all in the current of events, and we have no right to be surprised; but occasionally there is so sudden an alteration in the face of things, as to justify the sapient ejaculation with which I began the record of this Walk.

I went to see Uncle John ———— at the old Workhouse, the place which, when I first visited it, swarmed with inhabitants of all descriptions—young, old, and middle-aged, the depraved and the estimable, the shrewd and the idiotic. Then there was, a host in herself, the vivacious governess, who was always so glad when we came. A hundred times I have said I would sketch her for you, but, like Madam Blaize's deeds of charity, it is unknown what good things I should have done in this way, only for want of time. With all her official importance, there was an irrepressible youthiness about good Mrs. Treweeke, which made her pleasant company both to me and my young companion. It was the delight of her heart

YY

to have a laugh with Miss Kate in that snug kitchen of hers, and comical enough
to see the sudden resumption of authority, when any unlucky pauper intruded into
its dignified precincts. Yet she was essentially kind to those placed under her
charge, often abridging her rest for the sick, and her wardrobe for the ill-clothed,
piquing herself more on her popularity than on her supremacy in the establishment.
You could see she was proud of being called " my dear missus," a form of address
adopted by some from pure love, and by others for what they could get. I have
hardly yet reconciled myself to poor Mrs. Treweeke's death ; it came so suddenly
and unexpectedly, and the previous scene of suffering and depression assimilated
so ill with her buoyant, joyous spirit.

Active, scheming, vivacious characters are not generally amongst those of whom
it may be pronounced,—

> "No * * * life
> Became them like the leaving it."

I think of this with dismay sometimes, and recur with pain to poor Mrs. T——'s
few latter days, when her ardent, restless spirit, thrown back on itself, assumed
features of impatience and querulousness so foreign to her native character.

Well! she is gone, and the old women of the establishment (with the exception
of one) had their prayer, and died before the time appointed for their removal to
the Union arrived. Others, whose terrors, real and ideal, became more exaggerated
as the time approached, rushed on nakedness and starvation, by taking themselves
off the list of paupers. Childhood and imbecility made no effort to avoid their
destiny ; of the latter class were poor silly George and Catty Brand. In short, all
went but the few who were thought eligible to assist in the work of the farm, which
the parish determined, as a speculation, to keep on, under the superintendence of
the matron's worthy husband and survivor, John Treweeke.

Among those few A.B.s whom the parish magnates, the farmers, saw fit to retain,
was the heroine of a former Walk, Mary Stevens, long since tired of the convulsive
farce, of which I tried, you may remember, to treat you with a representation, but
who, I learnt on my last visit, had, true to her trade, decoyed away two girls of the
establishment, and decamped with them, the parish officers cannot guess where.
So this morning, as I said, the mansion that had been "vital and populous as the
grave," was now scarcely less silent.

Old Joanna marshalled me upstairs to her dying husband,—so she called him, but I think he will survive, in spite of her prognostics, to thresh more sheaves. It was in the performance of this surprising achievement, at the age of eighty-two, that the brave-spirited old man was seized with what all considered, he amongst the rest, his last illness. A beautiful example is Uncle John of that manly energy which triumphs over privation, pain, age—I should be sorry to say propriety—for yesterday, after he had been joining with the devoutest fervour in the prayers for the sick, Mr. Pascoe told me he suddenly started up from his pillow, on hearing a stir below stairs, and eagerly called out, "Are the rogues overtaken ?" Now this was said out of pure love of discipline, for Uncle John deprecates, no less than the fugitives themselves, being carried to the *Junion*.

WALK LXXXVI.

Gratitude of the poor.

"THE Lord have mercy on the rich !" These words concluded a soliloquy, into which I fell as I turned away from a cottage in Relubbus, wherein I held the following dialogue with a poor woman, whose family consisted of a sickly husband (and he walked ten miles a day to work for twenty-five shillings a month), a fine-looking boy of sixteen, with a cancer in his throat, three girls, of whom the youngest was a cripple, and a baby. "How is your poor boy ?" I asked. "Just the same in respect of health, ma'am, but, thank the Lord, beginning to have thoughts about his poor soul, and that is the main thing, after all. He never goes to bed or board now without bending his knee, for all, poor soul, he don't know a letter in the book." "He should come to the Sunday-school." "He do mean to, ma'am, so soon as he can git a flock (blouse) ; his do get very dirty by Saturday night," said the poor mother, in an apologetic tone, "and then it is too late to wash un 'gin Sunday; but (brightening up) he has got five little chicks, and when they are big enough, they'll fetch as much as will buy one." "Well! bring me your chicken, and I will get the frock; but there will be more than enough for that." The woman eyed me with such grateful and delighted looks as a poor curate might be supposed to bestow on a bishop who had presented him with a snug living, and with the same respectful hesitation as the same new incumbent might ask for a chaplaincy attached to the presentation, did the poor creature timidly suggest that "if—for eight-pence a-piece would be ample for the frock, as she did not desire anything very great—there *should* be something towards a bit of a shirt—winter coming on, and he might not be able to bear the cold as he used to—it would be clever, sure enough. The last he ever had was bought by money given her by a relation for the baby, but *he* wanted it more."

Was it strange that I should conclude my reflections with this exclamation,— "The Lord have mercy on the rich?"

FINIS.

BEARE AND SON, STEAM PRINTERS, PENZANCE.